LE PROJET

S

erret

C · P · SERRET

GRENDEL
VVEPT

TEMPEST & GAYLE⟨
PHŒNIX⟨
MMXXIII.

Published by
Tempest & Gayle
PHOENIX

Paperback cover photo by Jr Korpa on Unsplash

Design by C. P. Serret

Set in Seria, New Athenian,
Noto, and Phoencian Moabite

ISBNs: 978-1-7343234-6-7 (hardcover)
978-1-7343234-7-4 (paperback)

LCCN 2023911669

για την καλλιόπη

On the North Danes fastened
A terror of anguish, on all of the men there
Who heard from the wall the weeping
BEOWULF CANTO XII

For we struggle not against blood and flesh
But against the Rulers... the cosmic powers
Of this Aion's darkness
EPHESIANS VI:12

C·P·SERRET⸴
GRENDEL
VVEPT⸴
I.

★

N EMESIS WAS A YOUNG WOMAN. She'd pursued me to the seat of my exile, implacable and adamant.

—I require your keys.

I looked askance at this unglossed demand, and she read from her brown agenda:

—Three-five-three, delta. It isn't in the key locker, and Doktor Stender said it might be your keeping. I have an object to place in storage.

Amid the BBC accent, her shibilant *Shtenda* rang German. I said,

—Mine's a copy, but the original should be there. And that unit's for West Asia, not Egypt; are you sure… ?

—Quite sure.

Her condescension was incensive, almost daring, and I'd seen neither smile nor frown trouble her Instagram lips and Liz Taylor eyebrows, the hands holding her leatherbound papers as young and soft-looking as her face. Of course, we hadn't shaken hands; she'd ignored mine the one time I'd offered the courtesy, staring up at me like it wasn't there.

My fingertips pressed to my brow, I asked what it was, and she said,

—A figurine. It's in Receiving, and Doktor Röhm asked that I archive it.

—If it's West Asian, I'll take care of it. Receiving should've notified me in the first place.

She had a particular talent for looking down her imperial nose in the face of any differential in height and stood her ground as I rose from my creaky chair. Though she was taller than average, so was I.

The first sight of her had struck me – she was striking. Blue-chip. Twenty-something. Glasses a bold stroke framed by dark hair, her clothing quiet but expensive. She stood very straight, speaking to Mikkelsen within the skylit brightness of L3, no hint of deference – all the earmarks of a gallery consultant, the in euphemism for sales. The big ticket type. Some major acquisition in the works.

Persian, I'd've bet, walking by and away – I'd've bet a hundred lira on it and lost. But something stirred from its long dormancy, like a doubled pulse within my chest, and creeping fire illuminated the golden snapshot within my mind; till impelled by unwonted pressure, I shut myself in a private restroom and voided it like nausea. It wasn't till Röhm made the big announcement at the curators' meeting that I grasped my mistake.

The major acquisition: Doctoranda Maaike van Leeuwen, Associate Curator of Ancient Egyptian Arts. She floated in on the magic carpet of a new mega endowment, her ostensible foreignness courtesy of the Dutch East India Company or something current day like prescriptive fillers, Botox, and tanning sprays. Röhm gloated over her, and Mikkelsen waxed rhapsodic: a genius, she said a dozen different ways, and a coup for the Institute and its immersive near future – *immersion* the curatorial buzzword of the moment.

A new star shining over the Two Lands, Van Leeuwen had tailed me into West Asia and ground my underfunded efforts under heel – her wingtip's block heel. I'd brushed off her unsolicited critiques and maintained Minimum Safe Distance in the weeks since. She'd rated one of the two vied for corner cubicles, and even I'd caught the grumbling as desks were reässigned to accommodate her. But rather than leave her to that penthouse view of the historic college campus across the way, Röhm had offered up a spear, and Nemesis came to poke the bear.

She was gamine-slight in a sleeking black ensemble that showed little skin, the kind of urban chic that fit any blue-chip gallery in the city, not my shades-drawn office with its antique keyhole shelving and the dusty flat of the abandoned desk across from mine. Her blocky black glasses were a distraction from the exquisite delineation of her facial bones – I didn't have to like her to admit it. She could've been one of those Iranian royals in exile but wasn't; it might've been easier to accept her imponent manner had it hung from a Pahlavi tiara.

—Do you piss on the door? It's my responsibility – or do you feel the need to supervise another curator?

—Lead the way.

—You're joking.

I gestured at the open doorway behind her. It might be petty, but sometimes you have to face Nemesis and take one on the chin. I followed her out into hospital-white halls and the tonal discord of her fresh-from-the-beach fragrance; less department-store floral melon than niche iodonic mist, ozone, and the seaweedy wash of an ebbing tide – I bet it cost a fortune.

The conservation labs on L2 would be subdued with library-like activity, leaving L3 near-silent with shut-in administrators and empty cubicles. She fell back beside me despite my intention to stay a step behind.

—I have a few additional notes regarding West Asia if you'll allow me to finish this time.

—Assyriology, I misspoke in irritation – ancient West Asian art as a whole – is a different ballgame. We don't enjoy the lavish funding Egypt inspires.

—Then find more funding.

—You sound like Röhm.

—She's correct.

—Then what's the secret of your great funding success?

—Americans are fake. Appeal to the pretense, to the mask – make it about them – and they can't say no.

I gave her a considering glance as we reached the elevator. It would be worse if she was interesting.

—And Europeans? I prompted.

—Heritage. Patrimony. But if they wear logos, I treat them as Americans.

The elevator was empty, and I squeezed in alongside her waifish Audrey Hepburn frame and her overweening Dutch Superiority Complex. Maximum capacity: thirty-five hundred pounds. We descended in pressurised silence, the first plunge of the bathyscaphe into the deep. Next, the long fall into darkness.

L1 was lightless, other than in bleached fluorescent simulation, and as white and antiseptic as the floors above but with wider windowless corridors and slate-blue doors.

Apropos of nothing, she asked,

—Have you followed the murders?

—Pollock? No more than I've overheard.

—Pollock? An unlikely attribution; he's been dead for sixty years.

I shrugged.

—It sounds like the so-called art in our M 'n' C alleys. Abstract Expressionism with entrails.

—Judging by the leaked photos, there's a pattern: some mosaic structure or message.

—Conveying?

—You tell me.

The last was as humourless as the rest. THE GRINDHOUSE KILLER promoted by the press had staged over-the-top levels of exploitation gore across the city. A half-dozen works were discovered in as many months, multiple victims each; short odds on a pair of psychos painting in tandem. It was more than I needed to know.

A grey plastic cart awaited near the double-doored entrance to Receiving. A rainbow sheaf of mixed papers and a prone statuette of strange green luminance in a numbered ziplock rested atop it. Accession of anomalies followed the Institute's standard practise, but polaroids replaced digital photos, and paper forms the electronic ones. Unindexed, offline, and unsearchable other than in person, anomalies disappeared from the international catalogue and faded from memory; for it had to be anomalous: Δ353 was the Davy Jones' locker of ancient West Asian artefacts outside the story.

Van Leeuwen brushed her nape-length hair behind her ear and said she'd sign it out. She stepped inside and, released from the magnetic joinder of her earlobe and jawline, I flipped through the papers, which appeared incomplete, with key signatures obscured or missing. Then there was the fishman statuette, of which we had three good examples on display, but this was one glasslike, if subtranslucent, rather than clay. Glassmaking appeared in Mesopotamia some fifty-five hundred years Before Present, but the earliest glass sculptures I'd seen were Roman, thirty-five hundred years later.

Digging deeper, a construction project in Regensburg had unearthed it among a number of now-authenticated Caroline artefacts. Exploration and excavation of Mesopotamia hadn't begun till the nineteenth century, placing the object too far out of place and time to have been looted in the Crusades.

München had decided it was an unsigned contemporary knockoff and sent it to an associated museum in Nürnberg, which had returned it, declaring it wasn't, and further, it was radioactive. Some degree of radioactivity in objects wasn't un-usual; we had protocols, as would Nürnberg. The excuses had piled up as it shuttled back and forth, then across the Atlantic, leaving me with the hot potato.

A unique geometric take on the common 𒀭𒉣, abgal or "sage", sculpture of a two-faced fishman, a half-dozen inches in length. A grotesque in the style of a man merged crown to ankle with a giant carp, only face, hands, and feet protruding. Its beard and scales had been cast or carved with sharp Deco angularity, and a line of familiarish but unrecognisable logo-graphs descended the flat of the spine. I lifted it and breathed smoak, heavy, on cold and damp air; there were screams, howls – I couldn't make out the words – a great pillar of fire; and antlers, proud and crowned with dozens of points, stood black against it. Then a horn shrilled and shivered my spine, and Van Leeuwen's voice echoed hollowly at well's bottom:
—Is something the matter? Has it rung a bell?

She was studying me from the other side of the cart, her pa-pers beside the others. Her inscrutable gravitas deepened, an expectant tilt to her head. I set the statuette down.
—Something. It's… it's almost a classic example of the type, but this greenish glass, this amber mottling… It looks like volcanic glass, but analysis indicates synthetic. Not something you see in Mesopotamian artefacts outside of standard glassware or smaller objects.
—An early kiln cast? It's οάννες isn't it?
—Yes, the kinder, gentler monster.
—Interesting choice of words.

"Oannes", she'd said with Greek intonation – -ess, not -ez – and a minute narrowing of the eyes. I wasn't one to look at women like they owed me something, but I returned her unwavering gaze; it was outside her Græco-Egyptian wheelhouse, if nearby. One of two known tablets with the Oannes myth came from the royal archive in Akhetaten, and the third and most cited attestation was written in Greek; if in Hellenic Babylon, itself heir to Sumerian antiquity, as distant to it as republican Rome was from today.

In this story, before the philhellene story, Oannes gifted the means of civilisation – geometry, agriculture, architecture – to Palæolithic Man at the seashore between two primæval rivers, much as Prometheus had gifted fire. And no one could deny we'd gone from Shea's "wolves with knives" to ziggurat builders overnight, in anthropological terms.

⊅✳, *Uan*, now *Oannes*, had been cast as a sagelike divine figure by the ancient historians of Assyria, but in his miscegenated transhumanity, I saw a two-faced trickster. He'd receded with the antediluvian legends of the first Sumerian kings, and as Milton wrote, returned the mermanlike ⅁⊿: "Dagon, his *Name, Sea Monſter, upward Man | And downward Fiſh*", reaping in child holocaust what Oannes had sewn. Euhemeristic interpretation of legendary beings placed you on the outskirts of the irreturnable fringe, but I'd hunted the monsters through myth and time.

—Are we ᴏᴋ? she asked.

Of course, if I stared like she did, she'd take it the wrong way. But her οάννες spoke of advanced Assyriological knowledge; I had to concede,

—We're on the same page. It's all very curious.

—Now that you've seen it, you don't need to come the rest of the way down. Really, I'll bring back your precious key.

It was hard not to bristle at her attempts to put me off. Mindful that I was a head taller, with twice the shoulder width, I was short, saying I'd prefer to, and she left me a step behind, taking nonnegotiable charge of the cart.

The suite of freight lifts was a straight shot from Receiving, accessing the legacy quadrants of the basement level; two that also went up to the galleries, and two that only went down. In a less uptight era, post-frat interns had overlain the original Roman numerals with faux-bronze Greek plaques,

Α Β Γ Δ

but rather than reprimand them, old-boy Administration had reäffirmed classicalist hegemony and made the graffiti permanent. Leaving us the lonely Delta, from the Phœnician ⊲, *dalt* or "door". Van Leeuwen pimped her keys before I remembered mine, and I followed her into the freight cab. Ignoring the glass phallus in the room, we made the final drop into the oubliette and disembarked into the dusk chill of grey concrete: corridors of burnt-orange doors and sixties fallout shelter signs, yellow, black.

In contrast to the spotless, climate-controlled whitespace of the A–B storage, and more in line with the Γ-quadrant boiler rooms, it was in no way appropriate warehousing for anything of value, but where you might hope instead for the unwanted to decay and fall into dust, damnatio memoriæ. Overcommitted bayside warehouses held the bulk of the Institute's collection of 1.2 million *cultural assets*, as they were euphemised, while the alleged anomalies; disputed objects; and confirmed hoaxes of the four geologic continents were kept close – like trash swept under the sofa.

Van Leeuwen stopped at the rough 353 stencilled on a door in Krylon black, and I removed the heavy, shrouded padlock with my double-serrated key. The air was stale from passive period filtration – the gape of an open tomb – and I thrust one hand into the darkness and flicked on the inadequate lights.

The product of fifties colour psychology, the walls were the same questionable shade of teal as my old office chair upstairs, both sullened by age and neglect. Shelving packed the room, and I gave her the crash course: paperwork in the beige cabinet by the door, manila folders in that box on top, and anything hot in the shielded cabinets against the rear wall, per protocols.

She muttered something about naff facilities. I proffered a glorified Tupperware container of adequate size. Instead of taking it, she set Oannes inside, then gauged my eyes with hers.
—¿Julián? Devolverías…

The fluidity of her intonations threw me for another loop. No Dutch Spanish, but the sudden white-water rush of TVE Castellano, a questioning pitch unglossed by even a hint of microëxpression, throwing my name into doubt; she asked that I return the cart, not asking. Then she and her agenda made a smooth exit, and an afterimage glimmered against her oceanic sillage, 35 mm, pivoting in Hepburn's fifties Givenchy and raising a doe-eyed Hepburn smile, but the diaphane vision flickered out – a switch flipped off. Life on the margin left little tolerance for self-deception. No room for illusions of my own creation. My dreams were other.

Oannes was quiescent, submerged in charismatic silence and a plastic bin, and I shut him away for later study. After finishing up, I checked the key locker on L2 and found Δ353 hanging in place – only 340 was absent from the Delta set. Nonplussed, I cleared my head in the solo restroom, Maaike on my lips but unsaid. I flushed what'd tried to take root and washed my hands of it; then I retrieved my jacket in retreat to my smoking spot, out back by the fortified dumpsters, rather than the fumatory stand adjacent to the parking lot.

I squinted against the glare of a burnished aluminum sky. It looked like rain but wasn't yet; the cool autumn air unstirred inside the half-walled cul de sac behind the Institute's wings, where the administrators' German cars lined up like polished piano keys next to a privileged rear entrance. At the heart of midtown, I was alone, my relief silver-tarnished by a bittersweet kind-of regret; if not for Röhm's intervention, we'd not have crossed paths again and, henceforth, shouldn't outside of group meetings. But I'd riddles enough without Maaike – amid our cold-war tensions, we'd come to first names.

An electric snap! and my sigara, as they say in Turkey, ignited. The first inhale elicited a sigh, drawing out any tension and nostalgia that hadn't gone down the drain, Turkish tobacco evoking memories of Turkish earth: one between my fingers, the other ground into my skin. I exhaled a florescent blue haze.

I'd spent most of those days in the vast countryside, in and around smalltown Turkey; a longtime training ground for archæology field schools and home to the Neolithic wonder of Göbekli Tepe, discovered by Schmidt in '95 while I was doing my post. I knew the bright colours of Old Istanbul, so much like Greece, and a pace of life that placed tea first, leaving coffee a postmeal digestif.

The Aigilofling Foundation that backed my position at the Institute operated out of Belgium, and I could've taken my exile in Turkey. I'd blended with the locals and could've learned Turkish. The charism of the Record was always with me – as the glass statuette had thrown charismatic sparks, if not the all-encompassing flame.

The Institute's smog-sooted backside,

a grand edifice of marble and travertine fit for any prince and the fairest monument of Ferrara. Therein, the countess of my regard, born to a foreign princess; and widow to the late Count Ginori.

In nighted modesty and a cropped ruff of no hindrance to arms, I presented my self at a servants' door, as the countess bid all known to the Mysteries of the Kingdom, lest attending upon Her Ladyship's illustrious salon with such divers worthies as pleased her. A young page awaited me, alone, bearing light and clad in scarlet silks and cloth-of-gold, his gilt pomander cloying of clove, amber, and myrrh. A youth on manhood's precipice, of noble demeanour, lion-tawny, and turbaned as the Turk – or so Modarette beseemed. He had remained thus, unchanged, as Rumour had bent mine ear with her indelicate hand, a score year or more. In seeming service to the Countess Ginori, he watched o'er Her Ladyship and my self; for of all the mystes, we two were marked.

The mock page bowed in comely fashion, then spake in piping tones of twisted timbre, tuned to speech other than Man's:
—My lord Baron, Her Ladyship awaits you.

Then grinned he, baring the spiny teeth of his frightsome maw. Such familiarity did not become his office, but 'twas not for me to chastise this fell potestate of the LORD. In the absence of any witnesses, I made proper but secret deference.
—Your Eminence, I shall follow.

Modarette needed no light, and the lantern he bore was but Courtesy for my self. He led therefrom through black passages and narrow stairs unto a candlelit parlour that Her Ladyship reserved for certain intimates of which I was pleased to be accounted. 'Twas well appointed and rich in allegoric murals impenetrable to the uninitiated, disclaiming the Papal ostentation of the near salon, but such was the price of princedom.

I knew not if His Eminence feigned breath in mortal semblance, but on providing me with a suitable cup, he returned to the entry and held himself in immortal stillness, and within dancing shadows, the Numen shone forth from his eyes, for dusk unveils light. Her Ladyship should not fly to my side but arrive in proper course, and on me fell it to rest in readiness on the swift call to arms. Not to wait but to watch. I was without accord of Messire defunct Castiglione, who would each cavalier have cut short and fashioned a coxcomb, and every capon a Fool well roasted. 'Twas not for me to furnish Her Ladyship's table – my fathers exalted baron by the sword. Every gentleman knew IL GALATEO, but the cavalier was no player in courtiery, nor the countess an amoret to lead by the hand but a prince of Wit and steely temper.

I betook me an armless seat to my blade's unencumbrance,

the steel-framed antique better fit for some dowdy display of Americana at the Smithsonian. Creak! a jolt harsher than startling awake mid-dream; my heart pounded like I'd sprinted upstairs from L1, and I gripped the armrests against passing vertigo; against the elastic ripples in the here-and-now, till the quieting waves stilled. A familiar withdrawal but disorienting every time.

Charismata were more vivid than dreams: an oversaturated Ozlike Technicolor, the scents like curls of smoke. And time dripped or gushed out of the schism between heartbeats, and sometimes I fell through that gap to resurface downstream with the shock of breaking glass.

There was no doubting the fundamental prosëity of the Record, nor the chapters of other lives granted me in the grace of perceivance, of direct knowledge through perception. A charism not of prophecy but of the past, reaching back into thoughts and languages long dead. But once grasped, the tableaux shattered, and words blew away like dust – if dreamlike in that regard – leaving behind image and feeling, names weighted with meaning, and phrases in familiar tongues. Here and there, a diamond in the sand.

Or a handful of knives twisting in my gut: I'd taken no notes of what I'd seen in two failed attempts where I'd vomited on my first few scrawled lines, all the way down to gasping bile. There was no record but the Record – I could only see, feel, and know. From the simple life of a scribe, sitting crosslegged while pressing a stylus to a palmful of clay, to the cutthroat lives of hard men armed with stone, bronze, and iron. Fragments. Forgotten stories.

I could've pursued javelin from my undergrad track and field scholarship into an Olympic bid, but who was to say if it was latent talent or muscle memory brought back from charismatic saturation. It became an uneasy question, dripping blood on my heaped laurels, and I shied from fencing and the other combat sports, anticipating I knew too much there as well.

As I did the savagery of maneating þyrsas and their insatiable yearning for the human. The Old English þyrs, or "thurse", had followed me from an English Litt. course; for þyrsas, the raveners that walked on two legs, had been with us from our earliest legends. BEOWULF had unleashed a firestorm of charismata I couldn't forget too soon – waking nightmares of stalking old-growth forests, jungles, and dank alleyways; of places I'd never been or seen; of blood and screams.

But Modarette was no savaged þyrs, no berserker in torment, but deliberate, dolllike, and terrible… For the first time, my charism had revealed the face of the Other or one of their instruments on Earth. Not the chimæric metaphor of a clay fishman, but an incarnate power like Oannes, walking among us in Renaissance Italy, a short stone's throw across time.

Short enough to be on my heels or looking over my shoulder. I'd concealed my ongoing research into the intercession in civilisation, the enigma of the Record itself, and the Unknown Gods of our long Palæolithic night – of things, which in their aseïty, predated terrestrial evolution. But to stand in Modarette's presence, even by proxy… I could still feel him gazing back at me with abhuman eyes, a chill prickling my skin as if the centuries were no bar to his sight. I sat back and h'mfed, alone,

an indecorous exhalation, my hand rising in alarum from the balcony's balustrade, but the countess noted it not, taking snuff from a vermeil spoon whilst the false page presented her the salver. The fashion had come late from France, from the de' Medici queen, Catarina. It stung the inner chambers of my nose, and I knew not what virtue lay in it. The countess, too, sneezed, again wondering me.

A choral fluting rose from the edge of the garden lagoon below, unlit by the beclouded crescent moon, akin to the windless air of a wetted wineglass rim, massed in threnody: the embittered tears of our wintry prisonment. Serpentine writhings seethed at the edge of black water and failing lanterns' light, beckoning me, offering to draw me down to the Abyss in an ebon embrace. A vesper calling me home.

—Baron Orlandi, the countess called. Is not the choir all I said?
—Few are so blessed, Your Ladyship.

Lifting her heavy skirts of silver brocade and purple of Tyre with freed hand and filled cristallo glass, Issota, the Countess Ginori, did join me. A high, noble forehead; and skin of pearl;

her hair was the golden shade the ladies of Venice wrought by artifice, bound close and netted with the lesser pearls of the sea; and all the colours of the sea were bound within her eyes. She had a broad, smiling mouth and a merry tongue to match it:

—Blessing and curse are a coin, two-faced, and the proof of a coin is in its bite. I yet have teeth.

—Then mark I the Envy of Cosimo il vecchio: unable to chew his bread, dipped it in wine.

—What Envy in Man whose ears hear not and whose eyes see not? Dost thou not hear, my good Guiliano? Canst thou not see?

—I hear... I feel the Garden's slumbrous yearning, but Heims gives no relent. I fear... I know not what, and of late, my dreams are troubled.

—I am yeared twice thy score and two and can say Naught but our Summer comes not in time corporeal but in the Aion's span, and as we bound to mortal span from mortal span shall, in faith, know its fullness.

Countess Issota raised her glass, not to cloud-veiled Night but beyond.

—There, it approaches the intersecant of the spheres, a deluge; it comes but is not near. Not for such as we are now, but to the Rulers a day, the scent of rain on the blow. Be not out of quiet then, for all shall come to pass.

—What inquiet in eternity by your side?

—Have I then some small part of your Love?

—Were I a peer of Charlemagne, I serve no other lady.

—Not the Lady Moor?

—Fie. Such use is uncouth in mine ears and ill befits your esteem, madam.

—Maidens long – the one in skirts, th'other scabbarded. Her beringed finger alit upon the watery stage below:—Have not the very sirens sung the tale of Love at leaf-fall? On her coming from Florence? On a harvest-tide ball début? Did not the Moor, by her favour, smite and make prize Orlandi, as the Cathayan smote Orlando? Greatest peer of Charlemagne?

—Fie on it.

—There, sir! On your sleeve, an ermined heart, and against me, you take her part. O for youth's bloom that I might rival her. The Florentine has her champion.

Though played the Fool, I could not take up Her Ladyship's

hand. She was not my fieffal lord, yet above her, there was none, and in the eyes of the LORD, we were bound, beyond Death, unto the Aion of Aions. But fie on "Moor"; it rankled me. At his station, Modarette grinned.

COULDN'T SLEEP. The box beneath my bed emanated pulsing gravitation, and I rocked over the waves in a deadman's float. The vibrations were soporific yet electrifying, reëvoking the crystalline fluting in Issota's courtyard: a temporal crescendo that stretched and buckled the walls and windowpanes – they thrilled up my spine and over my skin, filling my skull with aching registers that bled into star-spangled colours of fire and livid flesh. And as trafficked midnight arrived at silent, small hours, I rose, dressed, and drove back to the Institute.

Blue-white light revealed a visage reaved from ancient ruin; the so-called neoclassical façade grimaced its flensed horror, hollowed by underlit shadows. Broadway's sparse streetlamps were wide of the unbroken treeline along the blacked-out river, a dark passage through earthbound constellatory lights. Parking was at its easiest, but a chattering stridulation troubled me as I walked from my car: *skree skree, skree skree.* Across the way, a blot flowed beneath drowsing trees, hyænoid but eyeless, where a predator's eyes might flash green in low light. My midnight inkblots were an old illusion, some congenital fault with my night vision, but that sound reached for me through dim nightmares, ill-starred and chilling, nearerby. I kept my pace steady and skipped the cigarette. Security checked me in with a wordless nod, accustomed to my insomnia.

Seeking repose in West Asia, I bypassed the baffling mass of paired papyrus columns, the talclike scent of plaster and cut stone betraying the changes begun in the templed complex of Egyptian galleries. I envisaged an underworld of pharaohs begging by the side of the road, robbed of their riches in and after antiquity, COMING FORTH BY DAY in rags. I'd shied from the relics of Egypt since my fifth-grade teacher and her New Agey adoration of the heresiarch Akhenaten. Irradiated by THE NAME, he'd yearned for the posthuman. Aten? The sun was but a shadow.

It was with an earlier king that I sought audience: Gilgamesh, on our featured relief in stone at the far apsidal end, a savaging lion clamped underarm. HE WHO SAW THE DEEP had beached me here, and I passed among the archipelago of plinths and glassed displays. Gilgamesh the slave, I said aloud to gypsum laid bare by time, and my words vanished as if unspoken, less than a murmur beneath the twenty-five-foot height of the gallery ceiling, a vast white cell divided by deep pools of chiaroscuro.

At the bottom of Oannes's trick gift box of civilisation, we'd found *empire* and fashioned the bronze spear and axe of conquest. Akkad became the first multilingual, multistate empire in our untaught story – after Sumer's fledging attempts at empire building had floundered – followed by a succession of empires too long to list: Assyrian, Babylonian, etc. On my appointment, I'd found the galleries a senseless grab bag of objects from the Ubaid period to the less-than-ancient Ottoman.

I'd undertaken a new syllabus, delimiting my galleries to foundational West Asia. *Foundational* was a broom, a buzzword used to sweep pre-classical – read, *pre-important* – antiquity into the Academy's corners. I'd used that broom to fend off classicalist objections from Röhm and the other curators, then swept everything after the xenonymed ἀχαιμενίδης, "Achæmenids", into storage and out of my corner. Three thousand years of diverse cultural heritage remained, requiring my narrative frame. It was a curatorial challenge to someone never intended for the job, but Röhm would've signed anyone that brought money into the Institute – even an archæologist on the skids.

Most art curators saw with different eyes and spoke in fantastical psychoëmotive terms of what they'd been trained to see. I was disinclined to dress naked emperors with interpretive phantasmagoria. Some archæologists wore the double crown of curation for national museums that backed in-house expeditions and had learned to spin postprocessural narratives for the curatorial milieu.

Outside, dawn reached my reverie from on high through squinting clerestory windows, and the key in my pocket drew me back to Δ353, the penetralium of my clandestine research. I left the door ajar to circulate the stagnant air, set my jacket aside, and rolled up my sleeves.

I donned gloves before removing Oannes from his doored cabinet, musing on the transglacial Holocene deluge that shrank the surface of the Earth, of those who retreated from a rising sea to settle the lagoons of Sumer's twin-river flatland, its rich flood-silted soil so like the Nile delta far to the northwest. I removed the abgal from its bag and stood it on end. Who knew what rose from the brackish reed marshes of ancient Urim? – or what else was stirring after the Pleistocene's two-and-a-half-million-year cold sleep? Like that chantant dirge four hundred years ago, yesterday… a few hours ago… Wanding Oannes, I shook my head. Some things are best left unseen.

The Geiger counter returned 4.2 millirems: I'd have to limit my exposure to half an hour or less. Under magnification, the matte surface was smooth and free of tooling marks, microfissures, or wear. Even the archaic-looking glyphs were crisp and undamaged, but they matched nothing in my knowledge of early cunéiform logography – the core of my PhD in Assyriology. They were alien to Mesopotamia or bullshit.

Under ultraviolet, the amorphous chartreuse, amber, and verdigris glass fluoresced an eerie yellow-green, confirming the presence of uranium. I rechecked the papers: München's fission-track dating reported thirty-two thousand BP, which would've made it rather young volcanic glass looking for an active source, but it lacked natural glass's occlusions and irregular structure. At all points, anomalous, and they'd marked the result invalid. I'd tracked the mystery cults that'd blown from West Asia like drift seeds, seeking lost altars to ἄγνωστοι θεοί, the "Unknown Gods", and their misshapen idols, and this cult object had come to me like an ominous gift with a dubious Hallmark card.

Not far behind the erect Oannes stood the drawered cabinet that'd held his perilous lyric, IN THE COMING OF SUMMER AND LIGHT, till I'd smuggled the tablets and their paperwork out of the building. Of fourteen per the colophons, eight baked clay tablets and forty-four fragments had survived; at their heart, an unblemished 𒀭𒌍 𒈨𒊏 𒀀𒃲, TABLET OF FATES. A mythic token of power bearing THE NAME in sixty syllables. Like all such names, it was an invocation, blasphemous and apocalyptic. The power of the beginning and the end.

Sumerian epigraphy placed the tablets in the Early Dynastic period, thirty-six hundred BP, in line with the limited contextual data on file. I'd drawn, transliterated, and translated it in secret. The unreleasable TABLET OF FATES aside, the manuscript was unpublishable as anything other than the driest fiction or fodder for Dänikenian alien originists to build their conspiracies on.

The mathematical proofs preceding THE NAME were dense and well beyond my level but, according to the grad student I'd bribed with pizza and Pabst, appeared to describe the geometry of sixty-dimensional spheres.

—An interesting conjecture, they'd mused over a beer, like poetry missing a few lines. Do you mind if I play around with this? I don't think anyone's gotten this far with sixty-spheres.

—Knock yourself out, I'd replied, but no attribution: it came to you in a dream.

Even now, mathematics was a blind spot in Assyriology. We weren't palæomathematicians by training, and nothing was more challenging to interpret, as I and my first grey hairs could attest. Those multidimensional proofs must've appeared heretical to the Euclidean faith of the nineteenth-century archæologists who'd unearthed them, far from the sea, at Sippar. One "eternal city" among several, Sippar was a cult centre of ⊢⊢, *shamshatu*; "the radiance", or "sun disk", guised behind the god Shamash.

A number of tablets in the Assyriological corpus attributed their authorship to Oannes, and they are typically studied as apocrypha, but my predecessors in Assyriology had locked this particular set of "nonsensical gibberish" away for over a century. With hundreds of thousands of tablets discovered but untranslated, it hadn't been difficult to scrub them from the corpus. My predecessors in curation had upheld the erasure, even after relocating the set from the Institute's prewar storage. Reburied, forgotten – as intended – till I'd opened the drawer like Moses the Ark, though the fire hasn't spoken to me.

Conjuring images of red ziggurats raised over the earth; the perpetual fires of sacrifice; and an everlasting supernal yoke; the remaining inscriptions did not bear thinking of, and I'd stashed it all under my bed like dirty laundry. I'd resigned from the University after defending a similar find, blacklisted from further fieldwork or academic research. The only Assyriological repositories outside strict academic control were private collections – like my deep-pocketed nemeses of the resident Bowen Trust – and large metropolitan art museums – whence the unexpected lifeline of an Aigilofling Fellowship opened the mausolean halls of curation, placing the key to $\triangle 353$ in my hand.

Alone, I'd stolen my first glances at those ahistoric tablets, breathing in their ancient dust, but unable to unlearn what I'd found in them, of a leviathanic Other beyond time or creation, moving unhindered across the outer and inner voids – through what we divide, in our naïveté, into reality and dream. Their abhuman shapes and godforms were only hinted at in those and other proscribed texts, and the metaphors of chimæric representation became clear. Some things are best left unimagined.

Most days, I could keep them and their dimensionless scale out of mind, alone in my apprehension that we'd evolved not with their aid, nor in their image, but in their sleeping shadow. And in the years that followed, I'd begun slowly, too slowly, to recognise my poisoning, drop by viscid drop; that my darkening dreams weren't subconscious Boschian hells but the bleedthrough of the Other; as if the veil between their transcosmic minds and mine had thinned, or worse, lifted. I could feel their drowsing weight as they slept through the final days of the Quaternary Ice Age while the polar glaciers cracked and faded, heralding the return of their millions-years reign over an iceless Greenhouse Earth. Like Atlas, I staggered.

I offloaded Oannes, reshelving him between a medusoid statuette with a vulval starfish face and the wide vaselike body of the primæval mother and a terracotta prism fragment regaling the ordained destruction of Edin by the three great lion-dragons of Sumerian legend. They'd risen in concert by the will of an entity invoked not in name but by the eponym 𒀭, En – or *Belum* in Akkadian – but most notorious in the Phœnician: 𐤁𐤏𐤋, Baʻal. All, in short, "the LORD". A rather Sodom-and-Gamorrahlike last judgement, from what little I could reconstruct – if you added three raging kaijū from a Japanese monster movie. Fire-breathing chimæra were part and parcel to Mesopotamian myth, but I'd found no other attestations for a city named Edin. Given the poor state of the prism, a missing name could've left the descriptor 𒂔, *edin* or "steppes", the only guidepost. I couldn't fathom what controversy had shelved it. Did it belong upstairs on display, or should I smuggle it out like THE COMING OF SUMMER AND LIGHT? Was it part of the story?

Without charismatic certainty, without manifest grace, my unwritten history of the Other would be as paranoid and delusional as any internet manifesto out there. I had no proof and couldn't measure grace in a lab.

There was no one to ask faith of – I was a comet passing

through, unable to match the orbit of family or acquaintances. No Don Quixote, I couldn't but doubt myself, and it was impossible to be sure I was apprehending some dead language no one knew the sound of or dreaming it up. Except that in the moment, I was sure.

I needed that cigarette I'd skipped, and I'd have to show my face upstairs before the Institute opened its doors to the public. I stepped out and aligned the padlock shackle; *skree skree* shivered me from down the hall. A bomb shelter door was ajar between me and the cross corridor, the freight lift, and the dim evacuation stairwell. There was no other way out and no other sound but the throbbing in my ears.

Step by step, I closed along the opposite wall, neck craned. A creaking thump echoed. I froze and waited, listening, then inhaled the cold air of the briny deep, inhaled its wrongness amid sepulchral stagnance and scabrous concrete. Sidling closer to 34… o, I watched a hunched figure, back turned, straighten to a familiar Persic profile. I exhaled the tension, and she glanced overshoulder.

—¿Julián?

—Sorting the rubbish?

I put on a bold face, shoulders squared, then stepped to the threshold, uninvited. Maaike looked at me over the top of her grandiose glasses, chin set, cradling one of those disturbing Atenist pieces in gloved hands: a golden-brown ivory head with an elongated skull, approaching Gigeresque distension, carved from what must've been a fossilised tusk of immense size. A small silver pendant hung on an ultrathin choker chain outside her high-necked dress.

—Not a fan of Egyptian art, then?

—"Thy pyramyds buylt vp with newer might | To me are nothing nouell, nothing ſtrange".

—And how long have you held onto that line?

—Five years.

She didn't smile. I didn't scowl.

—Aren't those Atenist pieces prized above all others? Why isn't it upstairs?

—The context indicated First Dynasty, not Eighteenth, and it was found in situ with.

Maaike cropped her sentence, turning it over in hand.

—It's apocryphal; the style and workmanship are wrong for the period, but the documentation lists it as ἄθωθις, the third king of that dynasty. The first depictions of human sacrifice in history date to his reign.

The last bit of "Atothis" trivia was a non sequitur unless it wasn't. I said,
—You prefer the Greek names.
—My thesis was on the Hellenic influence on Ptolemæan sculptural techniques. I majored in Greek art before specialising in Græco-Egyptian. I've spent a great deal of time studying κοινῆς sources, and I tend to look back on prior dynasties from that perspective. And convention aside, no one born in the last two thousand years knows how to pronounce pre-Coptic Egyptian.

I couldn't help her out. The hymns of Akhetaten had passed through my keeping, but the winds of time had carried them away, leaving irradiant splinters, piercing and overbright. But I could keep up with her overstated "Koine" affectation; it was the celebrated Babylonian hierarch Berossus, who – in his BABYLONAIKA – had attested the legend of Oannes in the Greek of the Macedonian era. I'd distrusted contemporary translations of the Helleno-Latin historians who'd cited him – I had to see for myself – but it was proving more useful than expected.
—What will you do with it?
—This? Nothing without more information. The fossil ivory aside, it isn't First Dynasty; it's far too sophisticated. But neither is it typical of the Eighteenth: look at the angularity of these lines, the geometric planes; it has more in common with your οάννες than with Akhenaten's reign. The mystery merits its display, but prior curators judged it unfit, and I have nothing additional to make a case with.

τὰ μυστήρια τῆς βασιλείας was Guiliano's gospellary thought, and mystery resonated, recalling it to mind: "The Mysteries of the Kingdom". To be learnèd in Greek in cinquecento Italy was far from common, but again, useful. And lucky. Holding on to snippets of Volgare was far more difficult with what remained of my high-school Latin. Unable to get closer, I said,
—Your pendant, Mélusine?

The silver oval bore a split-tail figure in relief and an inscription illegible in the spotty light. Maaike watched me with large liquid eyes.

—ἀβρασάξ.

I'd searched the arcane and occult for sightings of the Other, and I knew "ABRASAX": an isopsephic epithet representing totality: 365 of 365, or dominion over all time. Unique to the μέγας ἄρχων, *mégas árchon* or "Great Ruler"; from Jung's charism, "the thousand-armed polyp, coiled knot of winged serpents" and "hermaphrodite of the earliest beginning." A creepy but common eikon of magic amulets used to con rich Roman ladies in the place and time of mystery religions, rendered as a Roman centurion with snake-headed legs and a roost-cock head. Hers looked to be a bright and new replica, not daring but rogue in its sharp contrast to the bold lines of her curated style. She offhanded,

—O. I do have a few cunéiform tablets purported to be from ἡλιούπολις, found mixed with potsherds and other debris as fill between stone walls. Middle Kingdom. Why they weren't turned over to West Asia isn't clear, but I expect they would waste your time.

No such find had ever been reported in the annals of Assyriology. Couched near the southern vertex of the Nile delta, "Heliopolis" was the birthplace of irradiance worship in predynastic Egypt, the Aten the celestial barge of the original cosmic power, "Atum in his Disk". An irradiant starship, and from it, the irradiate power of life and transformation. Akhenaten hadn't discovered THE NAME, nor had his fathers, who'd established the public Aten cult. The secret had deep roots, and Atenism was its late, if conspicuous, flowering. I'd follow those connexions wherever they led – even under Egyptian earth – but most tablets were mundane: cunéiform letters, contracts, and other trivialities. A ten-lira bet it was something mercantile or diplomatic and as much a waste of my time as an obsolete coin. I said,

—I'll have a look when you have a chance.

She turned to set the bust down, and I left it there; she kept sorting the discards as if I'd left. There was no further sign of the kaijū cricket – some building sound, no doubt, mistaken for what I'd heard outside. I made my discomfited exit without calling it to her attention and sought the freight lift back to L1, caught by the tempest I'd thought spent. At that moment, I hadn't noticed, too in the moment, till she'd turned away.

There was no mistaking this pressure spike at windblown

heart. It was a cold place, and no one lived there. I'd seen spring across the looking-glass, and this was no vernal breeze, stirring late blooms and virid leaves, but a red storm under alien moons, and light would never cross between us. Charismata and Other arcana left no room for everyday enchantment, but I was blood and flesh and pressed the pained point on my chest till the doors opened.

Alone in this, I walked the white halls of the dead amid the disinterred breadth and wonder of our prized Ozymandian follies, the everyday objects we'd left behind, and the treasures we'd tried to take with us. Perspective on my folly. I was outside their comfortable walls and closed-in sky, with no way in.

I got out of the way of a custodian buffing the floor and badged into a rear corridor, heading back towards the dumpsters and my twice-delayed cigarette, when red and blue flashing lights stopped me short: DO NOT CROSS tape and black and white police SUVs penned and obscured my smoking spot, while navy uniforms cordoned news cameras from the cul de sac, press-van antennæ risen above the wall like periscopes. Security and an assortment of our contractors stood idly by, watching the police stand idly by, watching someone taking photos, a new dank odour hanging on the air. I caught rust-red patches on the concrete, a spiralling butterfly speckled with dollops of dried hamburger, and shut the door. Some art-schooler's grandstanding they'd overreäcted to.

Foiled again, I took the shortest path to my office – and my fail-safe nicotine gum – but ran into Röhm leaving hers. Iron-greyed, lean, and desiccated by too many years of air conditioning, she tried to fend me off, her iPad a raised shield:

—There's an emergency meeting for administrators in fifteen minutes. I don't have time for…

I cut to the chase, flanking her along the short walk to the conference room.

—Did you have Mikkelsen's assistant store a new Assyrian artefact that came through Receiving yesterday?

—I don't recall you submitting anything regarding a new acquisition. Your budget this year is…

—I didn't. Munich shipped it here without my prior authorisation – something I intend to investigate.

—And you say I had Patty handle this whatever-it-was?

—Not her. Van Leeuwen; the new one.

Röhm stopped at the conference room doorway, and I got my second hard-look-over-the-glasses of the morning. Like most administrators, she'd adopted the muted librarian mode of the W-2 staff, minus the curators' signature scarves.

—Micah isn't an assistant; she's Associate Curator. And while I did have occasion to speak to her yesterday, I don't recall anything of the kind. What is it, and what happened to it?

—A glasslike figurine: an anomalous artefact recently discovered in a German construction zone. We archived it, but something like…

—The Institute receives more than its share of divergent objects; they hardly merit your attention, do they, Julian? But I look forward to your completed proposal for an Assyrian special exhibition, news of your recent grant proposal to the NEH, and significant progress on your fourth-quarter fundraiser. Leave minor errands to the actual assistants.

—I haven't had an assistant in over a year.

Her mournful froggy face took on a pinched exasperation.

—And given your funding crisis, we can't afford to give you one. But there is some good news: I wasn't going to bring it up until our one-on-one Friday, but as you've mentioned her, Micah has offered to assist West Asia on a part-time Associate basis beginning next week.

"Micah" set my teeth on edge, though I was long accustomed to the inflective blanching of Julián. I enunciated:

—Doesn't Maaike have her hands full with the plans for the new Egyptian installations, et cætera?

—She assures me it won't be a problem, and Andrea has graciously agreed on the loan.

I could imagine Mikkelsen's gracious condescension; she would lord it over me for the duration.

—Be grateful, Röhm continued. Micah's talent for fundraising will be of great benefit to the Institute; we are already beginning the largest renovation and remodelling project this facility has seen since the Second World War. I won't allow for petty territorialism in this matter, Julian; we aren't the only major museum in the city. Now, if you'll excuse me, we can continue this on Friday.

Maaike's "talent for fundraising" meant she'd have top billing in West Asia, galleries adrift a dozen years before my arrival and second fiddle to the Assyrian section of the city's flagship Museum of Art downtown. Museums survived or not on the conspicuous benefice of the élite and the stiff markup on brass nameplates. Per Röhm and the Board of Trustees, fundraising was job one, but nothing had changed since the nineteenth century: enspelled by marble and megaliths, most donors and trustees remained aloof to the clay and bitumen of ancient Mesopotamia. Massive stoneworks, mummies, and denuded statuary dominated the popular consciousness and claimed lions' shares of the available antiquities funding. It's why Mikkelsen had Associate and Assistant Curators, and West Asia was a one-man show.

I splashed cold water on my face in the nearest men's room, but alas, it wasn't a dream. My misplaced human frailty aside, a Hellenist perspective was the last thing

nose to nose, Maaike's back to the wall. She was undaunted:
—You're easily amused, but you won't get what you want. Not now. Not ever.

Another blackout. Another leap forward in time, but I was taken aback, a full step back. I couldn't imagine what I'd been saying.
—Sorry?

Unbarred, she brushed past me and gestured towards Windexed windows.
—I must insist the shades remain up. Even Doktor Röhm doesn't have a view of the atrium.

As if I hadn't been menacing her up till that very moment. I wasn't one to look a gift horse of Diomedes in the mouth, but that didn't follow, no matter how you sliced it. At a loss, I said,
—There's too much glare on the monitors.
—Then we'll rotate the desks and shift the shelving. Now.

My office had become a pool of silvern brilliance streaming from the open-air atrium. For the first time, I could see into the lucid brown of her eyes, not doe-eyes but awake and focused on me. Affectless or unaffected, she remained poised, imperious, and peremptory; whatever discussion had ended had ended – hers, the last word. We'd moved on.

It wasn't even my office anymore. Years of dust had accumulated on and around me; it clouded the air with nose-tickling

particulates amid the fresh kick of Lysol and undernotes of the
sea. She or I had stacked boxes and crates of books and who-
knew-what-else beside already bared shelving. Less the Associate,
I'd lost half my office to Mikkelsen, and the soreness between
my shoulder blades suggested how much of the heavier lifting
had been mine.

Had I been alone, I'd've scanned through my phone, looking
for clues to myself: where I'd been the past week and what I'd
done. Who I'd pissed off this time. But Maaike hadn't moved
beyond arm's reach, mediæval eikon–lit centre frame, the silver
light transmuted gold; she was too close, now, for comfort –
an adolescent swell stumbled in, then took too long to realise
its mistake. Sleek and chic was her logoless brand, even when
turning my world upside down; a nacarat neckerchief banding
her throat, no anguiped in sight.

I'd dismissed her input twice, and with Röhm's backing, she
could reset West Asia within her Hellenist frame and add another
laurel to her cv before moving on. While working as a curator
served my purpose, curation had never been my end. I'd bide
my time and, facing her backlit halo, answered,
—You don't compromise much, do you?
—Why would I compromise when I'm right?

I 'D SEEN THE DESERT-PALE ZIGGURATS as a man before finding their photos as a boy – watched the sunset over Etemenanki. I'd dreamt of difform colossi and spiring temples, long forsaken, encroached by dunes of methane ice; the sulphurous warmth of violet oäses; and mercurious lakes that rang, howling, with emanant screams. The lodestar and the northern lights of my childhood wasteland. Unlike the Barone Orlandi, I was alone in this, and only silence kept and watched over me.

I couldn't say why I'd turned to archæology, chasing the "Sea Monſter" into the salted earth of lost Sumer. No Ahab, I'd no javelins for Dagon. Nor was I built low to the ground for all that digging. There was no money in it, to my mother's chagrin, and little in the way of celebrity short of finding the next King Tut. Fat chance, unless Maaike's tablets were a treasure map.

Putting my desk between us, I sat, then adjusted my monitor's brightness all the way up, offering,

—Anything else?

She proffered the open end of what looked like a roll of over-sized mints. Whether applied or innate, the indirect sunlight enhanced the olive tone of her skin, as it did the clear colour of her eyes.

—No thanks, I said.

Maaike didn't take the hint; staring with sphinxlike patience, she waited. I took the hint and removed one: it wasn't the tongue-piercing sting I'd expected. Less breath mint than minty candy. She placed the blue and white roll of Wilhelmina's on my desk, then put her hand out.

—I require your keys.

—Didn't we already do this?

—Your keys for West Asia. All of them.

I allowed myself the sigh.

—Check the top right drawer of your desk. The last assistant left hers there.

—These are complete?

—Well, I don't have a key to the secret room where they keep the artefacts from ἡ ἀτλαντὶς νῆσος, sorry. But your pendant will get you into our mystery cult lounge; try to remember it tomorrow.

Her look was sharp – an exaggerated, feline blink from the blinkless. Either she was humourless, or I was, or my pronunciation of the mythic "Isle of Atlas" really was that bad. She did that head tilt thing.

—Droll but dangerous. This isn't a private conversation.

I threw in the towel and apologised, sorry for even trying. Policy kept nonglass office doors open at all times, and no one had approved facilities funding for a glass one – thus far an administrator perk – but overactive passer-by imaginations couldn't misconstrue anything I'd said.

Maaike fished down the second-buttoned throat of her blouse to bring forth a mithril flash. She'd worn the amulet out of sight, which was creepier than before. She tucked it away.

—Be more careful. Please ¶. But I take it matters have become clearer for you.

—About?

—Us.

She was the boss, and I was her flunky. All clear, I said,

—Yes.

The rigid perfection of her posture may have relaxed a fraction of a millimetre, or I imagined it. Either way, no warmth, no smile. She said,

—Have you found aught of interest?

—Pardon?

—Three-five-three.

—Not that would interest you, no.

—Please let me know if you do – or if you're unsure.

I wasn't sure we'd shared the same conversation, but I nodded, as did she, before pivoting away. She shelved books. I investigated a week's backlog of emails.

The one thing Maaike hadn't moved was my boarded print of Redon's OANNÈS: MOI⁄ LA PREMIÈRE CONSCIENCE DU CHAOS⁄ J'AI SURGI DE L'ABÎME POUR DURCIR LA MATIÈRE⁄ POUR RÉGLE, but it now hung behind me, where I couldn't see it. She'd reduced me to staging, from her seat, and above her empty chair, Klee's unsettling WASSERPYRAMIDEN. Her addition.

She closed the office door, then leant back against it.

—Why did you leave archæology?

—It didn't work out.

I'd bidden my time. War had loomed over the years up to and following my dissertation on PARALLELS IN THE DEVELOP-MENT OF PROTOCUNÉIFORM AND PROTO-ELAMITE, awaiting news of the destruction of UNESCO sites in Syria and Iraq by one side or another in the perpetual struggle over Mesopotamian oil. After undergrad field school at Gordion, I'd worked seasonal digs throughout Anatolia – eating dirt alongside the excavators that did most of the heavy lifting and picking up some of their local colour, followed by a staff gig at a dig in northern Syria.

Most of my research was textual, derived from the backlog of tablets in the University's collection and the published Assyriological corpus, and my first book, DEMOCRATIC STRUC-TURES IN EARLY MESOPOTAMIAN MONARCHY, was received with mild interest outside of Assyriology. After publication, I started to organise the Virtual Gilgamesh project, following the open-access models of the Homer Multitext, Electronic Beowulf, and CDLI, to digitise the extant tablets of the epos using Reflectance Transformation Imagery. All to be available online, free of charge, glossed with drawings and critical notes.

I'd begun to wonder if my career would end there, reässembling broken tablets and publishing in pursuit of tenure while caught between charism and the new breed of virtual archæologists who'd never cracked a nail in the field, far short of becoming the next Woolley. But in 2012, the race was on to get in and out in the lull between bursts of gunfire and falling bombs.

My search for Virtual Gilgamesh grants and editors had raised my profile, and I was tapped as Site Assistant for a well-heeled German expedition to an unnamed tell northwest of Uruk, near the dry bed of the ancient Euphrates. The big dig I'd been waiting for. The surface survey by Iraqi archæologists on site suggested it might be a small nonurbanised sanctuary. Iraq's Department of Antiquities issued our permits, and we arrived that fall, one of the first teams in-country since Van Ess in 2002. We came in like buttoned-down tomb raiders out of a spoof action movie, with bad wardrobe and endless crates of equipment. The Germans never lacked in preparation.

They specialised in remote sensing, and after the magnetic survey, our palæobotanist identified the remains of a date grove near several strata of mudbrick structures. Our initial sounding was a gusher, dense with sherds and other objects, drawing us straight down, four meters, to evidence of the Middle Uruk period, six thousand BP; the early days of Sumer, and as good as it got for a specialist in archaic texts like myself. Iraq had banned the export of artefacts in 1932, and at the end of the season, we turned everything over to Bagdad: a laundry list of limestone statuary, glazed cylinder seals, and lapis-eyed statuary. Our job was to document, conserve, and publish.

We returned in the fall of 2013 to gopher holes pockmarking the findspot. Secondary markets in New York and London trafficked undocumented finds in the moneyed bliss of claimed ignorance, and Safe Harbor policies were a flexible back door that allowed looted objects to enter major art museums in contravention of AAM guidelines.

Winter. We'd settled in for the excavation, ferrying in from our dig house in Samawah. A familiar cycle of find-the-trash, sort-the-trash. A fired clay brick from the second sounding appeared to be my find of the season, featuring a keystone inscription in Sumerian, forty-eight hundred BP, Jemdet Nasr period. I drew, then with difficulty, transcribed, transliterated, and translated it: "For Nanaya, his bride, Meskingasher, son of the sun-god, King of Eanna, her temple hath rebuilt."

My reading would be dickered over for years, if not decades, to come, but it was the first evidence the enigmatic King Meskingasher was more than legend, with a possible correlation to Uruk III. "Son of the sun-god" was an epithet adopted several hundred years later by pharaohs of the royal irradiance cult concealed within Atum's temple, then by the all-conquering Alexander. Here in Mesopotamia, styled only by Meskingasher and his direct heir, for whom he'd abdicated by entering the sea, never to return.

The brick would go to the dig house for conservation and photography. The photographs would be wired to Berlin, but I'd have to wait on radiocarbon dating of organics, in situ with the find, before publishing stateside. A set of ostraca arrived at my tent, and as I sorted them, a schism into a Ranger's gun-slinging past cast me from the Texas frontier into the Iraqi evening. Outside my tent, I was alone with the moon and the unchallenged stars of the rural desert night. The trucks had left without me.

Unable to locate the overnight guard, I searched the site with an LED lantern. I couldn't contact Samawah without the team leader's satellite phone or the guard's radio. At a loss, I rested my eyes on a folding cot, then sat up, startled back to wakefulness. A scritchy sound like a cat in a litter box: *scritch scritch, scritch scritch.*

I stepped back out, waiting, my head cocked in the stillness. It came again, farther away than I'd thought. I ducked into the tent for my jacket and the lantern, then to the chase: a loping inkblot and the scritching led me across the trackless alluvial plain, silty with windblown erosion. My footprints were my lifeline back to the dig, a faint ellipsis fading into the murk. Near giving up, I caught the yellow flicker of an oil lamp, looters my first and second thoughts. *Scritch scritch, scritch scritch.*

Turning off the lantern, I climbed the shallow slope of telltale mounds; I had to see for myself. Had they found anything? I had to know. With my heart in my throat, I descended towards the beckoning flicker. He was in white, a luminous body fallen to earth amid a crater of spoil, a spread of small objects on cloth. I flinched at the steel ring of his shovel striking home, at the damage it could do. All to benefit brokers and auction houses overseas. He'd make enough to get by another day.

I couldn't see a vehicle or hear the grumble of camels; he might've split off from a group nearby. It was the wrong thing to do, but I greeted him in my tourist's Arabic, a tremulous raised whisper. He started like a gunshot, raising the trench shovel above his head. I halted my cautious advance and crouched on the slope. Relighting my lantern, I held my hands up in placation. He raised the black-bladed USGI shovel higher. I could see the whites of his eyes, the fear. I pulled a sheaf of twenties from my wallet. The Iraqi government was deprecating the U. S. dollar, but they still spent.

Among the sherds and other detritus, a single largish tablet had survived the shovelling. My pronunciation was worthless, but the money talked. I fled back across the shimmering land, lantern off, the tablet swaddled in my shirt as voices rose, receding behind me. I imagined how much more damage they'd do before dawn drove them away – before I could alert the Iraqi security force at the team's arrival.

The unlit tents silhouetted grey against the flat horizon, a nylon refuge. Light. Magnification. The rectangular, phone-sized tablet had been baked, and after a light brushing, the inscriptions were clean enough to make out. A tablet of Presargonic antiquity, forty-five hundred BP, incipit THE RUNNING MAN. I read it, suspended my belief, then began.

From drawing through translation, the laborious process had never been less tedious. I didn't work in some feverish frenzy, but with trancelike ease, as if I were under a compulsion of meditative diligence, till I reäwakened to myself, the tent flap fluttering in the wind, and dawn flashing through the gap.

A single palmful of fired clay with a wraparound inscription, front and back, would redefine Mesopotamian literature. Less a prequel to the Gilgamesh epos – if Bilgames in these Sumerian lines – than the belated revelation of his murky origin. Raw and explicit in the Sumerian manner, THE RUNNING MAN revealed Gilgamesh was an escaped slave, "son of nobody, | field-born, mountain raised… "

The twelve-tablet EPIC OF GILGAMESH was a pastiche that combined popular Sumerian poems with regional myths and added Babylonian narrative. The Sumerian king's list described Gilgamesh as the "son of a nomad", but it was a single unglossed line. In turn, the Babylonian compositors had legitimised him, a semi-divine prince born: the son of the hero-king Lugulbanda and the goddess Ninsun.

THE RUNNING MAN had fled the nomadic Guti in the Zagros mountains far to the east, but "field-born" suggested he might've been an Elamite taken from the region of Susiana just east of the Tigris. After the harsh life of a slave, he was little better than a bandit, robbing and raping his way across the floodplain to an oäsis where King Lugulbanda of Uruk's guard protected a rare and sacred 𒄑, mes or "hackberry", tree. In his hunger, Gilgamesh overcame the guard and took fruit and branch; thus challenging the king himself, whom he slew in single combat. Inanna's priestess anointed Gilgamesh king of Uruk, and in his awe of the great city and the temple-mounted ziggurat on the horizon, said,

> My father have I slain. No, by the light
> in mine eyes am I deceived: amongst the gods
> Lugulbanda standeth; for from a slave,
> a king made…

A Sumerian GOLDEN BOUGH to rival Nemi, it was the most important literary find in Assyriology since Smith in 1872. It would send my dissertation advisor's landmark popular work, GILGAMESH: HOMERIC DIVINITY IN THE HUMAN TRAGEDY, back to the drawing board.

The quiet was overrun by the sound of trucks and yammering – gruff, excited, sleepy – in German; Arabic; and English, our common second tongue. Iraq was a dry country; otherwise, there would be champagne. Or so I'd thought, but I couldn't've been more mistaken. Our government overseers from Antiquities and Heritage were less than pleased about the missing guard and my overnight stay on site, and by the time the shouting had stopped, my find faced the team's preheated skepticism, then disbelief. They were professionals. They published. They taught Gilgamesh at university. It was impossible, quite impossible, they said.

I led the team to the looters' findspot, trailing Iraqi security and their AK-47s. There was no stratigraphic record left to speak of, but the Germans argued the warren of badger holes was too shallow for the tablet to be Presargonic, as the epigraphy suggested. Thermoluminescent dating might… They handwaved that away. An ancient fake was their concession; at the absolute earliest, a propaganda piece from the Gutian interregnum – which wasn't without interest but neither revelatory nor revolutionary. A new footnote to the epos. In turn, I suggested the Babylonian compositors were also its censors, wiping the stain of slavery from the hero's journey just as they'd omitted the little-attested Sumerian DEATH OF GILGAMESH and its depiction of human sacrifice.

One overseer countered by claiming it was a contemporary Turkish fake, brought to foist off on a gullible archæologist for hard cash. Many antiquities and accompanying hoaxes were recovered from locals living near a findspot, and innumerable pseudocunéiform tablets had been circulated for two hundred years.

There was, in fact, a small cottage industry in Turkey producing cunéiform replicas for collectors, but original compositions were novelties made by Assyriologists for each other. No one else could read them. One of the Germans – Leichenberg – claimed

I'd made the fakes myself before the expedition and had faked finding it here to promote myself and my fledgling Virtual Gilgamesh project.

The other official suggested it might be an Iranian state ploy to damage Iraqi heritage. Ancient Gutium, after all, lies within modern Iran. He called my visa, and even the dig permits, into question. The Germans rubbished my reading of the Meskingasher inscription and insinuated I'd paid off or harmed the missing guard even though the security team found no trace of him or his weapon. The site workers were caught in the middle and given contradicting instructions by all sides.

It was chaos – and in that chaos, there was one chance. If I was caught, I wouldn't face deportation but an Iraqi prison cell. I rolled the dice.

After a few more rounds of shouting; sat-phone calls to Berlin and Bagdad; and general disruption of the dig; I burned my notes in front of them, claiming I'd smashed the "Iranian fake" – sorry, Iran – and discarded it in the spoil. The officials left it there, but to the Germans, I'd confirmed their story by destroying the evidence.

Little did they know. The tablet found its way into a crate packed with field equipment for the return trip to Germany, then out of a Near Eastern Studies school in Berlin. Nobody saw nuthen, but my erasure was in effect. There were no cold German beers of warm farewell.

I showed myself out, and nothing awaited me on return to the U. S. – excommunicant in absentia, the doors of Assyriology closing behind and before me. My Iraq visa was revoked at Najaf International. The Meskingasher brick was buried in a state vault and left unlisted in the initial publication of findings this year, tainted by association. The heretic, and his heresies, burned. Virtual Gilgamesh came apart at the seams as prospective editors dropped away, and the initial grants were revoked. My next book, MAN AND MUD: HOW CLAY LAID THE FOUNDATION OF CIVILISATION, VOL I. THE TECHNOLOGISATION OF INFOR-MATION, died in the planning stages, as the University Press suspended publication indefinitely.

The tablet had arrived stateside, shipped with a faux bill of lading for a replica, and Customs never gave it a glance. IN THE COMING OF SUMMER AND LIGHT now rests beside THE

RUNNING MAN, and Maaike holds the key to something else unforeseen, either treasure or trash. The odds were against a three-for-three, no bet.

—Didn't work out? she repeated.

—Politics, I said without lying. I didn't get tenure, and you get one bite at that apple. My Fellowship saved the day, or I'd be somewhere making lattes.

She straightened that fractional millimetre.

—Don't depend on them. The Foundation has mysterious connexions, and as soon as we provide you with sufficient funding, you should resign as an Aigilofling Fellow.

—That serious? They're not connected to al-Qæda or something?

—You'll be better off, she dismissed. Think about these strange murders. Something's changed.

It was no reason at all and another of her autocratic directives. It would be ungrateful to resign on less than hearsay, after their proäctive support – after the University made it clear I'd reached a dead end in my field and at their institution. I didn't cross my arms.

—Of course, Your Majesty, anything you…

—Don't, she interrupted. Don't…

Maaike took another moment.

—Should my feelings mean anything to you, never call me that again.

The door snapped open and shivered with buckling vibrations against its bumper, and across the room, the force rebounded – a punch to the heart. Maaike went to her desk and sat with smooth but rigid poise in her also-creaky chair.

In the sudden stillness, there was only the lashing of the storm cell inside, the ache of it, and the void between us – a passage of interstellar dust. I sighed without sighing. Her superior manner must've evoked similar snark for years, especially if she'd picked up her accent in the UK – the few Hollanders I'd met abroad rang American – and Brits were the masters of snark.

I took it on the chin: apologising and offering to buy lunch, and not at the Institute's odious cafetorium, which the staff had called the vomitorium for decades.

—Get me caught up on your CV. Your plans. Whatever you've told everyone else.

Frankly, she could conspiracy theorise about the news with

anyone else, but it wasn't the moment for that level of frankness. She looked past me at our grungy whitespace in need of fresh paint.

—I know a place.

The place was Italian and a little posh for my salary, but so was Maaike. She wasn't an aristocrat but had an air. It was obvious she knew money and the people who controlled it, the odd bird of some old bourgeois Dutch clan, I'd bet.

She ordered wine, but she was a European in a bistro; what else? The wine

was of exceeding fineness, but His Grace stinted not on a good cup; nor the duchess consort, for whom festivity was its own occasion, and all lavishness went before her in train, the candles alone the ransom of a prince. And all the princes and popinjays were come in their finery to disport as to some bacchanal of old; none more than a prince of the Church, red in face and habit, coming forth unmasked.

I had no eyes for the wheeling dancers, and low rouses lay below my state. Certes, made me known to my Marslike fellowes in good cheer, but on descrying the Countess Ginori, I took my leave of them. She was at merriment's heart, and her laughter rang as crystal, attended with all deference by noted peers and patricians; as in all such balls, their masks proved no guise but made greater the pomp and splendour. Waited me apart her party, taking such refreshment in the wine and music as I might, till the illustrissima condescended to take my part.

She dimissed her Court, and I bowed from my station. In her coming, she did Grace me a smile to make Winter yield and the very Alps kneel and doff their caps of ice.

—Ah, Little Flea, I have expected thee.

And in the Glory of her eyes lay Night before the dawning; and therein, arcs of colour leapt without radiance and melody danced without sonance. The Word rang as a shout, then an incandescence, blue-white, and the glistering expanse sprang forth within the interleaving foment of the spheres, and lo! The light was beyond reckoning, and I was seared by a great fire, and on my heart was burned THE NAME, but without breath, I could not speak; and light beyond measure filled me, and it knew me as water knows the vessel, and in it was ecstasy and Passion and

I wept comets in joy; I, the Word spoke and the unspoke Word, and every heartbeat a sonorant thrum, sustaining these Logoi within resonancy and reticence.

And knew me this no countess but entheos, and that I stood in the presence of the LORD. Great Ruler; "nameless, known by many names"; they oracled thus through Her Ladyship and my self, and she should recall Naught that passed hence. Gravely, then, I did bow.

—Dread LORD, have mercy.

They chuckled with Her Ladyship's throat, strainèd and too deep.

—Thy cherished rival is near: her scent doth betray her, but I cannot divine her in this crowd. The eyes of this race are weak, and these circumlocutions of colour... e'en I am confounded, but I have known stranger dreams. Indeed, I possess a store of ravishments beyond thy kenning and shall vouchsafe thee such Revelations...

Laughing, the LORD said, not to me,

—And so ravish my self ¶. I am legion, are we not, Little Flea? Come away, she durst not approach, foolish child. Peradventure, she will choose the lesser path and burn thee from me. I should savour the sting of it, but thou mayest yet sway her to thine end or her Glory.

I followed then, from the masked mob and into the columns' shade, behind the footmen's line, and there they put me to marble before kissing my mouth and, with a sharp bite, did draw forth my blood and lap therefrom. Libations, a rite of the LORD.

—The essence of thy race is sweet. How is it these drink wine and not those under might ¶? Fogh, but this flesh is pestiferous, and I am fevered in the drinking – I mark it upon thee, as well. Come, we will perforce vent this heat, and I take usure of thy debt to me.

We passed thence unto a drawing chamber in darkened disuse, but the candles lit with the wave of Her Ladyship's hand. I, no cavalier then, presst to the nearmost couch with immortal might and made lady's mount, in no joinder but taking. I had it in my heart the countess had been despoiled thus, and my face the mask. Thus was a rod made of the chastity of our division and stomach salted to bitterness, but the lightest of chastisements beside the lake of fire stoked withal by the Church.

By her teeth took they long draught of my wrist, her fine mouth besmeared crimson, and in her eyes, the Numen burned hot, like steel in the forge.

—Fie on these swoltrey loins; they cannot be borne. Fret not, Little Flea, for we collect penance in red coin. Spendst thy self in pearls, as thou wilt.

No word or deed without controlment, we who bore the Mark might not know each other and cling thus as a babe to teat; for under serpent and sun must each take the road of metempsychosis alone to the Tree of Revelations, and the wedding feast will receive us. We knew not of inferno or paradise, but in this pale purgatory should wander till Completion. Then in the Court of Summer, in anointed Authority, guide Man under the radiant light.

Our hundred passages were inviolate, and discourse of such forbid by the LORD; for as Lot's wife, we might not look back but onwards, ever onwards, to the parousia of the Kingdom. Be it, at times, midst aionic travel and travail, we allinëate as Phœbus and Dian, but the direst temptation lay in aurioled eclipse.

And the bastonet chafed, for 'twas not in me to bend, but all Justice lay with the LORD, and as they took with one hand, they granted hard absolutions with the other. And swift or slow came expiations for our trespasses gainst their will; for resiant orc held our hearts in thornsome grip, with claws to turn against us within, in kátharsis. Or in attack without, as a florin tossed, to claim the LORD's due – in offerings of blood and flesh upon the altared earth, and on our hands the rank smirch of it. If not Man in rightful liege to the Rulers, then orc and unrecalling servants of Death – so were we learned.

To my Shame, I lost my mettle, and in the superior seat, they laughed as she ne'er did, saying,

It's time for the curators' meeting. Are you coming?

Maaike waited at the doorway amid funhouse-mirror distortions, agenda under her folded arm.

—O, right, I replied lamely.

Gathering my wits, glancing at my watch, and walking the highwire of vertigo, I joined her in the hallway, a steadying hand against the wall. Another three or so hours cut away. The pace of visions and blackouts was increasing, and I was losing my balance. I needed more than a moment to digest what I'd seen, a breath to gloss a few fragments before they faded beyond recall, and too many resonances were floating up and flaring out.

κύριον, the "LORD", again, and always in the gender-neutral – a point I'd missed before. And that phrase, φοβερόν κύριον, ἐλέησον: "Dread LORD, have mercy." Like the "Kyrie eléeson" well known to Catholics, a ritual response suggesting those enthëasms weren't infrequent or unexpected. First the face, and now the voice of the Other. It took my breath away – theirs down my neck – but I was scrambled and missing something. Something obvious.

But a power above and beyond the creature Modarette had also been in direct contact with this mystery cult in sixteenth-century Italy and their peculiar Pythagorean μετεμψύχωσις, "metem-psychosis"; it cast a spotlight on the abgal from eight-century Regensburg. Something had been passing through the shadows of our civilisation all along, something distinct from the ancient irradiance cult of kings. As we came to the conference room, I muttered about having to wait on a cigarette. I needed time to think. Alone.

—You'll have to quit, said Maaike. We missed the announce-ment during our meal, but I heard someone complain about it afterwards. The Institute's campus, in its entirety, is smoke-free as of the admin meeting this morning. I forgot to mention it.

—That doesn't sound like you.

—No one's perfect.

—Are you sure?

With a sidelong glance, no quirk of her filler-stung lips, she led me into a gaggle of curators gathered around a long table, talking murder. I sat alone, waiting for stragglers and Röhm to bring the group to heel. I'd have to check Maaike's cv later; whatever she'd told me at lunch had fallen into the blackout, and I'd have to fake the rest to whatever bars she hummed. Of course, she sat across from me, with Mikkelsen's set, and kept giving me her profile – in the distance, trumpets. Not brazen but organic, primal, and resonant. Not now, but somewhere there.

I ducked into the safety of my phone, unsure of the Volgare orco, in retrospect. Googling returned "demon" or "ogre" and the Old English orc, also "demon" from the Latin. The Barone had felt intense fear and repugnance of orc ἔφοδος, a violent "attack" incited by possession or external influence; if not an aspect of archontic enthëasm, then something other.

Röhm took her place at the head of the table, and I listened for keywords as the side talk petered out, still following the old speech, from orc to the glossed orc-þyrs or orcðyrs, interpreted by Tolkien as "ogre". Interesting, but off track. I'd my fill of þyrsas, and homicides on the Institute's back doorstep – a very real crime scene – were shaking things up. I set my phone down, a gleaming black mirror reflecting a ghost of me.

Expectations to the contrary, attendance had spiked the past several days, but for the wrong reasons, and trespassing at all hours had become problematic. A typhoon of press and serial-killer enthusiasts had washed in for a post-cleanup peek at the crime scene from the driveway, wall, or gallery windows on L2 and L3, but only offices and Conservation had a rear view.

The Board had voted for a cooling-off period. The Institute would shut its doors for a week, security would be stepped up, and the cul de sac gated. Until further notice, regular staff weren't allowed onsite after hours: we would wrap the work day and depart as a group. The cul de sac itself was off limits to everyone except custodians, security, and administrators – they weren't giving up their parking for anyone. A smoke-and-vape-free museum campus, no exceptions; the fumatory would be dismantled next week.

The nameless, faceless killer or killers couldn't have done a better job of throwing a wrench into my works. Nameless. That cultic phrase, οὔνομα μὴ χωρῶν, πολυώνυμος. "Nameless, known by many names." It was their entheal voice I'd heard; their words already wiped from my charism's dry-erase board, leaving spectral shapes, though I was sure they'd spoken in Latin, not the vernacular.

Raised voices brought me back to the table, a futile rehash at higher volume, protesting this unprecedented weeklong closure. "Monster" was bandied about by those who knew only Man, however depraved at our worst. But I'd fathomed the þyrsas, and sensations of mercyful fleetness remained: a terrible gnawing pain, not in the belly but in the heart, a taloned vortex, chewing, grinding, great gobbets of living flesh swallowthemwhole... I wiped the corner of my mouth.

Why? they kept harping. Why here? How could they not care about how this affected everyone? –meaning themselves. Röhm stated the obvious: a serial killer was devoid of conscience, and, —A monster like this is incapable of feeling, but we are all deeply affected. The families of…

Grendel wept, I murmured underbreath. More a thought than said. I'd experienced thursic tears: a crocodile's tears for the lamb and cold tears for their own irreprievable anguish.

Only Maaike looked at me, and for a moment, we were alone in hard vacuum.

C·P·SERRET،
GRENDEL
VVEPT،
IV.
★

H IS WAS THE THIRD VOICE of the morning:
—Allo? Doktor König?
—Corbín, I repeated for the fourth or fifth time, but
never mind. Do you have any information on…
—Ja, Doktor, ve have no record of a recent transfer to your mu-
seum. Are you certain it vas dis Akademie für Orientalistik and
not anoder? Who signed the transfer, may I ask?
—I can't read the signature, but you might recognise it; if I
could fax it over or…
—Fax? Ähm, allow…

A few sharp notes in German preceded an abrupt handoff
and the fourth voice of the morning. An unpleasant memory:
—Herr Doktor Corbín, please, the prank has yone far enough.
There are no mystery fyurines that vere shipped to your Institute.
Please submit any future inquires through your Direktor. Tschüss.

A dead end and ringing disconnect. A reminder.

Maaike was in Ancient Egypt for a couple days. For me, no
cliff's edge creeping closer. I'd no wings, and it wasn't for me to
fly, but as Gilgamesh, to go under.

I set forth to Receiving. L3 was in its first flush of the morning;
artisans good at handling and caring for art hadn't yet dispersed
throughout the building. I was other, passing through, and suffered no lost time in the elevator down but the boxed stasis itself.
Receiving was as empty, and it took several minutes to locate
Faraz amid the transitional warehousing that held artefacts and
artworks on their way in or out of the Institute for any number
of reasons. He chuckled at something he was watching aloud
on his phone. Urdu? It made no odds. I showed him a photo of
the abgal statuette on mine. He frowned up at me, his brown
eyes a shade lighter than his skin.
—No come in.
—The new curator signed it out last week. Van Leeuwen. Maaike
van Leeuwen, the pretty Dutch girl. I was out in the hallway.
—You see the book? Ask Nasir later. He go airport.

I scanned the logbook near the entrance, caught in that lucid dreamlike feeling. Nothing. Waiting to awaken, I did a walk-through of West Asia. A nod for the gallery attendant; an eye on the drones circling with white antennæ hanging from their ears; and a passing glance for relics of the holocaustic reich of Ashur, self-styled Lords of the Universe. They'd had no idea.

On his return, Nasir told me he hadn't seen the fishman either, and he went so far as to go through the recent packing slips. Nothing. Conservation on L2 was another dead end of expansive whiteness and green doors. No one had gone down to Receiving to process an anomaly. The polaroids had taken themselves.

Leichenberg's word "prank" came to mind, but the glass fishman wasn't something Maaike could've pulled out of thin air or carved up in her free time. I'd seen the sixteenth-century mystery cult with mediate eyes; it wasn't improbable that acolytes remained. Someone could've put her up to it. There was no way Issota's ἄρχοντες, "Rulers", and Modarette had simply faded away.

The return lift to L3 did little to settle my thoughts. Röhm was riding me, but before I could arrange for dozens of international loans, enlist a circulating agency to organise a national tour, and compete for a spot in the exhibition schedule, I'd first have to woo rich old ladies for the money to pay for it. Even funding a fundraiser was more than I wanted to think about, but money was Maaike's game. I was just a pretty face – a moll – to hang on her arm.

On my desk, I found a dusty shoebox under an unopened roll of mints. Three conserved palm-sized clay tablets were inside: one missing a significant corner, the second complete but split, and the third fragmented but collected in a nested box. There was no note, but they had to be the supposèd waste of time she'd mentioned.

Paper. Faber Castell pencils – an affectation of my first season with the Germans. More paper. I began to draw, and unsought and uninterrupted, time lost its way in thoughts of her, our discussion scene to come, and the calligraphy of Old Babylon. Per the colophons, I had three of three tablets on long odds. I continued to work, my nose filled with incense from the salacious rites of Akhetaten, celebrated under a burning eye within the sunshade temples of THE NAME. Skulls elongating after

repeated baptism, they'd sought their Otherness; for it wasn't
solar rays in which they'd bathed, but the irradiance behind the
disk. I knew that light as it knew me.

They'd fallen short of their vision – as they'd depicted themselves – instead become incestuous and sterile in their irradiate
narcissism. I was ten when my charism dropped me into the
thick of their rise and fall. Fifth grade. Too young, it was impossible to shake, and I gazed through the night fallen atrium
window. I was alone but could hear laughter. A coughing, gurgling sound, like a throat cut and filled with blood.

It began, of all things, with the big eighties exhibition of
Tutankhamun's funerary loot, looted first by the reäscendant
priests of Amun from the woman pharaoh Neferneferuaten after
suppressing Atenism. I still had the glossy paperback catalogue
somewhere but retained no memory of the exhibition. I don't
know if my mother took me through the Assyrian galleries on
purpose, as an afterthought, or if it was an accident on the way
out of the museum, but it was there that I was first transfixed
by agate-eyed Gilgamesh.

Unlike many archæologists, Indiana Jones never resonated
with me. No Cyclopian structures were hidden in the river valley;
no impenetrable jungles full of snakes and spiders. No canni-
bals. The biggest dangers in the field were dysentery and war.
Instead, I'd sought to be a raider like Rassam and a scholar like
Smith. Lawrence was one of few adventurer-archæologists to
carry a popular legend out of Assyria – the only one, at least, with
his own movie. Steeped in charismata, I knew the harsh taste
of adventure, of earth and blood, and of war in its squalor and
sublimity. I'd no need of fantasy swashbuckling or so much as
a schoolyard scuffle since

his face struck not by a riding glove but bared fist, the Venetian
cur sent to; him, astagger mongst colours riotous and curry-
favells, his fallen cup a bell to the ears of the Duke's audience
chamber.

Death had seized upon him, and my hand its consummation;
'twas writ on his choleric face – this parrot would contend with
the hawk. I gripped my sword but did not draw; 'twas not yet
the moment, though not one but two seconds stepped forth to
my side: Messires Orsini and Cerchi. The one a fair Achilleus,

t'other an aureate Perseus, no less swart than the Florentine lady of our contention.

Twas a sore point this, these unseemly japes, trammelling the Honour of Leonarda de' Corsi, Lady Companion to the Princess d'Este. "The Lady Moor" spilling from the mouths of sots as too much wine, this strutting Venetian the image of Courage in his base assailments of one made defenseless by her very absence. Yea, the cavalier rises to such need, unbeknownst to himself, as any blade of quality bowed springs true – and to the point – and one flawed in its forging is ever askew. War made no game of gages.

Indeed, hands fell to swords on two sides of the matter, of limpieza de sangre as the Spaniards say, making much of it; for Charlemagne delivered Sicily but not Spain, and long did the Moorish boot tread upon the Spanish neck. But this, our Ferrara, is neither Spain nor Sicily and what then of the Florentine lady and her gilded skin? Do the vernant fruits not ripe thus in their season? Fie on it. Be it the duchy it self, I would make me Coriolanus and lead the Volsci to the town gate. Let these paragons of courtiery hold the wall as they might, and five prove lesser than three.

My blade bared not a hand ere Count Castelli interposed his martial personage, laying castigations about him like a pike, barbed and sore. Brought up short, I released my sword and did but nod to the bold gentlemen at my side. No word need be said. They would call on the knavish Venetian if his seconds did fail to call on mine. Let us settle the matter in some sleepy grove at the verge; 'twas not yet the moment. Turned me upon my boot-heel and

fumbled from my fingers, my forest-green Castell 9000 rolled across my desk, warping like the rubber-pencil trick while the here-and-now shuddered, then snapped back into our familiar illusion of straight lines. Not a distortion in space, I'd gathered, but in time or my perception of time. I was no physicist. I still smelt the vernage spilled on the marble floor, sickly sweet.

It was daylight. My phone screen indicated the passage of hours, not days.

—Is it big? Maaike asked.

The door swung open the rest of the way. She'd dressed to kill. Rosé tweed. Orange shoes. Landing another whale for Egypt, an easy wager.

—Quite slipshod security, she said. I shut the door on my way past last night. You were rather focused and didn't notice me. I thought to give you some extra time before they turned you out, but it must be big if you were here all night.

My rehearsed lines fell to pieces:

—It's the Oannes story. Well, first, there's a creation myth. The first two tablets. The third one – this broken one – is the Oannes story. I can read it, but I'm not finished with the drawings.

I couldn't have garbled it better. She came around my desk for a look without setting her purse down on hers; she wasn't staying. Too close, yet farther away, she said,

—Would that not be something of importance.

A sardonic tone, a nonquestion. Her orange tortoiseshell glasses were seventies style, huge but airy, and blocked less of her face. Snarky? Smug? You'd think she had a translation on file and was waiting for me to catch up. I could be catching up on her nuances or bullshitting myself.

—More so, I said, since it's an Egyptian creation myth recorded in Akkadian. It begins with a creator goddess named Mout – if I'm saying that right. The Oannesesque story describes the arrival of a fishwoman in the Nile delta, "She who is first among fish". It follows the same pattern of teaching by day and returning to the river at night; the same key disciplines: architecture; agriculture; and "numbers", it says, "and the division of numbers".

Maaike leaned closer. There was a sweetness in her fragrance I hadn't noticed before. Pollen or seagrasses. She said,

—They both originate in the delta. Mût was a mother goddess but obscure before the Middle Kingdom. There were a number of regional creation myths competing along the Nile, and within her cult, some early controversy over whether Mût could have been the sole creator of the world without a husband. After the first intermediate period, they married her off to the self-created Amun ¶. "Foremost of fish" was the goddess Hatmehyt. She was the highest god of μένδης, but we know even less about her than Old Kingdom Mût. Unlike the other predynastic cities, μένδης has no known creation myth. In hindsight, one might suspect…

—It was suppressed.

"Mendes" had never pinged my radar. It forced me to look further east, to the Indus and Yellow Rivers, and southwest to the Río Balsas. How many visitors had risen after the Holocene deluge; how many loci of civilisation seeded at fertile junctures, the stories forgotten or redacted over time? But like the fall of Edin, it wasn't clear why these tablets were in △340. As myth, they were uncontroversial – as far as I could see.

—Suppressed, Maaike reïterated, and absorbed. During the Middle Kingdom, Amun rose to preëminence in Upper Egypt, with Mût subordinated to him. Hatmehyt became an aspect of Isis. Whatever significance they'd held in Lower Egypt was sublimated.

—Was anyone else given the rôle of knowledge-giver, like Prometheus or Oannes?

—No; civilisation and all its arts appear ex nihilo with the first kings of Egypt – or so the story goes.

—Then how'd this end up as refuse in Heliopolis?

—One might suspect someone wrote down a story they weren't supposed to hear or transcribed a papyrus they shouldn't have seen.

She put one finger on my scrawl and said something I missed, hung for a moment on the inviting distension of her lips. A diamond sparkles even when you see it every day. I h'mmed? She repeated her question about "the serpent and sun". I h'mmed.

—There are a few lacunæ, but it says she brought the inheritance of those blessed by the serpent and sun: "those who ate not of the fish of river or sea."

—Ah. Predynastic Egyptians saw fish as unclean, but as the population grew, the poor ate fish while the rich abstained – I'm not a fan myself ¶. "The serpent and sun" brings to mind the New Kingdom iconography of the Aten, with its single uræus under the wingless sun disk. Atenistic ideas turn up here and there before the Amarna period, and if these date to the Middle Kingdom, then they could predate Akhenaten by five hundred years, and the myth itself may be Old Kingdom or older.

—That's fair. I'd confirm Old Babylon by the epigraphy. Sixteen to eighteen hundred BC.

—How many extant versions of the οάννες story are there?

—Three. One tablet from Akhetaten, one from Nineveh. And the Greek citations from Berossus.

—And his was a translation for the Macedonians. That's amazing in itself, don't you think, for the origin myth of the earliest known civilisation? Two clay tablets? We'll need to go over it line by line. Let's discuss it later, over lunch, and…

I couldn't say if it pained me to disappoint her or if I was disappointed, interjecting,

—I can't. I've a lunch meeting that…

Her look was sharper, drawn back to me.

—Is it a donor? If so, Doktor Röhm said I should accompany…

—No, no. More of a lunch date than a *meeting* meeting. I'm humouring my mother since she hasn't caught on – if it was going to happen, it would've happened by now. It's a complete waste of my time.

Maaike straightened, frowning, not with her uncreased brow, but in that minute narrowing of her eyes, in the pitch of her lashes.

—Then cancel; this is more…

—I can't, I repeated; sorry, or I won't hear the end of it. It's a small delay. We can go over these later today if Mikkelsen can spare you. Or tomorrow.

Maaike glared down at me a drawn-out moment longer, then stormed from the room in a lightning flash of bougie colours. I exhaled like a slashed tire. She was used to getting her way.

I began gathering the poker spread of papers when a pointed cough interrupted from the doorway. Röhm waited in her funereal best, no Johnny Cash, where I'd failed to notice her. The pregnant pause offering no relief, I asked,

—Was there… ?

—Be careful with her.

I gaped, then rose from my seat, removing my reading glasses.

—I'm not…

—Maintain professionalism, Julian. That's all I'm going to say on the matter. What's the status of the fundraiser?

It was my funeral. There was little recourse but a convenient if vague fib:

—I'm having lunch with someone today.

—Is Micah attending?

—She's busy, but it should be fine. We don't need that much more for…

Röhm crossed her arms as I extemporised, though holding an agenda made that awkward. She lensed the tablets with an evil eye.

—The Trustees toured West Asia this morning and are less than pleased with your progress. Visitage is down year-over-year, and they described it as dingy and demoded and more focused on Assyriological scholarship than art. This is not, after all, a collegiate museum ¶. Given the dramatic progress of the adjacent galleries, they will request a design brief from Micah in the coming weeks. She hasn't been advised yet, but she did volunteer. We expect you to place your full knowledge of West Asia at her disposal ¶. Needless to say, the funding goals we've previously discussed are null and void. The Trustees expect a tenfold increase. Tenfold, at minimum.

—Ten times? They might as well ask for the moon.

—Then bring them the moon. These are competitive times in a new technological era. The MOA is well ahead of us as a whole, and West Asia is our most outdated exhibit. Nothing less than a complete overhaul will suffice, and the new funding goal is modest at that scale and likely insufficient. You'll agree that fifteen or twenty is necessary to overtake them. We must look to acquisitions as well. However fascinating you find those little clay buns, they are not – strictly speaking – art. The viewing public requires something more dramatic and easier to understand.

The near galleries of L3 belied her usage of "art"; a collection of Modern and Contemporary con jobs with less art than a single clay tablet, but there was no way to open eyes closed to the refinements of scribal calligraphy. I said,

—No; Maaike found them in the Egyptian warehousing, undocumented, and asked for my help with interpretation.

—I do not think you have the luxury of time for original Assyriological research, *Curator*, see to the bills. It is time to plan bigger and better. I'll need a written proposal two days before our weekly meeting on how you plan to reach the new funding goal. Ask Micah for assistance; I'll be reviewing it with the Trustees next week.

Röhm stalked off in turn. The rescaled financial challenge was, in short, incomprehensible. Between stress and grogginess, midmorning escaped me. I stepped out early to return home for a shower and fresh clothes, then departed at the appointed moment, five unpunctuated texts from my mother in reminder.

The brunch proved poor on quality food or conversation, weak on coffee, and expensive in wasted time and money. I left the café and wiped a surreptitious hand on my trouser leg to cleanse it of the clammy sweat that'd clung to the slim but flabby palm I'd had, in all courtesy, to shake twice. I folded my jacket overarm and lit a cigarette, relieved but irritated; it'd warmed up for the walk back to my car, and midtown lunch traffic loomed between myself and the Institute.

"Undocumented" was now the story, and I'd have to update Maaike when I got back; in this, at least, together. She got the gap between events and the story, but again, she knew too much for someone without so much as a minor in Assyriology. I cursed losing whatever she'd said at the bistro.

I turned off Seventh. I'd lucked into a parking spot on a cramped side street most might mistake for an alley. Or looking for the street sign, it might be an alley after all. Remote unlock – *skree skree* – I opened the car door – *snap, crackle, pop* – I folded the wrong way, matchstick bones flaring heat, the celluloid hangs and melts through.

OTHING WAS BETWEEN US.

N   *Skin to skin, she moved over me,*
       A numinous breath over the waters.
The rocking waves pulsed and pulsed
Unto a convulsive arch and shaking still,
And I held a kiss to her flushed aftersmile.

I surfaced from the léa in which we'd lain, rising through
a thick foam mattress, into the gloom of my hospital room,
between white sheets and white walls, immobilised by the turn
of the screw gripping my skull, by tubes and wires mounted
to my arms, chest, and finger. A dream – as vivid as the Record
and all too human amid my otherness. Sotted with morphine,
I couldn't feel much beyond the itch of my cased limbs, held
together by titanium pins like a marionette.

A miracle I was alive, they'd said. A hit-and-run, they'd said.
In the insurance photos, my car looked to've been torn in half
with the Jaws of Life, not crushed by an impact, but I was found
across the alleyway. There'd been no need to extricate me. I'd
heard no engine, no squealing tires, just that.

No eyewitnesses, they'd said.

Torn from my life. Unmoored from self. Alone with the tempest, but within the storm's silent eye, a summer idyll. A woodland meadow. The air of pine and a NATIONAL GEOGRAPHIC
view of ice-clad mountains sinking into blue glaciers and green
valleys overhung with serpentine mists. Alone with Maaike,
but not Maaike, Romanticised in a faux mediæval dress, the
laced bodice revealing more skin than she'd ever shown, and
the warmth of a smile as I'd never seen. She'd sat in the pool
of half-unbraided hair, a rich leonine blonde, shades of russet
earth beneath wheaten savannah grasses.

We'd sat for a time within the vast hush, on a silken carpet, red
and gold, embroidered with elaborate but unfamiliar arabesques,
just near each other, our fingers not even touching. The great
castle behind us was bare of pennons, guards, or sound. Not a

spiring Gothic fancy but a moated fortress of dove-grey stone; the dirt road that stretched back beyond it empty of cart or horse; the wood, dotted with apple trees, too quiet, absent bee or bird.

In lucid freedom, I'd reached for her hand and kissed her without inhibition. And in the tumbled, entwining unreality of it, in the heated press of her body, I'd held back nothing. Everything I'd wanted, she was. Everything I'd striven not to think about or imagine.

By grace was I divided from myself – that was the price of it – but here, tied down and drugged like some movie interrogation scene, forced to look. Forced to see, not the Other, but myself and the faërie Alastor that'd sprung from an unwitting Dutch girl. The Waterhouse setting was odd enough for me; I was no mediævalist. No Romantic by sentiment.

I tried to doze, but a technician showed herself in to draw more blood, then a nurse to cuff and poke at me again; then breakfast arrived before I could drop off. I watched slivers of sunlight crawl over medical posters and whitespace, the voices on the other side of the door a ceaseless Babel on the edge of comprehension. A doctor checked in and out, saying nothing new but running up the billable interactions for my insurance.

My mother had come straight from the airport and staved off the first few calls from Röhm. Either way, my part-time Associate Curator of Ancient West Asian Art was at the full-time helm while I was indisposed; she'd stopped by once, all business. In blue, like the dream that'd followed. "Doctor Corbín," she'd said, widening the lightless void, and had rubbed it in: "You should've cancelled."

And as I thought of her, Maaike stepped into my hospital room, and the schism between reality and fantasy couldn't have been clearer – my subconscious and I could argue about it later. She didn't hesitate to approach my bedside, behind the blue-chip veil, agenda in hand.

—¿Julián? Were you able to get any rest?

Her wry note rang off-key. Something lost in Dutch–English translation, or it was me and the lack of strong coffee and sweet nicotine. I hadn't had a cigarette since landing here, but the greater catharsis had subsumed any withdrawal. I'd quit by default.

—Not when someone pokes at you every couple hours. No.

—I'll limit the poking. As far as what we spoke of last time, the plan...

Maaike leant over the bed rail, holding the sheaf at an angle better for herself; she rested her other hand on the rail, recalling to me the sensation of her palms and fingers moving over my bare chest. Her amulet hung at her throat, and I could now make out the chimæric anguiped and the crisp

ΙΑѠ · ΠΑΝΤѠΝ ΔΕΣΠΟΤΗΣ · ΑΒΡΑΣΑΞ

"ΙΑΟ, Despot of All, ΑΒΡΑSAX" without my reading glasses.

In certain heresies, ΙΑΟ was the seven-headed dragon and the least or greatest of seven powers seated across the near cosmos. Some heresiologists interpreted ιαω as an acronym for I-am-first-and-last, depending on which heresy and whom a given sect had cribbed from within the general apocalyptism of the Roman era. Often paired as magic words on amulets or in spells, or as here, an eponym for something nameless.

—¿Julián? she nudged.

—Yes?

—That was a question.

—O, run it by me again.

Her flat look was eloquent. She said,

So you've done after all.

—Done what, Your Ladyship?

I was ta'en unawares by her secret blow but now beseated and presented with a cup. I felt the staring eye of the near eikon, a mural of layered significance: The serpent and the tree, said in secret, "ΙΑΟ and lord almighty." The serpent both coiled the trunk and circled the orbèd crown, as a shepherd's crook, heavy with the red corbozzelo of Revelations, the gilt gloriole behind their head radiated seven rays with pointing hands in terminus, a sign rubricated at each fingertip:

ΑΒΡΑΣΑΞ

And stumbling away from the Garden's edge and unto desolation, the First Man and First Woman, their covered faces turned from the Tree and submission to the lord; the Mark upon their craven brows, and its burthen could not be voided. A fall not of Man but of the earth, and beneath white and fallow blankets, the Garden has slept, awaiting restoration.

It lay upon us, we who have passed hither from Eden, to o'ercome this Winter of our ignorance; to redeem all. And a great deluge shall presage Summer, and in the Garden's bloom, the parousia of the LORD themself.

—You have declared your chaste and noble admiration, said she. You are aware it is nothing less than that.

I withheld an indecorous sigh, the parlour empty of all save ourselves and the crimson page. My private audiences with Countess Issota came often but, for my part, too rare.

—Madam, know you not the heart that beats within my bosom? This bond... ?

Her tinkling laughter o'erran my protestations as cavalry o'er retreating foot.

—None durst forth but as hearts' beat, and thine with a most noble cause! And methought Chivalry all but dead.

—Chivalry is eternal; it is Man that falls by the wayside.

—O, well said, my lord. Well said. Chivalry in its fullest flower, mere but inspired by the Florentine lady. Here Baron, a kerchief for the nonce to wipe the blade of victory.

My sigh defied the chains of Jove, cold Tartarus betokened in my breath, not for my part, but for the despatch of the wretchèd soul in my proper hand. No other fancy would dress such zeal as mine – 'twas come to swords, in no contest but war, and war is ne'er a winsome thing. Yet such was my rôle in this: to kill, and if needs be, to die on it and pass again. So oft a slight proves doughty but stood me not for her Honour, I had none.

The countess raised one white hand, feigning a dolesome brow.

—Alas, the Court of Love is no more if e'er it was but THE DREAM OF POLIPHILUS. In thee alone is it given shape, fallen from the Forms of the radiant sphere, and thou wouldst duck and cry, not I, m'lady, not I! Be it my very walls stand undefended. O distemperate youth, he hies to the maid and leaves the castle to the birds.

—Good my lady, as I have breath, no maid shall languish undefended. This sword but one of your thousand, from the field of Troy to the duelling pitch; till Eden come again, and in Completion, I take your hand in mine.

Her Ladyship shrove her self of mock dismay and, in jesting dispensation, laid gauded fingers o'er heart. Such were her humours.

—I shall pardon thee, mine earnest Giuliano, and thou wilt bear my favour as yon caballarii of old and mete Justice in defense of this damosel.

Stonish Modarette stood apart, eyes closed, and from ungartered stocking, Countess Issota did girt my sleeve with care. We touched not, flesh-to-flesh, as the LORD forbid.

These weighty trifles infixed my bosom, and in plaza and Court came their remembrances in looks, smiles, and words of indifferent matter, but headlong raced the determined day and hither found it self.

Departed we on the dew-trammelled morn, the clacking of cobblestones under wheel our cockscrow, gaffled and flying before the dawn: I, in my silence; my seconds brazen with trumpeting courage; and our leech asleep since the crossing of the Po di Volano. Her Ladyship's coach gave no easement to the saddle of a good horse, but the countess brooked no refusal. Patronage bore its pennons aloft.

Twas a dun land by day, in the mortals' fall; here, without the vale in which Ferrara couched itself: the regimented lines of tilled field awaiting spring. A land of ancient groves and forgotten gods; more, a land of dreams. I was jerked from my cerebrations, each second first:

—Guiliano! Guiliano! A great day!
—The dastard shall see discourtesy repaid!

Gave me good countenance to their cheer, of little heart for levity, but of mind for a ripe and bloody deed. Soon but not yet the moment.

We came upon the lantern-lit field of Honour, neither first nor last, to await the fulfilment of such witness as agreed. I wore Her Ladyship's favour and bid it accompany me into the earth should I fall. My party made pavilion of the hundred-limbed Titan of a great tree, and taking refreshment there, I snapped the smallest finger from a louring bough.

Midst his plausive clowns, the posturing player jeered at me across the narrow glade:

—Think not to escape with some scratch, sirrah; that I will gift thee some mark to woo and win the black favour of the Moor.
—Think not, I returned him, a drop of thy blood will this grove depart. But dog's meat shall be carried hence – I have here the price of it.

Swords flashed free in the flickersome light, out of precedence for our just and ordered slaughter, but shadowed witnesses cried foul of the noble duel à outrance. Only shamed thus did these Court gentlemen bethink themselves, and swords put up, give o'er villainy.

Messire Orsini presented us not a matched duelling set of the strip swords favoured by gallants but ring-guard cutting swords of mine acquaintance, late proved in the Duke d'Este's gun-fouled wars; I, too, a veteran of strife in this and other lives, Death knew but did not hold me. Dawn's rosy quarrels descended, the first volley in vanguard, and the Venetian made his choice.

As reckless with steel as his tongue, he surged forth in all abandon, caution cast aside with Wit. Twas a goodly arm bound to this knave, and not without challenge did I counter his first thrust, for 'twas not in Agrippa's Art to take and not to give. Allayed to the eighth quartering and tempered in the Roman school, I rallied and brought forth a wanton song in ringing Toledan tones to give e'en the Muse pause, and a stirred hush fell o'er the assemblage.

I was in no ignorance of the Bolognese style fit to swaggerers but cut my way through its formulas in a Milanese mathematic of simplification: a quatrain made couplet, and the finer poem drew first blood: a most excellent line of red striping his satin sleeve. A mere scratch that left my blade clean.

The seconds and his leech clamoured to his side. Was fickle Honour satisfied with a bite of such slenderness? Stomach made of her a Cyclops, destroying men, and in his madded Pride, the rogue delivered himself into my low Justice.

His foot upon the Greeks, Agrippa saw through the octagon to the spheres known, too, to Spain; in this, a sphere 'twixt mine undying heart and the Venetian's dog-wormed pump, measured in the lengths of our swords, extended tip-to-tip. I strode the sixty spheres, and time shaped all geometries.

The villain styled a strip at Court and proved novice to a cutting blade forged for war; his arm worthy of a cavalier, he made sport of him self. Twas a child's art to traverse his swaggering line. Him, I provoked into the void of our sphere, my foot feigned back. Then a twisting cut to play him false, ripping bloodless satin, and his heart reached the centre. The final thrust did call it self home. Yea, Spain: el momento de verdad, his consummation.

The Venetian toppled to earth, no semblant of Grace, the red sash of roguery across his breast. Then did heart-blood spill forth as his seconds and the belaboured leech rushed again to his side. I wiped my blade with the appointed silk and let my lady's kerchief fall, acquitted, to the ground.

Witnesses murmured mongst themselves and quit me the field. In all, 'twas a foolish thing, but oftentimes, I forget my self and live a Man's foolishness. My seconds, bright-eyed but sombre cavaliers and gentlemen, offered salutations. Chivalry fair would not have us mock and mow the dead or his companions in their womanish dolour.

A mulled cup, and went we away to coach and steed awaiting us and those not yet in their departure, in witness to a callow deacon anointing the Venetian with oil – an outlaw Last Rites abridged of Viaticum. Twas but chance, as we passed mongst horses and lanterns, that I descried the shake of a window curtain, and breaking dawn illumed the image of storied Roxana: in the most regal portance of the Lady de' Corsi, and abreast her, the princess of her service. And no word or sign did pass 'twixt us ere the curtain drew shut. And the coachman stirred the horses, the Estense arms belighted in its passage unto the open road. Messire Cerchi braced my shoulder, and

It should go well, Maaike said, but you'll need to be fit enough for the gala in the spring. You are the host.

At the centre of wavering distortions that I could see but not feel, herself undistorted, she reärranged her agenda, the improbable Instagram face and raised chin in the carriage window. The same delicate frame of shoulders. Signora Leonarda's upbraided hair was the same savannah-blonde as my dream of Maaike.

Was it all... ? All I'd struggled and striven for... ?

A dream.

—I'm sure it'll be fine, I finally replied, with or without me. But I'll do my best.

—No; you will be better in time.

—I yield to your confidence.

I hadn't told her a wheelchair was the worst-case prognosis. Overshoulder, she said,

—Naturally. I'll bring more documents for you to sign tomorrow.

—Are you planning to visit every single day?

—We will see.

Maaike shut the door behind her. ἰάω κύριον παντοκρατές: "IAO and lord almighty", radiating "ABRASAX" – that mural sprang straight from the pendant she'd dangled beneath my nose not a moment before the vision. My so-called temporal distortions were some kind of disassociative vertigo. In the dusty grave of his forlorn irrelevance, Nietzsche laughed. These gods, too, were dead.

T HE THREE-LEGGED SHADOW WAS MINE. Like my imaginary hero Giuliano, I wasn't one to retreat, and I had business at the Institute. A reckoning.

I addressed the white marble stairs from the front, I, and my hollow aluminum medical cane, the matte-grey reward for my gruelling weeks of rehab. The Palladian portico made no concessions to accessibility. I could've had the Lyft driver leave me at the west wing's parking-lot loggia entrance, but I wasn't taking the easy way out. Not today.

Winter had passed me by, and I'd stepped into the city's new spring. The Grindhouse killings had stopped, not a one since the Institute's, and fear had receded with the new year; a black cloud, on the far horizon, moving away.

Maaike's maybe meant no. After the first fundraiser dinner I'd missed, she'd briefed me, telling the wry tale of an infamous patron with a pug named Sartre that piddled on everything. After that, she was gone, the Board's carte blanche in hand. It was all change in her grand but preliminary plans, and about what I'd expected: From my full stop with the Achæmenid empire, an expansion into Late Antiquity and the Macedonian aftermath in West Asia, with a preview selection moving into the special exhibition space for the gala. The Helleno-Persic Sellucids. So-called Parthian art.

I had bigger problems.

DON QUIXOTE, after all, I hobbled in her wake, the revenant of my mythos. My reckoning had come, but I could ignore mirages if I knew the real. Shrinks would only drug me into an antipsychotic stupor. A pharmal zombie.

Some nights, I'd heard *that* sound through the hospital room window, hearing things five stories up. My meliævalish dream had recurred, not once but twice in her wintered absence and in the absence of my quiëscent disassociations, lest I forget. Initial preparations were underway for the gala event next week. I wasn't back on the books till then, but first, I needed to face this alone.

The cane didn't help, supporting my injured and knee-braced leg with my injured and wrist-braced arm. I took a winding route through the Græco-Roman section, in my limping three-legged way, through clusters of middle schoolers amid classical learning. They would view the xenonymed μεσοποταμία, "Mesopotamia", through the Greek lens, if at all.

I stopped before a glass-cased black-figure terracotta vase depicting a þyrs that'd come from the sea, terrorising Troy as Grendel had the Danes: feasting on them, flesh and bone. Both hero-slain. The Trojan Cetus risen, in my mind, from the Sumerian 𒀊𒍪, *abzu* or "the Deep", where I'd envisioned sleeping unlife in geothermal citadels buried low in the lithosphere. I'd catalogued the undersea echoes of their abyssopolagic stirrings within a warming Earth; seismologists had given them poetic names like "the Bloop", "Julia", and "Upsweep". Mere blips after all.

Ancient Egypt waited, aloof to my lingering apprehensions and likely indifferent to its othering by the Academy's intrinsic classicalism – the exoticised Cleopatrine girl-next-door – preferring we leave the dead buried during their sojourn in the Silent Land. Amid the cordoned spaces, drop cloths, and scaffolding, the Aten remained, and even if I knew THE NAME was only discarded apocrypha, the sting lingered like stigmata on my heart.

The size of the building measured itself in mounting fatigue. My stomach a step behind me, I hobbled onwards to my own great hall, to a snake-armed bas-relief of the Typhonic 𒀀𒊕, Asag, akin to Maaike's silver ABRASAX. Known in the Punjab as the dragon Vritra, it was written in Lugal-e that the very rivers would boil in Asag's presence – like the boiling sea in the newish SHIN GOJIRA, which I'd watched in my hospital room. In ABRASAX and Asag, I'd seen suggestions of the Other; I'd envisioned our rocky blue-green isle adrift in an unimaginable black sea and the interstellar cartographer's warning, "Here be dragons", but that was no more than my story.

By the time I reached what'd become her office door, I was beat, and it must've shown; Maaike shot up from her chair, her voice cracking with uncharacteristic strain:

—You should've told me you were coming.

She came to me with quick stompy steps I could almost feel through the floor and took my jacketed arm in hand. I said I was fine, and she ignored me. As slight as she was, her grip was firm, and she proved a more than capable fourth leg till I sank into a brand new Aeron office chair with relief.

I didn't recognise the place. Repainted. Ultra-modern everything, juxtaposing fluid and flat geometries. Maaike hadn't mentioned it, and I didn't know what pretext she'd used to justify the outlay. Her mask softened for an eyeblink in the late morning light, like steel rendered mercury, or I wished it to be so. I squeezed her hand, not cool as I'd dreamt but fervid. She stiffened but didn't pull away at first.

—Don't, she said. The Tyrant is asleep, not blind, and the price is too high, even for us. The new moon will be here, this…

Frozen. Immersed in ice water. My limbs fell away, unable to respond in the repose of long dormancy, the spheres revolving around me in interlocked traceries of unlit form, the steady rain of particles a soothing hiss, and improbability crackled like lightning, near and far, teetering on existence.

A hole in my heart dripped a diffuse iridine mist; in and out, it breathed sparkling crystals of seïty, spiralling down to a small room lit with the yellow light of a single star. Gripped by a cobweb chair, I did not fall away – caressed by the shift of the near moon. It sighed to me its longing, shooting by within its lesser curvature of time. She-who-was-not "Maaike" stood between us, and I could not see through her. A lurching thump, here in my chest, another heart, I remembered.

—¿Julián?

The flow constricted like a tap closing, and "Julián" was I, alone with her but never alone, and for a moment, I felt when the next charismatic droplet would fall. Then it was gone.

—The new moon, I repeated.

A flash-heat rose on my skin, exposed, naked as I'd never been, but I hadn't grasped it. Hadn't caught up. Braced by the hyperspheric boundary, there was no vertigo, no up or down, all directions equal, every point the Beginning.

She sat on the edge of my desk, a vertiginous view, saying,

—Leave it at that, or the Tyrant will shut me out. They are nothing if not capricious.

"The Tyrant". Something familiar but not something I'd heard with my own ears. The image of Issota in the grip of entheos – that might well deserve tyrant.

—ἰάω, said I in Greek.

The mural. The amulet. The woman, alias Μααιke, shook her head.

—I don't cater to their megalomania: ἰάω, ἀβρασάξ, any of it. This… we're in THE HEART OF DARKNESS, and the Tyrant has become a god in their own mind.

—How long have you waited to use that line?

—A century, give or take.

Something in the air lightened. She should've smiled or laughed, like in my dreams, but didn't. My dreams of her. The new moon. The weeks that'd passed between: those mediæval dream-visions weren't mine but hers: something she'd done, almost succubine – but I'd been all too eager. She'd presented a mirror and shown me myself.

It was too much all at once. I was surfing the ragged crest of a giant wave, and when it landed, the crash would shake my bones – if I didn't drown.

I'd endured a Jobian winter, discarded even by her, it'd seemed, to regain everything tenfold. Grace with a capital G. For a moment, I'd inhabited the Record, beheld what it perceives, as if the Record was the act of existence itself: perceiving, thus reality. She was something else. She had no fangs like some movie vampire, nor Modarette's horrid mouthful of sandtiger teeth, but almost five hundred years had passed, and the Signora de' Corsi was in the room. It was no accident.

I was in the story, in over my head with her. She knew something about me I didn't and thought I knew what she did. All of her crypticisms… I had to keep her talking.

—Your name. Would you prefer… ?

—Not here. Not now. Remember what I told you.

Her tone had sharpened, but there was a sadness in her eyes, dark, ineffable. I knew that sadness, an ebon thread trailing back through my childhood dreams. She'd seen, but by her warnings, so did the Other: "not a private conversation" and "asleep, not blind". We were being watched somehow, adding an Orwellian charge to our pauses, to our choice of words.

—But, she added with hesitation, not naming names, have you found her?

And without lying, I said no. Issota shared these metempsychoses, but mystery and intimacy stood between us duellists, and I risked revealing my possible ignorance of *her who?* – and other things – by asking.

I bided and brought up the coloss shaking the building: the gala event. In lieu of a dramatic eyebrow, Maaike, as she would have it, responded with a fractional head tilt, acknowledging the change of unspeakable subject. With humour, I'd guess. I'd have to draw on any morsels she let slip.

—I'm still reeling from those ticket prices. Twenty-five thousand…

She stood and smoothed her clothes.

—I recommended thirty, but Doktor Röhm disagreed.

—And the five hundred tickets sold out. Even she can't sneeze at that.

—No, said Röhm from the doorway, I can't, but it means there's much more to come if you listen to Micah and follow her lead. If you follow through. West Asia could become the most visited Assyrian exhibit in the nation. If ¶. I was expecting you to return next week, Julian.

I'd've preferred to avoid her altogether, but at least we'd been talking turkey when she intruded. I claimed,

—I wanted to check in on the preparations before the big day. All seems well in hand, though the walk was a bit more than I'd bargained for.

—Stop by my office after you've caught your breath. Are you in much pain? You've lost weight.

—They gave me a patch. I don't feel much of anything except tired and nauseous.

—Don't let him wear himself out, she said to Maaike. He needs to put his best foot forward next week.

—I'll be fine, I interjected.

—You sound like you've caught your breath now; I'll expect you shortly. Micah, we'll meet at our usual time.

Exeunt Röhm, as abrupt as her entry. Maaike crossed her arms.

—I should have shut the door.

—Röhm would've had a cow. She thinks something's going on; otherwise, there's no reason to exclude you. This is your show.

—I'll accompany you. I insist.

—That'll confirm whatever story she's concocted. She'll send you back to Mikkelsen full-time.

—No, she won't.

The last carried the weight of a threat. Getting back out of my chair was a doozy. My back and shoulders had stiffened, and my knee let me know it wasn't happy. Not much of a miracle recovery. Leaning too hard on my cane, I said,

This riddle, Your Ladyship, inasmuch as I am accustomed to your jests, has the time not come to play it out?

Modarette had presented me to the warlike cabinet of the once Count Ginori, well kept but sober in its appointments and of modest comforts suited to no more than three or four intimates in counsel. Belighted by morn, the pennons, armours, and map table were relics of an age bygone, and beseated across from my self, the countess was as proud upon a campaign chair as on the seat of Saint Peter.

—It is not mine to do so, *inasmuch* as my salon should be the field. We have marched withal and hereat shall meet it. Some game is afoot.

—Then what... ?

The dread page stepped forth and announced the belated arrival of my good seconds, Messires Cerchi and Orsini, and Estense lady companions, Leonarda de' Corsi and Jacomina de' Migliorati. Fair of skin and red of hair, the Lady de' Migliorati was the gayest of a gay company, as spring in allegory. Countess Issota looked upon me with bright eyes.

—The match is aplay, and here is the board.

I rose, and Her Ladyship remained sitting. Red and gold, a cardinal of the LORD, Modarette made singular obeisance to the Lady de' Corsi on bended knee. I could not account for it, but she heeded it not. Her low curtsy to the countess showed to fine effect the gilding which had sent a viper-tongued villain to his consummate end, but she was no more the Moor than Modarette the Turk. The party presented themselves in a manner befitting their stations, and Countess Issota received them:

—It is to fulsome Shame, Lady de' Corsi, that our acquaintance came not heretofore, but herein lies a familiarity as one finds, mysterial yet affecting. We shall be the best of friends betime, an' it please thee, join us.

—Your Ladyship, I return the embrace of your Courtesy and the Honour of your most celebrated salon. I, like a child, shall sit by your feet.

—Lady, said the countess laughing, beseech you, sit at my side as should a sister.

The gentlemen kept their feet, footmen of jocund colours – and in conference between us, the Florentine lady looked on me not. My heart inquieted, for was I not since betaken in dream? In my heart's tale, we had walked arm-in-arm within the garden of the Hesperides: the white Atlas mountains above bemisted vales; and a fossed castle of silver cloud, apple trees hung with fruit, green-gold, in its demesne. Twas no High Mystery, but the common weakness of Man, which methought my self apart, but folly brings low such Pride as mine, from the falcon's heights. I clung thereafter to the pure service of mine admiration, for the Countess Ginori stood above me as the storied Mongibello.

I had neither ears nor tongue for Court gossip and left it in their mouths, lest I be bitten in the taking, and mine kept its pocket. Yet a feigning beckoned at corner sight: I should know this lady. Beyond dream or cupidity should I know her, and it worried at me, a hound worrying leather. Memory descended its pitchy course from on high, like the lofty channels that once watered Latium, laden with promise and misgiving. This ichor of mind reached back across the Aion to our very Genesis and all the perfumes of Eden. Twas the LORD's to know its ebb and flow, I a cup beteemed a thimble. Or 'twas a false conceit: Man, wont to excuse his faults, as to relieve his debts with another's purse.

These barren agitations bound me till the quartet took leave of Her Ladyship and my self, leaving us to the resumption of our prior parts.

—I cannot recall, said she, but a shadow troubles me. A shadow within the shadow, but be certain of this, my lord: the Lady de' Corsi doth know us of dim anciety.

Her bright countenance stricken on a sudden fell she aswoon from her seat, a cry catching in her throat, and her name leapt from mine. Fell me to her side, and in all presumption, upheld her in mine arms; for sobs racked from her heaving bosom as drawn forth under direst torment. Orc claws did rend her thus, in the LORD's kátharis, and I called not for aid, for there was none. The servants without stirred not, though her cries echoed and ran their shrill courses in the halls.

—O, gasped she, my betrothèd…

Again was I troubled, for 'twixt the widow countess and a

baron of no note, there could be no such union. But as Rumour would sup and break fast on one shank, was I well fed upon: in my championage of the Lady Companion, made adventurer; and gallant to the Countess Ginori, absent husband, both. Of these and more had Her Ladyship sung a merry song, but upon "betrothèd", no – her cries redoubled, lashed by ghostly afflictions, such that I was agonied for her sake. O, the Pity of it.

Then she screamed as one cut to pieces by the guns; for the marked, such is our penitence; such was the vouchsafement of the LORD's Revelations. Modarette waited, impassible, the marker of their observance and supremacy.

Her limbs fell limp, as one lifeless but in afflicted breath, her skirts capsized in silken ruination. She wept then for a time, heeding me not, till midst her weeping did say soft,

—I know thee, mine immortal, but there is no Mercy in what they have shewn. Soon, methinks, thou wilt know me. The LORD, this Báal cannot forgive us, and only in knowledge is there pain.

—I pray all easement of your grief, madam.

More the Fool, I kissed her forbidden hand, and she raised her face to mine and kissed me with tear-stained lips. I expected the orc to rend us both, but no claws came. Ferrara it self might suffer requital, but let Báal, as Her Ladyship benamed them, make of it a burnt offering as of old. I whispered to her in turn, though no word could escape the ken of the mighty:

—This doom you herald, what then our service to the Rulers, are we not mystes sworn?

—And if the canons of Rome held Cain in their sway, ignorant of himself, and made of him a priest in their keeping? We are deceived.

The rogue himself could not better have run me through.

—And Summer itself?

—Summer comes upon the earth, but I fear it a despotate beyond our image. Thou liest on the crux of an enmity eternal in its Spite, and forevermore will Báal keep us cagèd birds. Defiant or broken, all the same.

—A sword may be broken, but its edge remains.

Her dry and hoarse chuckle rose to my bravado.

—Well said, my lord. Well said. Chivalrous to the unending. Thou wouldst challenge Olympus with Daniel's sling.

—Gentle, my lady. You have said o'ermuch and perforce will be deprived of life. Repose thy self, I prithee.

A rivulet of crimson spilt from her corner lip, for she smiled though spent and wounded.

—Betrothèd, I shall say...

You should rely on Micah, not use her as a crutch.

Röhm was indignant. From its glass door to its extensive walnut appointments, her office was a black-and-white contrast with mine. Waiting-room prints of the Impressionists filled the whitespace: Renoir et al., in all caps. I was seated in one of the new and little used side chairs coupled before her broad desk.

—She's obstinate: she won't take no for an answer.

—Which is why I'm successful, Maaike addended.

Ma donna la Signora de' Corsi herself, her gaze crossed mine as she graced the adjacent seat, and I could believe she'd seen each and every one of those years with those eyes: that she'd seen too much and couldn't escape what she'd seen. But Guiliano's κῆπος τῶν ἑσπερίδων, "garden of the Hesperides", rang too close to my dream-vision: she'd enchanted him by the same means, and I tasted jealousy for the first time, hot and bitter.

I bore the brunt of Röhm's glare. The older man, as I appeared, was always at fault in these things, one way or another. Hell would have time to catch me later, alone. I cleared my throat.

—So you wanted to talk money?

—Funding, Julian. Funding. Money is never discussed. Especially with donors. You would do well...

After that stressful if chaperoned conversation, after we'd reëntered our office, I did the unadvisable thing and closed the door. Maaike looked askance at me, but I remained standing and made no move toward my desk despite my redoubled aches. I was done playing along and said,

—The Oannes statuette. Why the fake transfer?

Still gripping my good arm, she looked up at me in silence for so long that I almost repeated the question. She looked away; in her words, accusation:

—You said you remembered.

—There are things I know, things I've seen. But that castle, where... ?

She cursed, something I didn't recognise, but the tone was unmistakable.

—It was too soon, then. I cannot tell you. I'm not the one who will suffer.

—You opened this door.

—I know.

—You came here.

—I know.

—You found me.

—I always know. That's.

Maaike released my arm and went to her desk, retrieving her purse.

—I'll be helping Doktor Mikkelsen for the remainder of the day.

—Leonarda, please. I'll risk it.

Even with a cane, I was a wall. She was undaunted, as before.

—Leonarda? Recalling your life as the Barone Orlandi doesn't allow you to ignore the consequences. That's what makes monsters, my lord.

—My life?

—I'm not going to abandon you. I'll continue to assist with the gala, but we require some distance until the memories come – until they permit you to remember. Otherwise, it's too dangerous.

—You said…

—Don't! I must go. I've said… I've done too much already. There will be blood on my head again.

—You wanted me to understand, ma donna.

—I shouldn't have done.

Maaike brushed me aside, a cheerleader shunting a linebacker, before opening the door. I lost my balance in surprise; against her irresistible force, I was no immovable object. One thing was clear: she was something else.

—I shouldn't have done.

There were tears in her voice, if not her eyes, and a few passers-by caught her parting line. Rumours would burn their way down to L1 by closing time. I left the door open and three-legged to my seat, two words bleeding as if she'd carved them into me with a knife. "Your life", she'd said. Your life.

Guiliano's "metempsychosis"; Issota's "to mortal span from mortal span". I was the story, and the prohibition of touch widened the stage as it leapt forward in time, right under my feet. Maaike,

whoever she was, was part of the game, and "Hesperides"... ? –
we'd done all this before, and the spark of jealousy had burned
no one but me.

Worse, I'd an inkling: the lost time, the blackouts, were my end
of those enthëasms – at least some of them. I was being used.
Toyed with. If not by Maaike, then by the Other; if not by both.
I needed to discover whatever she was searching for: those "answers". More, the question. I had to revisit Δ353. Review every
fragment, every idol. Every verse of IN THE COMING OF SUM-
MER AND LIGHT. Recheck the transliteration, syllable by syllable. I started at the jab of twin needlepoints behind my eyes,
which spread into a persistent aching throb.

"Consequences", she'd said. Consequences, she'd reminded me.
Guiliano had known – no, I'd known. I'd seen Issota's suffering,
not second but first hand, and this was nothing in comparison.

I'd never feared the coming titanocracy – the Greenhouse summer of their archontic allegory. There was reason, I'd thought, in-
tent behind my insight into the Record. I was by grace a witness,
and if there was a cosmic war, a great struggle, it would come
long after my time. Would've, but now there was this palpitating
pressure... I would see its arrival. I'd be on the front lines.

Unable to take anything else for the pain, I rubbed my temples
and sat back in my soundless suspension chair. I paged through
my charismata scrapbook, my Othered memories: the lives of a
single marked man, over and over again, crossing the ages. So
many, yet so little matter till Guiliano, till Maaike née Leonarda
stepped onto the board.

It dawned ever too late that these memories, these ἀποκᾰ-
λύψεις, "Revelations", had been pruned. Manipulated – even
falsified. "Permit you to remember". I sat up.
—Kyrie, eléeson me.

The Record was self-evident. That eikon. Those epithets.
"Nameless, known by many names", and the Βάαλ, "Báal", of
Issota's denunciation. Jung's "coiled knot of winged serpents"
dealt me these snippets like clue cards in a game. Only then did
I see the bars of my cage against the light.

T HE CARNAGE RESOLVED INTO A SKELETAL TREE
as the shaky cam zoomed out: a lumpy impasto landscape of bones and flensed tissue. The driver's child-
like wonder rang gleeful till the light turned green: Gen Z-ish
and doubtless too young to drink. They'd grown up watching
beheadings on their phones, and viral videos like this were the
new normal.

Fifteen seconds. An imaging clinic midtown, the driver explained, eyes on the road; though he didn't remember the facility's name, he knew where it was. So did I.

—I was there three days ago.

I saw the whites of his eyes in the rearview. An openmouthed
Youtube-reaction thumbnail.

—Bruh…!

We were approaching the Institute, and I didn't have to field
too many of his run-on questions before exiting. I remembered
the faces of the staff, going about their routine. Professional,
friendly, unremarkable. I was sure the sensationalist newswires
were lapping up the blood like Ba'al, but I had no desire to see
more, no desire to know. The eikonography of the tree wasn't
lost on me, but it evoked flashes of blackened Aztec priests painting temple walls with human blood, moments of Grendel and
Modarette. An odd triangulation. These weren't thursic murders:
Grendel didn't paint pictures, but Modarette proved there were
other things in service of the Other. My kaijū cricket might be
as sinister as I'd thought.

Maaike had passed into obscurity like the moon, out of sight
but unmistakable in influence, in the dull ache for those vivid
nights of the unreal. She'd turned the gala preparations upside
down: hordes of Sassanid heavy cavalry, the ur-knights of antiquity, had expelled the Hellenes and the Hellenised from the
temporary gala exhibition as if pursuing THE RUNNING MAN
west, out of Iran. On all sides, bas-reliefs of mediævalesque war,
jousting, and horses. I hadn't taken her for a horse fancier, but

they were everywhere. She'd worked the art movers and in-house exhibition techs overtime, but she'd remained a step ahead of me, and I'd been unable to catch the why. Nor had the syzygy of the new moon invoked her cyclic dream-vision. She was closed to me.

The recurring pain in my eyes was the latest thorn in my paw. κάθαρσις, "catharsis", likely, but an unidentified skull injury from the purported hit-and-run was possible. I'd been waiting on the results of the CT scan, which I now knew might never come.

I was early for the shindig, as required, but so was night, already draining the last wash of red from the jagged horizon in the bloodied blush of spring. The purple carpet rolled out; the sidewalk was cordoned with police cruisers on both sides. Violet GOD-KINGS banners hung between the Palladian pillars, a nightlit black eye for the White City–era civic centre turned museum fifty years later, leading to the addition of a third wing and its civic-minded bomb shelter. A pair of rented spotlights were in position but not yet searched the sky. Little expense had been spared, given the expected take.

My also-rented tux was ill-fit over my braced arm and leg, at best, a comic effect paired with my drugstore cane. Event organisers with tablets and headsets walked in and out the open doors, doing something or other with NASA-launch faces, the Brandenburg concertos in rehearsal somewhere inside. I had to find a chair close – but not too

perplexed.
—How long?
—My lord?
—Since Her Ladyship took the road.
—Nightfall, my lord.

The countess had grown pale and fretsome, for the Mystery of the Florentine lady remained unillumed, a blot across our passages. The deceit of the mystes, the Elect of this false Authority, unmasked by Her Ladyship, did I contemn; and in bold affront, they enjoined we should fall upon the Mercy of the Innominatum, and make a penitent offering of a suckling babe to the altar fire, else all face retribution from on high. The Duke's Court was rife with their rank corruption, but my sword's point returned my refusal, and these minions and their venomed smiles made a watchful retreat, for Modarette hung upon us as the sword of Damocles. No evil had befallen Ferrara in aftertimes, and I could speak no ill of the Lady de' Corsi's devotions to Her Ladyship.

This fearful vespertine flight was without reason, but foreboding set its spur to me and I to my horse, down the stinking empty streets and unto the town gate; then a trot o'er open road, lit us by the gibbous moon. The coach ahead must needs walk its paired steeds and knew not of the chase.

Gave me rein to my steed's superior sight, and no Brigliador to be left behind, his great heart carried me to mine; for I caught sight and sound of a lanterned coach, paced by footmen. Blue and gold by day and befitting the carriage of any prince, but night made murksome all colours and purposes. I drew abreast, calling upon the coachman to halt.

—M'lord! replied he. The countess has bid onwards unto Dawn. No less!

—I would speak with Her Ladyship!

—Forgive me, m'lord!

I would not return injury to duty fulfilled and withheld harsher words, and drawing my strip sword, I struck thrice upon the coach with the pommel. The curtains fluttered and swayed, and the dutiful coachman brought the horses to rein at the knock of Her Ladyship's hand. The outrunners attended the coach door as the curtain drew open. I dismounted, calling,

—My lady countess!

—My lord, what madness has seized upon you? Put up your blade lest you be ta'en for a common highwayman.

How many poets of ages innumerable have made the sun of their lady's smile? And so 'twas again, and doubly so, for its absence deprived me of the sole light in Winter.

—Your Ladyship, Rumour, that scurrilous messenger, came on swift feet to the ball of the Count Ubaldini where I, in attendance, heard tell you were fled to Austria midst some stain.

And where, said I not, the Princess de' Este and her ladies-in-waiting, in attendance, heard the same. Said Countess Issota,

—Guiliano, thou art a Fool, but betake it, thou art my Fool.

—Then... ?

—Then thou hast but lent credence to the noisome tale that I am your mistress.

I fell to one knee in all Contrition and my parlour blade to the dust of the rutted road. A Fool I was and well named, bringing upon Her Ladyship that which I would give chase and a ruesome reckoning. Said she,

—Ill hath come to Ferrara, and I fear it lies within the sorceress who spelled thy service and seeks e'en now to spell mine. I doubt not her pursuit and shall draw her along, for from Eden she hath come; I know this in my heart, though I am forgot to the Garden ¶. Return not to Ferrara; a noxious air doth lie upon it. Embark thee to Verona or otherwheres. Away now, the witch is at my heel.

—Forgive me, Countess. I would not be parted from you, not to any peril, but make of me the Spartans' wall. Ride on, and remain me to bar the road. By my life, she will answer to't.

—Feats of arms suffice not to cosmic powers, and gainst a feigning lady in all her meekness art thou disarmed. Go along with me to Padua or Austria if thou wouldst. I would not part from thee, my Guiliano, but prithee, flee my company ere her coming.

—If the road cannot be held, then your sword and shield shall I be. Let Naught stand 'twixt us till this cloud should pass, and no adversary approach you, Countess, lest I, the threshold, be o'erstepped.

A footman opened the coach door, inviting entry at Her Ladyship's command. I gathered self and sword, and t'other footman took lead of my horse as I climbed within. Countess Issota was alone, without maids or other attendment. Asked I,

—And Modarette?

—The Bastard is gone ahead. He awaits me in Padua.

—Caged indeed. And what of the black acolytes of this Innominatum? Will they not… ?

—The Báalites cannot defy the Bastard, and in his vanguard, they cannot prevent us. It will go hard with them must he return for me; I am his ward, and to him, they, less than vermin. Thou wilt know all without my telling, for Báal's game is to play us thus: the apple of our ignorance to bait the mare. This may well be the road of their choosing.

—And the Lady de' Corsi? Should she follow… ?

—Then we lead her on a merry chase to the land of the Tsars and far Cathay. You marked the homage paid to her by the Bastard?

—It marvelled me.

—He is no bar to her will.

—Then she is no common witch.

—I purpose to the Biblioteca Antoniana in the answering of it. She is without the Mysteries as given us, but the ancients in their learnèd annals may have vouchsafed our deliverance.

The Basilica of Sant'Antonio held a library of great repute, and as Her Ladyship said, 'twas a struggle of pneuma, Logos, and arts most occult; of secrets withheld or couched within lies. Any cavalier knew the sword was not the sole means of war.

—Then, my lady, if you are to the Basilica, then shall I to University, and offer up such aid as I…

Ferrara! Ferrara! cried the servants. I would have leapt from the coach, but Countess Issota held fast mine arm; all could be seen therefrom, the curtain yet drawn. Eerie flames billowed above the Po vale, blue-white, flashes like mute lightning in a clear night sky – a brightness hard to look upon e'en across the many leagues of road and field behind.

Thrice commanded the countess all haste to the coachman, and

I stumbled midstride. I could feel it echoing across the centuries, like an ice-cold dagger in the gut. I took a deep breath, unable to shake it. Issota. Something… Something terrible. She and I were being pushed – groomed across the ages – into participating in the subjugation of Man to the Other and blood sacrifice in the name of some supposèd redemption.

My arm was still held. Not tight or alarmed but unyielding as iron.

Sorceress. Witch. None of the Above. Maaike stood unexpectedly tall in an emerald-green evening gown cut close, pedestalled by gold sandals. Her dark hair was gold-clipped back, complimented by chunky gold earrings with heraldic lions, highlighting the elegant line of her neck.

Blackout? Enthëasm? She wasn't talking. A sirocco from the near east warmed my face, bearing with it not the scent of the sea but an attar of jasmine, clove, and frankincense. ABRASAX hung, dousing her hidden navel, and without intention, I spoke my thought:

—You can't take it off.

If there was a yes, it lay within the dark liquidity of her eyes, the fractional parting of her lips. A blink of stillness before drawing me along, she was all business. I'd missed whatever she'd had to say about the renewed Grindhouse killings. I knew she'd said something.

Around us, the rich and fabulous weren't above taking selfies with each other, milling about West Asia, trying to interpret antiquity. The galleries were a dramatic contrast to her monumentalist maquette plinthed and spotlit at the entry, conjoining a scaled and full-colour Gate of Xerxes to the great apadāna, or "audience hall", of Persepolis. The numbers needed to pull it off were eye-watering, but pie in the sky was her problem. I was another prop.

Maaike's cool aloofness cast its own spell on the eminences of deep purses, and her recall of names and faces was unerring, but the riot of clashing perfumes left me seasick. She presented me with all due ceremony to an ostensible oligarch, Konstantin something-or-other and his modellike second-or-third wife. He asked if I'd played American football, and Maaike's grip tightened when one of very few faces familiar to me appeared: the dandyish stateside rep for the Aigilofling Foundation. One of those fawning lawyers that didn't practise law, per se, but whose nose for money was unerring – the bar a priesthood assuring privileged confidentiality.

—Doctor Corbin! I was so disappointed not to hear you speak.

—I'm less than presentable at the moment, I said with a broad sweep of my tailored dishevelment, and Doctor Röhm favours the podium.

—O yes, he drawled; the hit-an'-run. We were all so concerned...

Insipid blandishments went on and on, and the smileless Russians departed with a parting nod and unsympathetic disinterest. The rep was too effete to be gay, but Maaike's look could have taken an arm off when he placed a careless hand on my recently dislocated shoulder, saying,

—And if you haven't yet, you absolutely must meet the Bowens. Their endowment to the Foundation was generous. Most generous.

—The Bowens of the Bowen Trust?

—Yes! They're here! And Liza's just your biggest fan!

I knew the Bowens by reputation, by the vacuum left in their wake. Insatiable and nigh rapacious collectors of Anatolian and Mesopotamian antiquities, I'd lost a number of rareties to them in my short time as curator. Even whispering anomalies of questionable merit vanished into their unseen vaults. That the Bowen Trust contributed to the Fellowship, which supported my position at the Institute, was no surprise but galling nonetheless.

He hooked my sore-shouldered good arm, and his puffinlike proboscis led us on a circuitous but unerring path through the puffed-up crowd to an odd couple, tippling champagne, each striking for different reasons.

—Doctor Corbin, this is Wesley Bowen and his sister, Mizz Liza.

Nape-length coppered-auburn hair and that peaches-and-cream complexion common to born redheads, her eyes gleamed like polished blue granite within their crystalline clarity. Ms Liza Bowen's strapless beaded dress was simple but glistered money, her bared shoulders and fingers free of ornament. A solitary armlet, the colour of bullion gold and inset with smooth but matte stones, set off her fair skin and the Chartres-blue beading. Thirty-something with unretouched laugh lines. Unusual for this crowd.

He'd drawn the short straw from their shared gene pool, a pink-faced boiled lobster in fluffy black tie, hand bowknot, and tinted bug-eye glasses. His grip was firm; hers wasn't, but neither was it boneless. Her smile crinkled the corners of her eyes. He didn't.

—My sister's the collector. I just hold her purse.

She elbowed him, beaded clutch in hand.

—Our father made him gatekeeper of the Trust, so I have no choice but to keep him around.

—He was impressed by your ability to shop and wanted the money to hold out.

—Don't be gauche; collecting antiquities isn't shopping.

There was something familiar about her, and I said so, though it was wishful thinking; I'd've remembered. She smiled easily, absent the tells of dissimulation.

—We've never met, but I did attend your lectures here – when you gave them.

—Yes! was interjected with excess flamboyance by the Puffin. I was just telling him how the Foundation would very much appreciate a return to his prior form. Very much.

Maaike spoke up at my side:

—Doctor Corbín has been working on the renovation of the West Asian galleries while organising a national Assyrian exhibition and, of course, recovering from his injuries. But if the evening is a success, you can look forward to his lectures in the future.

To the point! the Lobster barked, laughing, but the look Liza gave him was far more pointed. Her full attention bore down on Maaike.

—I'm sure the Bowen Trust will offer its full support, Doctor…?

—Van Leeuwen. Doctoranda.

—Leeuwen; that must be Dutch for lion.

—It is.

—Of course, it is. We were all very concerned about Doctor Corbin's injuries and that hit-'n'-run. Who would do such a thing?

I pointed out,

—Doctoranda Van Leeuwen is the prime mover behind this gala and the architect of the ongoing renovation of the Egyptian section.

Liza looked at me, then the space, asking,

—And the planned renovation of these galleries?

—She'll be at the helm. The gallery maquette is her design.

—Interesting. Bringing us to that matter we discussed, Wesley.

The Lobster responded after another barking laugh.

—Up at bat! Well, you see, it's two matters…

—Wesley.

—Your pardon. Through Liza's efforts, we've acquired a significant collection of relevant doodads and would like to propose an endowment for a rotating display under the Bowen name. A permanent addition.

—And? she prompted.

—And we would like to hire you and your expertise to create an illustrated catalogue of Liza's collection, to be published by the University Press.

How exciting! the Puffin flapped, etc. But I blinked at that. Through the lenses of the Academy's Truman Capote glasses, I was out.

—And they've already agreed?

—When she wants something, Liza can be very persuasive.

—I'm certain Julian will be more than pleased to catalogue the Bowen Collection, said Röhm as she stepped forward from where she'd been eavesdropping. It's a rare opportunity for a curator to access an extensive private collection. Regarding any endowments or bequests, please contact my office anytime.

She proffered a card, using it like a hook to draw him away from our momentary convocation.

—Do you have a card, Julian? asked Liza.

Surprised, I checked my pockets, but Maaike slipped another from her clutch and palmed it as she had countless others. The issued cards weren't up to snuff, and she'd had new eggshells made. It was my first time seeing them.

Liza excused herself in turn, saying she'd have her PA arrange contract negotiations, but as she turned away, Maaike asked,

—That cuff. Is it Eighteenth Dynasty?

—Good eye. It belonged to the woman who became king.

—Hatshepsut.

—Yes; she reminds me of someone I knew long ago.

—That should be displayed in a museum.

Liza gestured to the space around us and smiled.

—It is.

T HE EMBER OF WRATH smouldered within my bosom, and as I lived and lived again, would it endure till I might set the Tree it self aflame and cross all purposes of the abysm-wight that named them self Ruler. This usurping Typhœus, this abhorrence mongst Titans, could not be o'er-thrown with a sling, as Her Ladyship alluded, and sought she elsewhere the namings of all innominata. And from the rabbins of Padua, I sought lore and legend of Báal and in orators' halls and profane texts for the key to the bottomless pit.

Zabarella's discourse was in vain, as a diviner of THE COMEDY, facing e'er behind him self, and I departed therefrom without gain. Our Latin forbearers had done the Greeks too much hon-our, and by succession did we.

We back to yesterday, ever back, and advance not; were it some deceit of the Adversary, that the high of Chivalry falls behind, forgotten. I perceived the expansion and rotations of the spheres, and oftentimes a bitter chill from I knew not where, but if they be music, Aristotle knew not their measure; the cardinal number sixty, not fifty-five, but the fullness of their weaving lay beyond my ken.

Thrice on the road hither had the earth groaned in shudder-some dismay, the horses betaken with mounting fright, and grievous word followed Her Ladyship's reception: Ferrara lay cracked and strewn, scores dead; the living left without refuge in the Po vale. Such was the Spite of the Adversary, a false Authority but not without might.

December's morn frosts had come, the cutting air fouled with signs of beast and Man; these and the ready clamours of industry made a town – an empty wall ringed round was none. A wolf knew track and trail and scented the marshy damp of the market square near yon basilica and abbey, I no perfumed lady's pup with a stoppered nose of odorous pome.

I betook me under a stone archway and into the warming sun and adjusted my hat so, whereupon a maiden voice called me back under shade. The moon had waxed and waned o'er Padua, and from the far horizon, a storm of uncertain course was upon me, lax my watch.

The Lady de' Corsi awaited, hands in folded modesty; so was I disarmed, as the countess had warned, with no recourse on this field but Courtesy. Green and gold her colours, as Summer in her arrival, the lady made no profferment of her hand, and I bowed with a flourish of my hat, whose adjustment had lasted but a moment. Said I,

—My lady, are you alone?

—No, sir; my maid stands close by.

I followed her hand to a demure mouse in Winter cloak that bobbed a curtsy, not so close as she should be, but an archer ranged to o'erwatch a conversation 'twixt intimates. A boreal gust chilled me in the stern and salted breath of the sea, though Venice lay a day's ride from Padua's Venetian walls.

—'Tis well. I would not wish Rumour to blot and stain your skirts with coarse aspersions – the low would make lead of gold, for base themselves, must all be so. How chance you to University?

—But your self, my lord. I heard tell you were of studious bent and sought to meet you thus, and I have.

Whilst her words bespake earnestness, her countenance retained the noblest reserve – a model for any gentleman – but she spoke not of bestricken Ferrara nor of her office to the princess in a time of great trial. I played out a few canne of rope that she might ply it:

—To what end, Lady?

—Your hasty departure at that pitchèd hour did weigh upon my mind, that I might be its cause, and came I in all haste to make amends; for your friendship esteems me, though we are little met, were you mine own cavalier and defender in a minstrelled romance of old.

—At times, a gentleman is called upon to beat a cur, but trifling matters should not trouble so fair a damosel.

—You are the picture of Chivalry, my lord. How does Her Ladyship, the countess?

—She is hale and well, I thank you.

—Good sir cavalier, if I might press upon you this service, a letter to her hand alone.

And ta'en up, the rope wound a noose, by her self hung. I a

footboard that she may step up to Issota Ginori. Perchance 'twas always so, I twice the Fool. Sealed with the device of a standant lion under the sun disc, I took up the folded sheet as a poison cup, with smiling dissemblance for the poisoner. Said she,
—In heart's ease, I take my leave and beseech you to call at the Ragione palace, where I guest.
—My lady does me too much Honour. I am unhorsed and, yielding to your gracious hospitality, pray heaven will stay my ransom.
—Give you good day.

The Lady de' Corsi departed with the Mouse a proper step behind and looked back not. A red coach awaited her, armless but royal, and pulled by two matched roans of notable breed. The clack of cobbles under wheels again measured out the breadth of my perturbations, for there was Justice in Her Ladyship's judgements. And with the image of Countess Issota came Modarette alongside the shadow path behind. The smirking thing bowed in mock propriety and said,
—Her Ladyship bids you attend on her in all haste, my lord. Her coach awaits by the crossroad left, forestalled by the Lady de' Corsi's departure.

He spat black bile on the cobbles, a spumy befoulment that reeked as if the creature were filled with rot, his clove pomander a mask of no avail. My gorge rose

Downtown. Charcoal overcast. I was holding the rear door of a sedan I didn't recognise. The Lyft driver said bye, and I shut it and waved. Why... ?

The antiquities broker across the street dealt on both sides of the table, but that was across the street. There was no appointment on my phone calendar. Nothing in my call logs.

I headed that way. Standing still was like asking for a collision. I merged with the riches and rags, divided and inseparable, in the pollenless fume of April à la diesel and concrete; shamblers staring down at their cupped hands; and the brisk, speaking emphatically to the air.

Weeks had passed, stuck on the starting blocks, waiting for the gun and another killing to grist in the mill. At this rate, a Grindhouse mural for my living room. I'd heard little of the Bowen endowment and less of Maaike. She was sifting through the Institute's warehousing, thousands of Assyriological objects,

looking for something. I was uninvited, and during our one-
on-one, Röhm claimed it was to research and refine the reïn-
stallation plan for West Asia. I didn't contradict her. No bet,
Maaike had searched △353 top to bottom, though everything
was where I'd left it.

THE TABLET OF FATES suggested itself, an H-bomb in the
hands of a chimp. It was one thing to possess THE NAME, but
the means to use it was either lost with the missing tablets or
unknown. Inert as a plutonium pit, I looked upon that sheet
of clay and saw an unspeakable fire, a white-hot needle in my
heart. A threat – a potent threat – and a temptation, I couldn't
offer it to her at unknown risk, to an unknown end. It might be
safest, for everyone's sake, to destroy it.

Budgeting for new acquisitions was still fluid, pending Board
approvals, but I was here, so I went in. Past the portcullis awaited
a darkened shrine rather than the typical overbright art gallery,
with museumlike spotlight staging. It was free of the clutter that
defined run-of-the-mill antique shops, though the offerings up
front were little more than that. The good stuff was in back, past
locked doors and a wizened Armenian woman not to be trifled
with. She rose to meet me.
—Doctor Corbín, I should have expected you to appear as soon
as the Bowens emptied my storeroom.

It was a pattern established over the past few years, and as the
endowment negotiations wore on, the Bowens remained a step
ahead. I asked,
—How long?
—Not thirty minutes.
—Liza Bowen?

The publication contract was settled, but her PA contacted me
again to delay my initial survey of the collection. Ms Bowen had
gone overseas, and her return date wasn't fixed. The Armenian
said,
—No, the tomato with the name like a law firm. He has no
discernment and takes everything. She's choosy and drives a
hard bargain. I'd prefer she keep him away; he always insists on
confidentiality. Now we must move all the pieces to a separate
room. My sons have better things to do.
—Ah, I would've…
—Liked a look, yes, but we must respect the client's wishes,

however foolish. We can at least find you a better cane than that thing under your arm.

She opened the door nearest her desk and yelled something that echoed, drawing a chesty bellowed response.

—A temporary medical necessity, I explained. I don't expect to need it for much longer.

—You cannot be seen leaving here with such a thing. It would harm my reputation.

A silver-mounted ebony stick presented itself through the doorway, a momentary impression of broad shoulders before it shut. The opera handle was shaped like a stylised gargoyle, reminiscent of Jaguar's leaping hood ornament from days of yore. Art Deco?

—Tiffany, she said. One of my boys won it in a game of paston. Far more suitable for a man of your bearing. You may rely on it.

I set my aluminum cane against her stout antique desk when she proffered it, surprised by the weight in comparison, if anything, a touch long despite my height or because my length of arm. She knocked thrice on the door with the adjustable cane, and it disappeared in an eyeblink. I bowed from the neck, offering no other thanks, but said,

—A pleasure. Major renovations are in the works for the Institute's West Asian galleries, and the door is opening for significant acquisitions. Please contact my office if anything of note comes up. I'd like to get a drop on the Bowens for once.

Her poker smile was set. She said nothing further but gave a small nod as I took my leave, vintage walking stick underarm. Outside, I loaded Lyft, but the tingle of watching eyes brought me up short. I was anonymous, I'd thought, beside parallel conduits for steel, rubber, and passing bunches of strangers ignoring each other – all but for an unsettling flicker of motion, an alley fifty yards down the sidewalk. A cat or a stray dog? I didn't check; I wasn't a twenty-year-old with a killing blade and the feudal sanction to use it.

Two hybrid cabs loitered in front of an upscale bar on the next block, in the other direction. The first drops of rain began to spot the sidewalk. I skipped the Lyft and took one back, enjoying the nostalgia of a metered ride till I had to pay.

I slept on the problem but awoke bemused by a song like a blue whale's, thinned-sharp by miles of ice: ice that creaked, groaned, and cracked in accompaniment. Less a dream than listening to the traffic outside when you're not quite awake and it's cold and damp and no, not yet. A fanciful image, not so distant as memory, not so close as the Arctic. Mine was the white linen expanse of the real, blank, absent her olive limbs. Absent her dream.

My re-search had turned up nothing but a few typos in my transliterations. Nothing of substance. No nonnuclear weapon I could use against l'Avversario, "the Adversary". No leverage with Maaike and no new insights beyond a suspect reality TV narrative with a nameless editor, but Issota had fled "Leonarda" under the same limitations. As in the flight from Ferrara, even if "Maaike" was out of sight, she was on my heels.

Or waiting in ambush. A silver ring bound the loop of her red-and-blue scarf, horses depicted in varied dressage. Red glasses. The corridor behind West Asia, first thing in the morning, she demanded to know where I'd been yesterday, the zing of ozone on her ocean air. My arm hairs lifted without goosebumps, reaching out to the lightning strike. I was glib:

—Why bother with fake glasses?

—Why does anyone?

I'd found no trail to myself, and her demand hung, unanswerable other than *ask the Tyrant yourself*. I was a horse on the chessboard, played by both sides. Played by her, but her nearness stirred murky waters, warming my skin.

I asked why she wasn't in mediæval studies if she had a thing for knights in shining armour. Her exhalation was as sharp as a train venting steam, and I started in surprise: there was nothing human in that sound. The flexion of her crossed arms tightened.

—If you have to ask.

She wasn't going to explain. She was keeping tabs on me, knew more of my whereabouts than she was saying, and had penned me in; while working around me. A pen had two solutions: through or over. I tried to step past her, but she held my sleeved arm – no contact. She said my name, but that lever – this name, this life – was too short to move me. I said,

—You can't have it both ways. All in or all out.

—That's impossible.

—You want to take but won't give.

—I cannot.

—Two new moons: you've shut me out.

—I can not! It's too…

I kissed her, pulled down by the lift of her chin, and her words broke against my lips.

I didn't know who she was.

I didn't know who I was.

Glass-eyed, she'd frozen, and I raised one hand to the soft, fevered skin of her cheek and kissed her again and bounced off the wall and bellyflopped on the icy tile, my cane skittering away; my injuries reäwakened in all of their punishing glory.

Maaike held one hand to her lips as if scalded.

—What have you done? What have you done.

She stalked away, leaving me alone on the floor, my cane out of reach. Two screws of pain bored into my eyes and through the back of my skull as spinning saws cut into my jaw from behind my ears. I held my head, unable to even scream on the inhale of rasping breath and chattering teeth, spittle frothing wet on my lips, and I grasped then Issota's agony; her in my arms, transfixed on the talons of their unstoppable reach.

A pair of contractors screamed on my behalf when they found me in my fœtal curl, too weak even to crawl. I blamed the emergency stairwell, saying I'd fallen, then fallen again. Röhm arrived before the stretcher and told me the new cane was silly before they wheeled me away.

The scent of the sea clung to me in the ambulance as if Maaike were the wellspring of the depths; it'd carried from Leonarda on the cobbled pavement of Padova – a synthetic odorant that hadn't been invented until the nineteen-nineties. I mulled in the scent memories of clove and incense. Her at the gala. Modarette. Una maschera, I'd thought back then, "a mask".

The hospital staff was less than pleased to see me again, bruised everywhere and unable to hide the lingering pain in my head. They asked if I'd been hit by another car, and I stuck to my story; they blamed the opera cane and told me to stick to one with a rubber foot or have one added.

My X-rays and CT came back clean. No new fractures but a "mild concussion". Take the rest of the week off. My prescription for the patch had run out, and they wouldn't give me a new one, sending me home the next day with a vial of Vicodin, no refills. One step forward, two steps back.

That afternoon, I disembarked an over-friendly Lyft and

hobbled to the three-family townhouse, redbrick and yellow, where I'd mortgaged the third floor. The climb since the not-a-hit-and-run was a pain but beat physical therapy – or that's what I told myself as I ascended endless Escher stairs. Catching my breath, I opened my front door to shambles; everything was thrown this way and that, as if struck by Ferrara's 1570 earthquake. I'd looked it up.

The intruder or intruders had taken the trouble to relock the door with their lockpicks; I didn't expect to find a lurker, and smugglers didn't call the cops. Holding my metal-shod ebony stick like a club, I went corner by corner, room by upturned room. The adrenaline was bracing, but my bedframe was bare of boxspring and mattress, and my palpitating heart fell: gone, my cache of tablets. My notebooks. Nothing else.

Aching, I sagged against the wall. This wasn't Maaike's style – I knew it in my gut. She'd stick her hand out and demand. There were more players in this game, and they'd made an open move. Even if she wasn't an enemy, I needed to keep her close; even if

she is proved no lady, said the Countess Ginori in Greek. The Church would burn a witch, but stands she above all powers temporal, an Olympian amongst men, and could lay Padua waste if hand be raised against her.

The guest chambers were rich, but few candles held back the coaly fingers of duskness that would close about us like those ensnaring serpents that sting not but steal breath. Modarette stood in deep obscurity, marked by numinous coals. Said she, —All was revealed to me by an ancient scroll from the inmost crypts of the basilica, where I may not tread. Torn and difficult it was, woven of the rushes of Ægypt in the age of the Cæsars. Bore it THE REVELATIONS OF THE RULERS: of seven angels, natureless and oppugnant, risen from below the spheres; and of Astaphe, the seed which walks amongst men in mortal guise – a winsome maid with houri-eyes ¶. Said it, IAO the Great hath placed the Earth in the palm of her hand, and as she turneth her neck from Man, ascendeth she Astaphæus; the final throne of eight to sit above the Summer Court, and the Garden shall be sown with lamentations ¶. Hark, there is no Leonarda in the House of Corsi. This papess is unknown to Florence, a false coin gilt without but black within; her patents counterfeit; her letters held in suspect.

At his station, Modarette smiled at the behest of his masters. Not his impudent imp's grin but a missive.

One hand to her head, Her Ladyship pointed.

—Look'st thou at the papers there, all is within them.

—And the scroll of the ancients?

—Burnt, for the bishop received intelligences of my inquiry and of heresy, hidden serpentlike, within the old library. Ta'en from my hands and is perforce no more.

In her page's delinquent office, I poured and presented her cup.

—Why speak you in Greek, madam?

—We have received Greek and Latin across the Aion, and me-thinks they will yet endure, but Latin is of the Church, and we are not. It may be that in the passages hereafter, thou wilt have need and bethinkst this time and remember. As the scroll was Greek, so must I speak.

—Surely, 'tis forbid us to transmit so across the Aion.

—I fear not Death but purgation without end. The Rulers are gaolers of souls, and Báal is without Mercy, but Astaphe hath such power, she can divide First Man from First Woman; and in the binding of one soul, destroy – for all eternity – the other; and nevermore shall they be one flesh. On the moonless night last, she did enter my mind, e'en from Ferrara, and therein made free.

Countess Issota sank into the nearmost seat, betaken by press-ing malaise – it hung upon us as chains a slave, again jerked to.

—Forgive me, I o'erreach my self.

—Forgive me, Your Ladyship, for I have failed to bar the foe. Jacob wrestled the angel, and as I am blood and flesh, so must I contend or stand facing Atropos' shears as they cut the puppet's thread. If the Abyss take thee, then let it take me as well. Come lightnings, together smite us.

I knelt before her and to her hands bowed my head. She

★

HE'D BEEN MORTAL ONCE; everything telegraphed it.
S   Per her self-projection, I put my chips on a mediæval
Faust caught in a devil's bargain – Tyrant a slur nothing less than personal – but she wasn't talking. Her goals, her
reasons, were her own.

If anything, the cold war was at a crisis point. I didn't look at
Maaike. She didn't look at me. Eight thrones circled within my
mind like a diadem – ἀσταφαιὲ, "Astaphæus", would complete
the ὀγδοάς, "Ogdoad", if that scroll was credible. If my broken
reels of memory could be believed.

She'd put a hook in me, then pushed me away to pull on a short
lead. In Ferrara, the same hook to climb over me and grapnel
Issota – and that lingering gut ache I'd felt before, verging on
nausea, resurged.

Maaike's maquette, since returned to the office, was an island
caught between a superpower and some guy. Itself a work of art
in progress, if realised as intended, West Asia would become
a tourist trap in its own right, antiquities aside. Röhm talked
with dollar signs in her eyes, and she'd have to spend the money
to make it, but visitors would be stepping into Persepolis in
recreated colour – if cropped to gallery dimensions – from bull-
headed columns to a cedar-panelled ceiling and wall treatments
simulating glazed mudbrick. Resin castings of new and legacy
wall reliefs to be faux unpainted but viewable in colour via an
augmented reality app in the works.

I'd no doubt Maaike could take what she wanted – whatever it
was – without playing nice, without all of this creative effort, but
she rolled like an operative who left no opening for suspicion.
Every i dotted; every t crossed. Mouse clicks and the drag of
pen on paper interrupted the clacking of her clicky keyboard.
I'd seen no blood on her manicured hands, but l'Avversario had
shown me what they'd wanted and nothing else. No glimpse of
themself but a puppet show.

In my mind's eye, a seething Gordian knot merged with the

wheeling eyes of the Hebraic ophanim, and they stared back, unblinking. "The thousand-armed polyp" was alien to our notions of the alien, to our terracentric imaginations and nothing so definite as the chimæric dragons, titans, and kaijū of our depictions. But kaijū, "mysterious beast", had tipped me off to kaijin, "mysterious person". First attested in eighteenth-century Japan, describing an Oannesesque fishman, I'd gathered that in contemporary Japanese entertainment, usage of kaijin extended to any humanoid monster. There'd been Modarette, not þyrs. I looked at her, not looking at me. Not þyrs and not yet Astaphæus.
—Excuse us, came a deep voice from the doorway.

Two ill-fit sack suits with belted badges. Cheap shoes, cheaper ties. The muted body language of authority, shoulders bowed under pressure from above, their flat eyes cataloguing everything in the room, and a combover too grim to be comic.
—Yes, replied Maaike.
—We're looking for Doctor Julian Corbin.

I signalled with my cane. It'd become an extension of my arm despite or because of all the criticism. They entered without invitation, identifying themselves as detectives on investigation and saying I might be a witness. Brown Suit mentioned the antiquities broker I'd visited Wednesday last. Beige Suit said,
—Doc, you notice anyfin' unusual when you was there? Anybody out of place inside or hangin' around outside?
—I was the only one inside the display area when I entered, well, myself and the proprietress. I believe one or two of her sons were in back, but I only glimpsed one of them. Outside, I can't say I was paying attention. I caught a cab at a bar down the block.
—Was there a robbery? Maaike interjected.
—No, said Brown Suit. Triple homicide – there'll be a new conference later today. We're talkin' to all the known clients of the establishment.

They repeated variations of the same questions to which I gave variations of the same answers, and they left with my card, leaving theirs and requesting I call if I recalled anything else. They didn't mention THE GRINDHOUSE KILLER by media name and didn't confirm or deny when Maaike inquired; itself confirmation. They hadn't mentioned the bodies plastered across my smoking spot last year, or in the imaging clinic I'd visited last month, and that wasn't an oversight.

Telling a suspect they were a witness was one of those things they did on cop shows, but I was in no condition to take down a couple of men the size of the Armenian's sons. On top of everything else, I'd have to retain a lawyer – stupider things than accusing me had happened. L'Avversario had left me there, baiting me to go in, and I'd stepped into the trap.

—You should have listened, snapped Maaike before walking out.

Her too. If anything, she was the better suspect. She

Issota is dead.

Belovèd the final word from her lips as the Adversary gripped her life's breath. Smothered under a wanton and luxuriant cruelty, permitted a heaving half-cry but denied succour again and again, her beseeching hands upon her throat, were they the very stranglehold that pressed her so; her eyes flashing green, then to amber gold; her skin tinct azure; for the Adversary did paint the unlightsome orc o'er her fair aspect.

For this serpent cast no lightnings of Judgement from their deep throne, but as the dun boas of the field, oppressed in black coils. Till frozen, till freed, till breath be reborn.

Now vail me the blue eyes of her repose and the fading warmth of her lips do kiss. Kiss the cold tears driven so. Sleeps she in the arms of Love and of my burning heart doth not partake. She will not awaken.

Say I,

—The one and only lady of my heart, this life is dead to me, for I have no other life but thee ¶. Wolvish fang, gilded misericord, thou art well named. Speed'st me to Her Ladyship's side anon.

Freed by two lines of fire, life's blood runs its course away. Be it I shall seek her a hundred lives of men, a thousand; be it India, the Japans, or Peru; and put foils to the overgreat Despot. Hate is born anew.

With a mocking bow to the play spent, Modarette departs the stage at his master's beck, shuddering the Abyss at his coming. O piteous pit, already thou groanest under the serpent's eyeful coils.

The last, this kiss to my lady's white hand, for the benighted curtain draws close about us. Like Ero, I leap to catch

Mizz Bowen will be with you shortly. Please have a seat.

The Bowen Trust sublet a suite within their extensive corporate holdings. Tax reasons. The top floor of the hôtellike midrise presented a decent view of downtown, a few blocks too far from the Museum of Art to spit on it. The depth and breadth of dead space in the reception room was as much a part of the veneer of money as the Peruvian marble; African burl panelling; and the real, if contemporary, art.

The lawyers had done their thing. Square footage was allocated for the Institute's new Bowen Endowment, a shiny brass plaque in the works, and a piano-black wedge

Julián Corbín, PhD
Bowen Curator of Ancient West Asian Arts

back on my desk. I'd updated my cv.

After the physical blow of Issota's death, of our deaths, I'd needed a personal day, caught up in the prescient grief that'd haunted me for weeks. Maaike was a wild card, but l'Avversario had shifted the spotlight with a sadistic murder. Yes, *murder* – I'd finally grasped the word. They'd stoked the fire, l'odio è rinato, "hate is born anew". I needed a weapon, and somewhere in the Bowen Collection, I imagined a sword thrust into a stone, foolish as it was.

Liza stepped through the bright wood doors before I could step away from the glass. Her red hair tucked behind her ears, she greeted me by the familiar and extended her hand; she walked with them in her pockets, the old school preppy casual of chinos and a pale blue blouse. Her aldehydic floral scent was lighter and fresher than the full-bore No. 5, like silk on the air, and her white point-toe pumps zeroed on me like missiles. We shook hands again. She said,

—We'll head down to the collection. It's in the basement levels. With boilers and other waterworks, conventional basements were less than ideal for antiquities. I said,

—No light? No heat?

—Climate controlled, HEPA filtered. You'll see. We're in office twice a week, so I'll give you a key card of your own.

She looked at her assistant.

—Molly, Doctor Corbin is a priority contact.

—Yes, Mizz Bowen.

—I'll be back.

Liza led the way out of the office and through the almost-as-posh corridors, past a prestige law firm, a hedge fund, and a crypto something-or-other.

—What do you do for fun, Julian?

—Old movies, when I have the time.

—What, eighties? French New Wave?

—Golden Age. Even Pre-Code. I don't mind New Wave for contrast, but only in black-and-white. Hardboiled.

A wink crinkled one of her eyes.

—Ladies and gents, there is an old soul among us; I may have to join you at the talkies. Here, we'll take the cargo elevator all the way down.

Liza flashed an RFID card before hitting the down button, then handed it to me, saying,

—This one's yours. You can also use it to access the parking levels. Use reserved section B near the elevator. You have my number; call anytime, but if I'm not available, it'll ring to Molly like before, and she'll know how to find me.

We stepped into a bare steel elevator large enough for a Bosendorfer Concert Grand and the pianist playing it. Her eyebrow quirked.

—That's a rather natty opera cane but too much for shirtsleeves. You need some blazers.

—How do you know I haven't any?

—If you did, you would've worn them to your lectures.

—I'd've noticed you in the audience. You weren't really there, were you?

—The right hat and sunglasses work miracles. I didn't wear them to hide from you – I didn't think I needed to – but that Röhm woman smells funding opportunities like a shark. How would you have known what I looked like? Google?

—I didn't, but I would've noticed.

—You noticed my shoes upstairs but didn't comment.

—I wasn't sure it was appropriate.

—It's appropriate.

—That ballistic shape...

—Zanotti.

—I hope you own more of them.

—I do. Your assistant doesn't like me. Is it going to be a problem?

—No; she'll stay in her lane. Did you wear that armlet just to bait her?

Liza chuckled.

—Her reputation preceded her. This is us.

We stepped off on B5, far below the parking levels, into the echoing clack of her shoes and my cane on polished grey concrete. It recalled the Institute's acceptable A and B quadrants but with better lighting. The few doors along the grey corridors were widely placed, and it wasn't long before I discovered why. She unlocked one with her key card, then waved me in.

I stepped into a room the size of an indoor basketball court, including space for the stands.

—You're kidding.

A triple-mezzanine storage structure of freestanding industrial steel, with stairwells and walkways, filled the centre of the enormous room: a ziggurat of objects. Monumental statuary was spaced along one wall, with ample space for new acquisitions. I looked to Liza, bemused.

—Cataloguing this will take years.

—Which is why the contract included an annual salary.

—There's enough here for a team of Assyriologists.

—And how, but Wes is quite the miser with information, and not everything will appear in the print catalogue. He prefers you to be the only person on the project or in this room. No assistants. Will that be a problem?

—Not as long you don't mind having me around.

She smiled at that but didn't reply directly:

—Temperature and humidity control are here by the door. Make any adjustments you deem necessary. Gloves and analysis equipment are stocked in the desk drawers and those cabinets. Let me or Molly know if you need anything else.

—This is a little too good to be true.

And it was. Half of Assyriology would give a kidney for the opportunity.

—Why me? Why not De Staufer at the Museum of Art or someone from the University?

—I prefer your interpretations. Your voice.

Liza touched my arm, bringing me back to earth from the baffling scale of what towered above us. Blue, her eyes.

—It gets better. While I was away, I closed a deal on a new acquisition…

She trailed a stirring hand across my chest, then dropped smoothly. There was no chainsaw buzz when she drew my zipper down; a surreal turn into a surgent pressure and flash heat. But it was her eyes that held me, a clear, unwavering horizon, and all the angst and frustration of Maaike and the Other lifted on the pulsing crescendo: it welled up, erupted, and blew away. I was on the shore of a new world.

I lifted Liza to her feet, but she stepped back and away from my intentions as smoothly as she'd knelt, wiping the corner of her smirk with implicit punctuation.

—It's something important. Something I've been searching for. I won't say how I came by it…

—I won't ask.

—But are you well-versed in Luwian?

That ball was deep into left field, but by reputation, she was more a collector of Anatolian than Mesopotamian antiquities. I said,

—Luwian? It's a little out of my wheelhouse. If it's cunéiform, I can transliterate, but I'd need several reference works for that and any attempt at translation.

—Then bring everything you'll need and keep it here; there's plenty of shelving. I'll leave you to it for now.

Liza's abrupt move to depart drew an involuntary step towards her, one hand raised. Wait was on my lips, but overshoulder, she said,

—O, you'll have dinner with me Thursday, won't you?

T IS COLD, BUT I AM RESTLESS. The orb is yet rimed
I   with frost, but the little flea niggles me. It jumps and
jumps in the cold world and dies, yet it cannot die, and
forgetless sleeps. Little biter of my blood, thou hast become my
blood; I am the flea, but the flea is not

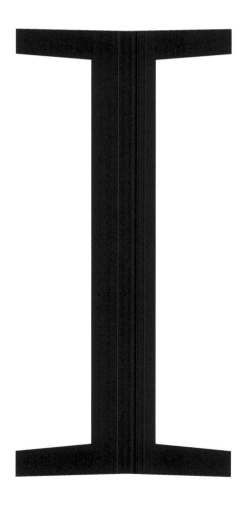

T IME FOLDED IN ON ITSELF, and Thursday night arrived with alacrity. Liza wore a third-date dress, wholly self-possessed and as at ease in her own skin as anyone I'd ever met.

She inducted me into the performative rituals of her social vocation, a cycle of charities, foundations, and other events which defined the annual "season". We enjoyed an ordinary dinner for two – if at a restaurant I could never get a table at – and a gallery opening full of strange objects and stranger animals, bandying the emperor's new adjectives among themselves; it was dinner and a show. We'd already clicked.

The black car that'd picked me up took us back to her spacious uptown loft, "You'll join me for a nightcap?" no question. Our lovemaking was nostalgic with the normalcy taken for granted by other men; it'd brushed past me at times, ungrasped, unheld. She was nothing if not assertive, and a woman that knew what she wanted was all the more enticing.

Liza was something of an "old soul" herself, eschewing the Millennial addiction to text despite her oversized smartphone of the moment. In the ensuing days, I found many excuses – most transparent – to call. And as I began my assay of the Bowen Collection, our lunches, dinners, and sultry nights became most. And my new dinner jackets, pair of tuxedos, and assorted blazers took up residence within my corner of her suitelike walk-in closet, my opera cane at final rest in her umbrella stand.

The change of wardrobe presaged a change in Röhm: from tolerance to something resembling deference. Deference not to me but to the money I represented as the Liza Bowen's plus one. I settled into mornings at the Institute, with Röhm's consent, and afternoons at the Bowen Collection. Spring warmed to summer, and while I found several artefacts suggestive of the Other, I hadn't reached the host of tablets shelved in drawered cabinets. But for the first time, I was sure my answers lay within reach. Somewhere, somehow, in their arrogance, l'Avversario had shown their hand.

Maaike tried to elbow her way in, but the contract was airtight. I offered to give her a signed copy of the catalogue after publication and got the cold shoulder.

The stridulant kaijin remained quiescent after the gallery slaughter, and the detectives didn't return to question me. No lip from them or her.

Then with the first ginger leaves of autumn, West Asia closed for renovations. I wasn't involved and focused on a bimonthly series of Assyriological talks – to keep the Foundation off my neck – and the national exhibition of Assyrian art I intended to launch at the grand reöpening. Lots of phone calls, emails, and Zoom meetings. A few hostile faces from the good old days.

This morning had progressed like most, but with Maaike in Egypt, I had the place to myself. A light knock on the open door was a welcome respite, accompanied as it was by salon-sharp copper hair and a pert smile.

—All this time, Liza said, and I've never seen your office.

She strode in, in her direct way, closing the door behind her. Flared skirt, strappy sandals. She sat against the edge of the other desk, the grandiose maquette between us; she set her purse down, then went Golden Age vamp:

—C'mere, Mister.

—What, there?

—C'mere.

—What'd she ever do to you?

—Don't worry your pretty little head.

It wasn't my kink. In my dissociative isolation, I was too far behind the curve for public nooners. This was Liza's game, and she was wet in anticipation. In my urgency, in my anxiety to avoid detection, I was far too rough with her, but she only spurred me on, refusing to break in half. And in the rise and fall, in the fresh scents of her hair and perfume, the flutter of fear quickened. Fear for her and of l'Avversario.

Fear of thursic memories, for those were also mine. That momentary yellowing of Issota's eyes, of ultramarine-blued skin, a warning – a Kalilike gold-and-lazuli reflexion of terrible potentialities, but there was no blood on these hands or under my nails. A potential that hadn't.

It would be easy to drift in the lullaby, in the months-long absence of rebounding time and the novel peace of dreamless sleep, but Liza could be ripped from me in an eyeblink. I could be taken from myself. From humanity.

Somewhere, somehow, there was a non-Pyrrhic solution to Other malice. A way to sever the cord of immortality. I wanted this life with her, not otherworld ravishments beyond mortal ken, but this devil couldn't simply be denied. On the geologic clock, Greenhouse Earth was imminent. Nothing stood between Man and an apocalypse.

Smoothing her skirt, she chuckled in throaty tones, here and now in the human drama, unaware this puppet show was set on a larger stage.

—I hope we didn't traumatise your assistant.

My stomach flopped, a transgressive twist deeper than any adolescent embarrassment.

—She saw.

—You were… preoccupied. She started to open the door, then closed it.

Liza's smile said it all. I deflated. She was just getting started. I couldn't say what we had for lunch, someplace downtown, not with her bare foot snaking up my trouser leg under the table. A teaser leading to the big reveal back at the Collection, but I was more into the swish of her skirt than the Luwian mystery she'd been waiting on.

Nothing resembling tablets greeted me. I sat before splinters of bleached driftwood and a jigsaw mound of yellowish chips. Hundreds – no, thousands of wax fragments inscribed with broken lines of cunéiform. Once upon a time, they'd been wooden tablets inlaid with a thin layer of beeswax. Clay was less common in Anatolia, and the locals had adapted local materials, including wood and ivory. Given the low survival rate, they were rare but not unknown.

I was no stranger to puzzles, but this would require working with gloves, tweezers, and magnification. The most delicate touch. Liza squeezed my shoulder.

—Thoughts?

—I'll need more tables to spread these out. I'll start with the wood fragments and try to get a sense of the tablet sizes and how many we're working with. I don't see any rot, mildew, or charring. Do you know where they were found?

—Tall tales. Nothing to hang your hat on.

—This won't be in the catalogue.

—No; it's a pet project. I'm relying on your discretion.

I looked up at Liza from my seat. She was teasing and gave me an air kiss at the cheek.

—I'll leave you to it and see you at home for dinner. You'll sleep on the couch if you're late.

Her overstuffed couches were comfortable but had little appeal without her. I set a phone alarm; then, lit magnifier and soft-tip tweezers at the ready, I

mounted the first wall. Innermost, and at fifteen paces, the highest of three that set in stone the division 'tween castes and the city of winter from those without. Llys, the old capital and eldest shahdom; ancient, even in its declination, and unsurmounted. And by Law, fief to her, the heir of Ymerodraeth; though it was said she was loth to leave the fastness of Fedvvyd and had let its reins to lesser hands.

Alone, pennoned Henllys, the golden keep moated within the first circle, stood above all. Fount of Law and seat of the shahanshah, who guesting, captained the table.

—Marzban, sir!

—Sir!

Two sentries of the watch saluted my arrival, wingèd spears at rest, round shields slung, and cloaked in the shearling of woolly mountain sheep. In the elder fashion, their helms were enamelled red; first forged in alchymic green flame like their polished spear tips, which shone an amberous gold.

These mild morns frosted naught but breath, and it was my custom to walk the battlements under embered dawn. I nodded to my azad brothers in arms, the limestone beneath our feet worn with the long centuries of our service to the empire. This, the first bastion of order. This, the final bastion of our retreat. This, the very wall between myself and Her Imperial Grace – it was for me to know it and my place. Awash in the restless wind, resinous pine, and the thousand hearth fires that cast their grey pall over Llys, the last beacon of Law in the night of superstition.

The embattled walls were washed with yellow lime, where it was not befouled by moss or vine, where it had not been scathed by wind or negligency, baring the stone beneath. Limewash brought from beyond Coedvvig Ddu – the evergreen forest that stretched south – to this, the rock of our union in ballad and campfire tale. Every stone contested 'tween vispuhr houses. Four thousand years? Five? The learnèd made tourneys and duels of their numberings.

But four royal houses endured, for Danyal and Lleon fell to the Div, and the horridity of their subjection, no less than of my blood, was not to be spoken. Gorg and Vardan had not departed Caers Siddi and Goludd, the easternmost holdings or their spring grazing, far northeast, beyond the Div advance.

What remained of the western oxherds grazed now upon the meadows of Cymoedd Glas – the white mountains ranged eastwards – below ascending sun. Named for the creeping vales of blue ice, the high wellspring of the Stiffrvvydd, which descended to the city's canals and into the vast waters of Llyn Tvvyll, the western expanse. The far side was beyond sight, where Caer Fedvvyd, the new capital of contested dynasties, lay in Div clutch.

I was not called on to patrol this day, only the practise fields and bath-houses awaited, and I remained past the changing of the guard, under a grey eagle's ranging wings and the half-disc of the snow-bright moon. It was said that the sun cast the veil of day over the sphere of cloud and rain and that the starry vault lay ever behind it, but by unanswered circumstance, the moon might pass on either side of the veil.

The spearsmen abreast myself snapped to rigid attention, were the shahanshah himself arrived for the watch; and a repentine audience with the Banbyshn of Llys, foremost heir of the Kian Dynasty, was upon me. She stood tall and straight before her veil-faced maids-of-honour, mobled up in the richest furs of Fedvvyd's woodland estate, her braided hair the blonde that few kept beyond childhood – her brows the faintest dusting of gold above dark eyes – her glance sharp as any spear.

I bowed before the princess afar, a dream of spring that never was, my first sight of her in the shahanshah's party at the meeting of the two armies; I knew then the bard's golden lance through the heart. A marzban might attend court, but the banbyshn was ever aloof and heretofore had no cause to speak to a vassal's retainer from the northwestern reaches – I was no vispuhr knight palatine to shine in her regard, but the dazzle of the stars was not lessened for being out of reach. I said,

—Your Imperial Grace, forgive my rude presence. I shall depart hence, and yield to you this high place as befits your worship. And good morrow.

—Good morrow, Marzban, but stay, I pray you. How go you uncloaked?

—Uffren was my charge, ma'am, along the moors and reindeer barrens. Where the 'Scarp whelms forest deep and dark, and by winter, we hardy few went on snow-skates, unhorsed lest our steeds perish of cold. Llys is yet new to mine eyes, and these are the warmest days of my memory ¶. But you do me too much honour, ma'am: a marzban holds the march, and I left Uffren ungarrisoned. The prince-consort is Marzban Palatine of Llys, and in this place, I am but a humble horseman. How may I serve?

A hooded court lady spoke out of turn, her eyes bright blue against brown skin and hair, as sometimes said of the eastern folk.

—Illustrious Knight, is i' true Caer Fandvvy be hewn of ice?

—Nay, Your Highness, it is a rude fort and rough-framed, and its lichenous stone may not be seen for a hillock – and ice near upon it. The white bears range south and lard the stew.

The banbyshn made a curt gesture, a silver signet of Kian's lion-and-sun proud on her hand, amid other jewels. Her maids-of-honour were the daughters of vassal shahs. Rival houses. Hostages to custom.

—Sir Gvvyn, then, mean you to enter the lists of the tourney in preparation?

—Aye, ma'am. I would not do but at the bidding of His Grace, Shahryar Rhys. I am better fit to barbarous march, the clash of coldmetal and stone, and the tilt with brutish unycorn.

—But you bear no lady's favour: no ribbon; no ring?

—Nay, ma'am. Even so, I am commanded. I do not covet the tourney prize, but it may be that such sport will lighten the hearts of the people for a time.

The arena lay below us, a circle within the azad circle, adjoint the practise field but open to all in times of contest. The ancients made much of circles. Built of red stone but here and there in tumbled disrepair, the image of Ymerodraeth itself.

By long custom, the victorious knight dedicates his prize to the vispuhr lady of his admiration; their chaste bond akin to retainer and lord, many were the clashes of fealty recounted in lyred lyric for the ladies' savoured tears. Its first practise lost since to the ages, it had become a game played 'tween them. Too oft to mortal outcome. Too oft in azad blood.

Her ladies rapt in their attention, the banbyshn said,

—Has no lady of the court found your favour that you might seek hers?

—There are none to your gentle grace, who outshines each and all as an emerald does the sand. There is but one Lady of Ymerodraeth, and would I, the least of His Grace's knights, besmirched by failure, should I be one to grasp the sun?

—The days have grown fell and strange, and you have won much worship, your deeds sung in court and commons. And of five named *grivpanvar* by our father, are you not the sole azad to bear the silver gorget on your breast? But few worthies could claim such in all the nine dynasties ¶. Failure, sir? Of what do you speak?

—Look you, ma'am, this gilded parapet declares it. Every winter, the 'Scarp closes, the earth freezes under foot, and in summer, does not thaw but to scabrous and pockmarked moor. Its mossy fingers leprous spread, and the grasslands diminish, and so are we diminished, the arts of old forgotten, the ores of adamant exhausted, and we remake what remains with lesser craft. The hoary bull totters and hyæna gather to despoil ¶. Here we stand, our crumbling castles abandoned, our herds and peoples hewn by flints. Our little ones in the blood-matted grass, lying still. Their blood calls for vengeance, but my sword hangs at my side unwet.

Encamped out of season, Llys was but lightly held. The weavers of silk did not sing. The tanners of pelts did not laugh. Too few, the golden-haired children to play and run. But the pompery of the gathered princelings went on unabated – the hunts, banquets, and tourneys – in all desperate cheer, ringing hollow as an empty cup.

The banbyshn was sharp in her reply, saying,

—Could you have held back the red flux, Sir Gvvyn, with your spear? Or sundered the great escarpment of ice with your sword? But how many have you delivered with sword and spear, throwing back the Elder Foe in his hosts and reaving the very lions of the steppe?

—Too few, too few.

I raised one rough-calloused hand: there, the rutted track which passed between the great lake's forested edge, northwest, and the broad steppe, north. The deathly furrow of the

Long March. Routed by spring storm; flanked by raiders and fell beasts; winnowed by sickness, frailty, and the great clash at the bloody fords; the line of weary townsfolk had stretched parasangs in the wake of horse-drawn vispuhr wagons, the horse and oxherds, and ox-drawn raman industry. Unaccustomed and ill-prepared for a hard march, the keens of mourning were followed by long silences.

—There, I said. Ymerodraeth lies slain on the battlefield, and I have brought forth her empty cloak. Llys holds her remembrance, and the images of the dead hang upon me. Here, this silver gaud is the weight of it. All I have failed.

And displeasure seamed her smooth brow

—Kneel, sir. I am wroth with you.

—Ma'am?

—Kneel!

I fell to one knee, and the nearmost guards, her liegemen, raised their shields and lowered the bitter tips of their spears. I said,

—Your Imperial… ?

—Silence! she snapped. Humble? We have never met a more prideful knight: you have taken all of Ymerodraeth unto yourself. Would you take the White Crown from our father's head? ¶. And yea, even the humblest flower will reach for the sun, but you are too proud to feel its rays. Know you, the sun you have spurned shall bind you. Pray, sir, you do not burn ¶. Before these witnesses here, we claim your life; it is forfeit to the crowns.

Numb as in the withering, vaporous wind over the glassy blue cliffs of Uffren, I withdrew my scabbarded sabre from its carriage belts and laid it at her feet. The foremost guard saluted, knelt, and presented it. Then, before her whispering ladies, the banbyshn drew White-hilt, an heirloom of my fathers, said to have passed across three dynasties of shahs. Sunlight played across the leaf-pattern temper line; for as limber as yew, it bore a fearsome flintful edge. Hilted in ivory; silvery alcamynium; and pommelled with an ancient white jade as rough-hewn as me, brought along from the farthest east of legend, beyond the brackish barrier lake. An alcamyn rod fit to mete my justice. I bowed my head, so let my failures end. I was ready.

The banbyshn laid the bare blade to my shoulder but drew it not against my neck.

—We hereby dissolve your allegiance to the House of Arman. As you have claimed Ymerodraeth from Kian, henceforth, you shall serve at our pleasure until your death or the shahanshah release you ¶. You are reborn, O prideful one. Rise and retake thy measure in our service ¶. Sergeant, report to His Imperial Majesty that we have chosen our knight and champion. We will inform the shahryar directly.

She returned the blade, and the standing guard put up his spear and descended the wall. I, a thunder-struck tree uprooted by her storm, said,

—Unworthy though I am, I pledge my life and death to Your Imperial Grace. Let me be the spear that scatters your enemies, the sword that flies to your hand ¶. My liege, call forth the charge.

—Are you too proud to rise, Sir Gvvyn? – too proud to serve by imperial command alone but must place your oath above? Indeed, you may be too much for the sun itself ¶. Here, take this ring and give it unto your intended, for we have it from our ladies that you are unwed. We must needs claim her service till the nuptial binding join you.

—Ma'am, I am unbetrothed. I was not recalled to Caer Pedryfan in my commissions and spent my youth afield ¶. My kin fell to the Elder Foe, and with them, any counsel held for my despon-sation. I am the last of my line.

The shahs had stricken "Div" from all tongues and ears, but the Elder Foe remained. The blue-eyed lady-in-waiting who had spoken so boldly stepped forth.

—Llesa! Sir Gvvyn must take…

The banbyshn's keen eye silenced, and her voice cut:

—Your place, Prin-cess Es-sylt.

—Yes, ma'am.

The cowed lady curtsied and withdrew, and the guard returned to his post. Llesami ap Lleu drew down the silver-fox fur at her throat, revealing her well-shaped mouth.

—Llys needs sons and daughters, not maiden knights, and all men look to champions such as thee. Get thee a bride. Love us well, but under the Law, we cannot be thine. And it may be that Vardan will gift a suitable dower to bride a grivpanvar. The ring, sir.

The maids-of-honour tittered among themselves, and I ac-cepted the proffered ring and the commission it bore. In emerald and gold was I indeed bound to the sun. All emerald was in possession of the vispuhran, found amid the ores of adamant and prized above all other gems.

Out of the ladies' ken, the guard tipped the edge of his helm, signing caution: dying ground ahead. Where helmets ring under blows, and there is no retreat but victory. The banbyshn said,

—Away now, Illustrious Knight. Take up thy sword and do us some honourable service. Bring us a worthy token of thy love before the fullness of the moon, whence the tourney commenceth.

—Ma'am, my courser is a great champion who has suffered to bear a knight as poor as myself. But as you have my love withal, he and I shall prove it on the very giants and raise your worship.

Sheathed sabre in hand, I bowed for my leave. And smiling, she added,

—Away, and know our good champions do not fail. Com'st thou by the first flag of the tourney, or we shall not see thy face again.

—Ma'am, I

was out of room. A half-dozen wooden tablets, once three hinged pairs, though there was more grey desktop visible through the lacunæ than there was remaining wood.

"Llesami ap Lleu" gave name to Maaike's dream-vision, for they were one and the same. A queen pulled from the sleeve of l'Avversario. Llesami frowned and smiled; her hand was cold; in that time, in that place, she was mortal. It was her beginning, if not mine. Her story. Hers, and perhaps Issota's, if she was there, somewhere, behind a different face. A different name.

The sword and spears looked like polished bronze, but as far as I knew, neither tin bronze nor the arsenical bronze sometimes found in Mesopotamia could be tempered like steel – I was no metallurgist. There were other copper alloys out there, but however steellike, it wasn't steel, which at best guess, moved the early mediæval scene back to the Bronze Age. I had memories of the Palæolithic night, and if my origin still lay in mystery, this appeared to be our first meeting – and in a place I didn't recognise. Not exactly.

A walled protocity like Llys would be a significant find to the field, if of little interest to the nonspecialist, without monumental architecture for tourists to gawp over. But if I were looking for semi-settled pastoralists with her Indo-Persic cast, I'd expect to find them somewhere along the Eurasian steppe, from the Caucasus to the Stans, braced by mountain ranges and inland seas. Central Asia. Llys would present an idiosyncratic site like Sanxingdui, if not so far east – I'd have to check the literature. If not documented, its ruins, stripped or intact, might lay undiscovered. Waiting.

After months of peace with Liza, I found myself troubled by words. I couldn't remember the dead dialects of the Stone Age, only moving pictures: the flashes of fire, obsidian, and blood. But I could remember everything Llesami said, everything Gwyn – I – thought.

My alarm went off.

L INES OF HORSE CHARGED⸳ SPEARS RAISED, on hanging tapestries of civil war, of the clash of riders and foot; our spears sharpened against ourselves, for always have we sewn our own division. Splintering, there, to three shahdoms, then eleven. Wars I knew not the names of and gaping anarchies where Ymerodraeth did not know itself. Spun before them, to my left, hung the Clanstrife.

Clans unified by Cayo Mardd, poet and image-breaker, said the first Padshah and Lawgiver of Llys. The confederacies of tribes made one people, one speech, but in three castes new divided; all rights and duties constituted, according each their place; the daevas banished and their idols cast down.

THE RECORD OF DYRRAITH, so known to the shahs; I had but glimpsed it in the Henllys and Pedryfan. The light of hearth and oil lamps was dim and smoaky, and much lay in shadows. Much of it was strange to me.

I would not number their dynasties; these hearth fire tales of the vispuhran: the idols upon which they hung their names. I had known my father's father and learned his way, his azadagi, but the aforetime is unanswered. And "dyrraith", a word uncertain: *fate* to the foolish, and *jeopardy* in all else. It left little enough record.

There, any of a thousand shahrdaran quelling the hundred tribes. Let them lay one stone upon another, we pulled them down; let them smelt one copper blade, we fell upon them and put all near to the sword. Ymerodraeth suffered none else to rise above flints, and the outer barbarians chewed their bitterness like rawhide.

And there, the Div, a steppe adder struck in twain by Padshah Fereydun's sword. And sundered, the wyrm multiplied, untold. I said,

—Your Grace, I am compelled from your service, but you remain ever in my esteem and the memory of my fathers, whose fealty to Arman did not waver. I sought no other liegance.

I proffered a skin of koumiss to Shahryar Rhys, as horsemen may offer fraternity to horsemen, himself knight palatine before his beard and hair turned silver and his crowning in Pedryfan. He took a deep draught, the joints of his jewelless hands swollen with rheum, his face cragged and burnt by the sun.

—Such is the hazard by which all live, and so Dyrraith is revealed. Pressed championage is not unknown to custom but ill-done and out of form with the courtly game. He coughed, then said:—I thought to see favours thrown to your feet when you took the tourney field; it is the least debt I can pay Lludd's faith to me ¶. It is within my right to contest the banbyshn's claim, but this day's loss may presage the morrow's gain – and thus is Dyrraith revealed.

In purple and blue silks, the shahryar was well cushioned on the rich carpet and leant upon a lacquered armrest, a single attendant waiting on our audience. No ministers or captains. Nor Her Grace, the shahbanu. Private audiences were not accorded even to a marzban, and I rested on uncertain ground. I matched his drink, sparkling and sour as the day, in my felt jodhpurs and quilted gambeson, harnessed for the field.

The window looked in upon the glassed-over winter garden and shadowless noon, a rainbow breadth of flowers in spring bloom. The window lattice bespake the decline of ancient Llys, the lucid glass patchworked with plates of plain mountain copper, weeping green. I said,

—I know not the ways of the winter court. I am of the blown summer steppe and the stony clash of the frontier. Thus, Your Grace and my fathers have made me.

—A colt is not taught to run. He knows the grass beneath his hooves, meadow and dale, the day his eyes open. How many summers have you?

—A score and twelve, sire.

He stroked his beard with one hand, his gaze as clear as ice melt below a clouded brow.

—The sharpest sword finds little rest in the sheath; I am remiss, and the banbyshn perspicacious. You are well seasoned and in want of a household. Did she make tender of a bridal match?

—She made jest of the House of Vardan. I am no prince.

—Should Gorg and Vardan return south, h'mf, or break away, and a struggle of three shahdoms, h'mf... We are rid at last the

ruinous cost of pastureless Fedvvyd, and the rot takes with it
too much of the limb ¶. But come, I would fain return you to
my house – if not Marzban of Uffren, then mayhap my son, and
we will thank the banbyshn and her empery yet ¶. My youngest
is nineteen, once trothed to Danyal but no more. She will be a
ready bride in two years and bear you many fine sons. Illustrious
Knight, what say you?

—Your Grace, my station is…

—Of the very highest: grivpanvar and champion of she who will
be banbyshnan banbyshn. She is wed these five years and proved
barren, and on her choice lies the hazard of all Ymerodraeth. In
dynastic succession, Sir Gvvyn, and needed reformation.

Any might gossip over koumiss, mead, or the autumn beer fer-
mented from hearty grasses foraged south of Llys. Any might gossip, but with princes, imperilous ground lay ahead. I questioned,

—Reformation, sire?

—You were not the first marzban to report the rise of the Elder
Foe in Mazandaran. Of their conquests of the hundred tribes,
the slaughter and slavery of the pari, and the spread of foul
rites. Since I first took saddle as a boy, it has been so. Some new
cunning seizer upon them and forged a nation in three generations. This Pretender among them names himself Gueyumar,
shah of the world.

I pressed the koumiss on His Grace, for he had grown hoarse.
He drank, then said,

—It follows, as Shahanshah Lleu sallied forth into Mazandaran
to suppress the foe in his young reign, that in their long strat-
agem, they did not trespass the green marches of Fedvvyd nor
trouble the red deer of the shah's fine hunting grounds, not till
the fullness of their preparation ¶. Time draws veils of doubt
over clear courses, and enmity is oft near at hand. A single household has its partisans – a dozen warnings might go unheeded. In
this, I fear, came the fall of two royal houses, the sack of Colur
and VVydvvyr, and the retreat of Arman and Kian ¶. Deprived
of the west, of three parts in seven, must we look to reformation
if Ymerodraeth is to endure. First, a council of state to guide
the throne in its course – the moderating hand of the best men.
The Law must be amended.

—Your Grace, these high matters are beyond my ken or reach.
"Watch and be ready", as you commanded; this, I understand.

Shahryar Rhys had sent no other reply to my reports of Div action in Mazandaran, the dark continent west of Mur Mvvr, the rocky range of mountains one hundred fifty parasangs north to south. Three fortress towns had watched its bounds and the east–west riverine passage, and in the bard's telling, no tribe might pass into our domain. But in a single stroke, the pillars had fallen; for the Div host had not assailed the walls we'd raised against the wilds, against ourselves, but the oxherds late returned from Llys and the southron pasture. Not to steal but to destroy. Not since the Clanstrife would azad raise hand to kine or colt; this was our azadagi. This was our temperance of war. His Grace said,

—You have proved the bold folly of the Elder Foe on the body of their great general, but they are not broken, only cowed for a time. My spies tell that they regather their strength and, stoking the flame of hate, will come again – if not till winter, after fatting their cows on our summer prairie. After devouring our flesh ¶. We must be fixed in our preparations: let the five armies face them as one, united, and reclaim what has been taken. And with my daughter's hand, Sir Gvvyn, I should bequeath five stallions, ten mares, six… no, twelve bales of silk, an incense brazier – alcamyn, not low copper – and an armour fit for the first knight of Llys.

He spoke of five armies, but of my troop, few remained in the saddle after driving the Div from the field, and less than one of the two armies that met at the fords came unto Llys. I knew not Princess Carys, to me, but a veiled girl in the shahryar's attendment. It was not for rough men to know the refined.

—But your daughter's sons would be counted azad, not vispuhr, and lack the privileges thereof.

—The greatest honours of Dyrraith lay within the ancient service of the azadan, and my grandsons of the vispuhran will not forget their cousins. This, I promise you.

—Done then, Your Grace. I yield to this gilded honour, but pray you hold this counsel 'tween us. I leave this day on quest and would not have the princess troubled should I not return.

The shahryar lent forward, a hand on his knee.

—How now? The tourney lies but a fortnight hence.

—Such is the command of the banbyshn. I must go and come ere the tourney flag flies – bearing such tokens as befit Her Imperial

Grace – or look not on Llys again, my bones lying forgotten. If I find no worthy prize in a sennight, I am lost.

—O, but she has a heavy hand – a grivpanvar is not so lightly let away. Take with you companions?

—Nay, Your Grace; this duty is mine to discharge, and I will not lead others into mortal peril without uttermost need.

—Away then, Sir Gvvyn. Away my countryman and return my son.

—I wish nothing better, sire, and

Eh, like, excuse the interruption.

—I got it, Louie.

Brown and Beige were back from wherever they'd been lurking. They might've swapped colourways, but I couldn't remember anything except the bad combover.

—Doc? We've got a few more questions, if you got a moment.

I didn't, but that didn't matter. This time they weren't looking at everything. Just me.

—We understand you were checked into the hospital the morning after the murders at the antiques place.

—I fell down the stairs.

—Witnesses state you were found in the hallway.

—I fell down the stairs, then collapsed in the hallway.

No one would believe a girl half my size had bounced me off a wall. Brown and Beige did their bit:

—The docs at the hospital said you was worked over pretty good. Couldn't've been easy to take down those two by yourself. You're a big guy, Doc, but is you ex-UFC or somefin?

—My medical information is private.

—Unless a judge tells 'em to talk, and then they talk.

—Louie, the doctor's just a witness.

—Yeah, and no Grindhouse vics back when he was laid up. Sure. Coincidence.

—These things happen. Doctor Rome sez you're working downtown on Fifth in the afternoons. That correct?

I relaxed my clenched hands, then affirmed. Beige was bland, saying,

—We'll let you know if we have any more questions.

—Don't leave town, Doc.

I'd have to call the lawyer I'd retained and forgotten about – Police investigations dragged out longer than on TV, it seemed.

My hypothetical kaijin's blood trail had ended at my doorstep; then stopped. If they had no better leads, I was holding the hot potato. I was too preoccupied to be angry at more than the interruption but still a little hot under the collar.

My preliminary investigation had fizzled: Bronze Age development in Central Asia had centred in Turkmenistan, and the walled city of Altyn-Depe, with its ziggurat temple complex, had paralleled those of Mesopotamia. Neither its construction nor its geography matched my memory of Llys; and the hundreds of kalas, stone "fortresses", that dotted the Stans dated from the Iron Age or later. Though there was an outside possibility of an undiscovered stratigraphic layer beneath a younger site, I'd have to step back and start over.

I'd seen no evidence of writing within the extensive murals and tapestry. No pictographs, glyphs, or other script. No glimpse of scrolls, tablets, or codices.

The presence of silk required proximity to the Silk Road, but there was little overlap between the trade in silk and the end of the Bronze Age. Most early civilisations overestimated their antiquity, and I could discount Ymerodraeth's mythic dynasties, as I had then, but the absence of steel and agriculture felt backward, given the remaining context. A steellike bronze; pastoralist kalas; silk; and judging from the tapestries, classical κατάφρακτοι, "cataphracts". The puzzle pieces didn't align.

I decided to step away and

looked back and watched daylight fail against the invict ramparts of Llys, the fading glow of golden stone, the banner and throne of Her Imperial Grace; this, the sunset of Ymerodraeth. The children of the north told tales of an eternal city covered in alcamyn, but it never had been so.

Black snorted his impatience and shook the reins. A touch of heel and we were away, the wretchèd earth of the Long March beneath his hooves.

I had doffed the surcoats of Pedryfan but not yet donned that of Llys. And my heart was pained in the banbyshn's absence, as in her presence, but a calm settled upon me. As any, this quest might prove my end, and it was meet I determine west, though I would not reach the bloody fords in a sennight, nor the lonely cairn I raised over the little ones. Aye, north would be certain;

the olyfant and unycorn bore winter lightly and did not turn south, but leviathans were not the only game.

Aye, olyfants had trampled the pride of Ymerodraeth, but Div scouts were bold coneys of worth. I doubted not the attendance of hostile eyes. His Grace's spies had gone west; so too, I, Black, and a packhorse that followed on meek halter. A spear on my shoulder and two on the mare, along ample provend.

Three days of wind and butterflies over long grass and spring florets, the flight of ground squyrels and antelope, but no leviathans and their heavy tread. Even the lions gave way, out of measure troubled by the stormless horizon. Restless, they paced, then into the long grass.

A horse patrol I treated koumiss with bid me onwards west, for thence had they driven the passing game with their horns – away from our winter pasture – a great bull marked by the horsemen, his tusks said four paces long. But four days became seven, then eight, return forfeit; for the banbyshn willed she should not see my face again. I saw only hers, smiling; those of our dead, crushed, torn, staring; and of frenzic Div as they fell beneath my sword.

Life behind me and death before, I sought no ivory or trophy royal, released from liegedom to errantry and the end of my choosing. And my heart lightened with the redolence of spring grass and pine trees along the water, the great plains and rolling hills, the azure veil blinding the vault.

As the twelfth night fell, my mind turned to camp, but a pillar of light beckoned us onward. The forest thinned beside us till the waters of Llyn Tvvyll lay bare, a broad shore open to the steppe, and the moon cleared the horizon at its gibbous fullness. These, the bloody fords: the meeting of two rivers that descended the steppe from the farthest north amid the fanning of their streams. Where the Div had gathered them to a great slaughter, their sun-marked shields a thousand eyes fixed upon me. How they had laughed and sung. How the hyæna had laughed, glutting themselves on the fallen.

The horses were first to scent the unspeakable fire and snorted their aversion; then it came to me, a sweet smoak not unlike scorched boar but not. I knew the depravities of the D iv; here, again too close upon Llys. I dismounted atop a grassy knoll by a leaning tree misshapen by the wind. Tail tucked, the mare's feet and ears were restless. I gathered up the halter rope, then set her footloose and away homeward.

His ears fixed on the fire ahead, Black was caparisoned head and chest in a chamfron and peytral of polished alcamyn, and by feel, I checked his harness and my saddle-mounted sabre, making no light. Then I buckled a bevor over my throat and chin, bringing helm and cuirass into adamant union. Some southland knights palatine girt themselves cap-a-pie, but coldmetal was a thief of life in the white of the northern winter, and we bore the least that we might.

Secured over my gambeson, my coat-of-plates had passed from my father's father, the old leather without scarred, weathered, and oiled black, the alcamyn rivets flecked with worn gilt. With bright helm and bevor, I was no fine paladin for the tourney field. I mounted again, by the loop hung on my spear, and took up my teardrop shield, yet the purple and white of Pedryfan. In the distance, a baying, but not of wolves.

A fair parasang beyond the bonfire, the lesser lights of an encampment in force on the steppe. Not yet an invasion, but by the shrill cries round the fire, a convocation of their witches:

Ια Ια!
Ια Ια!

Spectre and delusion ruled the Div, in the blue smoak of herbs, in the tinctures of flowers and fungus. They called to the shadows that haunted their minds; they spat, hissed, and cackled, glutted on flayed and burnt offerings to their figmental daevas. A vengeance rite for the wolf-shirt general; here, nigh where the Div vanguard had broken. Where the banbyshn's knight palatine had fallen, and I, come again, was given his place.

They danced before the waters, in hides or naked to the night, raising meadow vipers and howling at the moon. They offered the lake to the dragons of the poison sea that circled the earth: Come and claim it! Come and pull Llys into the Deep!

Amid them, the Great Charlatan stood proud under the stag crown. I knew him by it, from the fluting song of the ridge-browed pari, not seen a five year. We had traded them black flints from Mur Mavvr, which they prized above all others, for intelligences of Mazandaran and the disposition of the Div:

deer rider! deer rider!
the sun war rides –
on olyfants, it rides!

So they had sung to me, my report of the Sun War but not olyfants, for who could halter leviathans?

And the olyfants had trumped its coming, scattered our spear lines, and all around me, my azad brothers had died bringing them down. None foresaw ten thousand Div descending the mountains, a baleful sun on crescent shields of bark or cowhide – the pari did not know such numbers. It was not a thing to be imaged but of night terror.

The Pretender was a big man, aye, but no fantastical giant; he who thought himself Cayo Mardd come again, this Gueyumar. The master magush of the Div; and said oracle of anamaka, the phantasmic "nameless one" of their obscene venerations. I thought not to mark him with mine own eyes, in the reach of my spear, of my life. Surrounded not by warriors, by flint spears and axes, arrows and olyfants, but by seers and sacrifiers. Some two score or more.

Across the river, the forest came thick to the water's edge. They had crossed to the open bluff for this fire sabbat, leaving their force encamped behind. This the place of their rout, where I smote their general down. With twenty horse, or even ten, I could trample them into the ground. For even in their madded frenzy, a lone knight should be well overmatched, but there was no time or second chance. Black and I would fall together, or he might win free if I alone were pulled down. This was azadagi, not the arena – the spectacle – of love and honour. This, one spear against the foe, in the darkness, unmarked and unrememberèd.

Banbyshn Llesami's fortuitous charge had loosed me like an arrow towards the Great Charlatan himself. Yea, it was well done. And my eyes filled with joyous tears at this final service to Her Imperial Grace, for those refuging in Llys and those sleeping under stone. There was no forgiveness for my lapse, but I kissed the silken favour she had first bound to mine arm. My life had reached its zenith; my burden its end.

I placed my leather-gauntleted hand upon Black's shoulder, my stalwart comrade these many days of trial. Then I lifted my oxhorn and thrice blew my challenge ere raising my spear overhand.

—Now, come death.

Both heels I gave Black, and forward we flew towards the mindless howls and cries of alarm, the Div night-blinded by their bonfire. Along with me charged the memory of my fallen fellows, and dozens of hands, with mine, upheld the spear. Ahead, Gueyumar roared in their debased tongue, rallying the witches to him. He brandished a great mace, and four slumped at the fire's edge leapt to their feet. Not captives awaiting sacrifice, but bear-shirts forbid the sight of occult rites. They freed their eyes from binding and took up plundered arms in my path, but I was upon them.

Black reared, scattering them with his flashing hooves, and over their ducked heads, I cast my spear full upon Gueyumar and smote him through. A great cry rose as he listed, then tottered, choking an empty curse upon me, and many Div fell to their knees, moaning their dismay.

I grasped White-hilt, then wheeled Black on the rabious bear-shirts, taking one from his feet as they made to strike at him or the phantoms of the air, taken too long by the rank smoak. Known to flint javelins and axes, they were strong but artless with alcamyn lances. None worth my name.

Shielding their looted spears, I hewed their limbs and cut them down. Then, we rode down the skin dancers, for I would let none live and returned the fray in all abandon to any who dared stand.

We caught our frosting breath amid the flight of screams, death cries, and the roaring of the fire. I blew my horn thrice again, proving life amid those trampled or sabred, the sands begored. What spectre had we become in their haunted minds? Their number gathered should have pulled me to earth, but I forgot not the near encampment, marked by numerous dung fires. Without the river's intervention, a parasang afoot was no great distance to their warriors. It was said they could run ten in a day.

Gueyumar lay like the great bull of a free herd, taken in the hunt, his defenders fallen before him. His mouth snarled, even in death, his teeth cut to points; his face deep-scarred by foul blood rites. One staring eye was blue against his brown skin and hair, as Princess Essylt of Vardan, for the Div were our nearmost cousins. Outcast without kine or colt or the arts of alcamy, and for their death, driven into Mazandaran – heavy with forest and spare of forage, to the verge of Modrvvy Ddu. Their idols consigned to fire; the magi put to the sword.

His other eye was the bright orange-yellow of the flames, its lids cut away. A defect of birth taken for the mark of their daevas.

The first token, for the shahanshah and empire: the charlatan's grizzled head and stag crown; a toothy wolf skull bored and mounted with three antlers, then worked with lumpish silver. Second his stone mace, stout and well-halfted.

I gave his carcass to the bonfire lest the surviving witches return and eat of it to claim his illusory power. Too, I burned their wood and bone idols, taking only a fish-man carved of a great chrysoprase of a like I'd never witnessed. It was most grotesque, and I laughed aloud, a hollow sound beside the waves and crackling fire.

But quickly, trumps in the distance; I could not gather up the defiled and lay them to clean rest. Nor might I reclaim the rings of gold and silver ravished from our dead, nor the shining plunder of alcamyn, the coveted auricalke of their fallen tongue, made trinket, trophy, or raised against me. Neither Div nor the hundred tribes drew coldmetal from stone, and alcamy, the changing of copper into arming gold, was kept even from the shahs. It was said the ores of adamant were deathly poison, and I knew but that the great foundry of Llys might not be entered without the alcamystres' strange helms.

I secured my tokens and took up my blooded spear. Nay, we could not linger.

Olyfants and seashell trumps of the Div sounded the pursuit behind us but fell away as we feinted northeast, along a narrow streamlet, and agore-blood, we stopped but to cleanse him and me. Black flagged mid night, and I dismounted and walked him southeast till dawn when we took our rest. I knew not if the Div searched the night in vain or fell to among themselves. I had cut a second head from the wyrm, but as the heart beat, hate did not die but renewed.

We came upon the packhorse by the doggèd track east, cropping grass, midday next. The stillness pressed me on, the calm of warning, in sight of free bison and the wild horses of the southwestern plateau, in the absence of pursuit. At the limit of provision, I laid camp a sennight to hunt and to rest the steeds.

I heard the trumping of olyfants but did not sight them over the tumulose steppe.

The moon waned into nought and waxed crescent ere we attained the commons gate of the third wall, ten paces high. It would be for Banbyshn Llesami to mete my end, but His Imperial Majesty must have word, and with this duty quit, I would yield to the Red Crown. A knight is but a servant, the banner taken up and on command lain down.

Shuttered windows and the lanterned night watch. Seven bridges across quiescent canals. From the commons gate to the martial gate, then the royal gate, unto the high doors of the Henllys itself, I rode to fulfil this final charge.

In peaked red caps, the imperial guard stood forth and made their just demands, and I, in turn, mine for a present audience with the shahanshah. It was my right to demand it as grivpanvar, at the pain of present death should his displeasure smite me. After a modest delay, ten guards led me through the Hall of Judgement: two bearing lanterns and four the covered tokens to be presented. The darkness within was heavier than night, and the mosaicked walls, pennons, and pillars could be little seen by the portals of moonlight above; the imperial trophies unlimned, too, the great stone bones of dragons taken from the earth.

Statues of the twenty padshahs waited in sightless procession. The incense burners sat cold but by day bathed the towering images in pungent fume, for what have we made of the shahs in our veneration but daevas? The entry to the Hall of Gold was aglow at the far end; for out of custom, the doors stood open between tall triumphal urns.

Through the doorway, hosts of candles cast drawn shadows over the stepped platform and two seats. One high and one low, and about the dais, seven gilded lamp stands and seven lamps of the oldest fashion. Said the Lamps of the Poet, but the first Padshah of Llys'har knew not the seven shahdoms – now, but four of seven lights burned. The walls were not hung with tapestry but clad with a wealth of alcamyn, graved and coloured with THE RECORD OF DYRRAITH, a glitterance of emerald leaves over lazuli waters. A circular map of the earth was set into the flagstones, encircled by Modrvvy Ddu, the poison sea alive with rank things.

The captains of Fedvvyd and Llys stood at attention in their regimental colours beside an assemblage of Kian's officials, taken from their evening pastimes or their beds. All beardless, the grandeur of their moustaches ranked below the shahanshah's imperial tusks; azad below vispuhr, each in his station; and three bards who kept the Law at their recitation.

I travelled not in the first circle and knew not their names, and Shahryar Rhys and his servants were not among them. Nor were the istandar: ears for the raman of the third circle. Nor were the banbyshn's maids of honour, but for Princess Mina, noted to me for her pallor and raven hair.

Many looked upon the horns of the covered skull crown and marvelled upon them, though all looked askance at me and my presumption, and another head would have rolled had their gazes cut deeper.

All knelt as Shahanshah Lleu and the banbyshn were announced. His broad, upturned moustaches were burnished below the alcamynium White Crown; he had fewer summers than the shahryar, but they weighed more heavily upon him, and he on his cane. The wound to his thigh was taken in a boar hunt, and as some, treasonous, whispered, no heirs had followed his firstborn, Llesami. She walked a measured step behind, the Red Crown of cupreous gold on her brow, and besat her the low seat after her father the high. Her aspect was stern if no less or more than her sire, her regalia red, his yellow. All rose, but myself, and the shahanshah said,

—Illustrious Knight, the pennons of Kian and Arman have flown at half-staff, in doubt of thy return. Our final report of thee that thou hadst journeyed west, upon the track of a great trophy for our heir, but set alone against the wrathful leviathans. The banbyshn absented herself from the tourney, and all were disheartened. And as we welcome the Hero of the Fords, stag horns, however fine and notable to our eye, are no cause for emergency counsel with the two thrones.

I said,

—Your Imperial Majesty, the banbyshn charged me to return by the first tourney flag or not at all. In this, I have failed and submit myself to her judgement without plaint, but I bear word and token from the battlefield which I must needs discharge ere the sword falls upon my neck.

—Battlefield, Sir Gvvyn? We have no report of interdict with the foe.

—Sire, beyond the boundary of my quest, one hundred parasangs

west, where the shore of our sweet watered lake was befouled
by the bloody fording, I came upon a witches sabbat, and chief
among them, the person of the Great Charlatan. My matchless
courser, Black of the Sea, trampled them into the despoiled earth
amid the wrack and ruin of their obscenities, scattering the last
like craven squyrels into the night. I offer Your Imperial Majesty
these tokens: the Pretender's head and stag crown.

Two guards stepped forth and, at the shahanshah's gesture,
unwrapped the head of Gueyumar, preserved in pine resin, and
his silver-mounted skull crown. The murmur of princes became
uproar, but the raised hand of the shahanshah restored order.
Banbyshn Llesami was standing. All standing knelt.

—Illustrious Knight, she said; how many were the foe?

—Your Imperial Grace, I accounted some two score and ten,
though I attest that, in the darkness, it may be some few more
or less and but few warriors of note, bearing our forgèd arms.

—Alone, you charged them?

—Nay, ma'am. Black of the Sea charged them. I had the honour
of his saddle and gathered up the proofs of his victory.

—And how many were slain?

—No more than a score, ma'am. The witches flee well.

The Shahanshah Lleu's laughter drew that of the vispuhran,
and the banbyshn, bemused, resat. And all kneeling rose but
myself. His Imperial Majesty said,

—Black of the Sea, the name of a great terror.

—So the foe found him, I replied, and yielded up two more
tokens. The mace and sceptre of the Pretender, and last, a jewel
idolet of their fire offerings. It is as foolish as a child's toy, and
I bethought to hear Her Imperial Grace's laughter. But sire,
beyond the black sabbat, the foe was encamped in force, with
olyfants. Look, I pray, to the west.

—So it shall be, sir, on the morrow. The stag crown and mace are
worthy tokens and shall be heirlooms of our house. Castellan,
place the head of the Pretender in the Jar of Traitors ¶. Now,
what say thee, daughter? Sir Gvvyn has brought thee a token
like none other. In it, we see the error of the Elder Foe and the
fault of their ways. Wilt thou take this prize and forgive him
the tourney's?

—I shall not take it, Father, for it looks to be both fish and man,
and I hate fish.

There was some laughter among the princes.

—But, she said, leaving the fish, I shall keep the man. Sir Gvvyn, rectify thy tardiness.

And the laughter spread. I raised one hand to my breast.

—Ma'am, I bow to your mercy and place the gem at the shahanshah's pleasure.

He was of good cheer and gestured broadly.

—Sir Gvvyn, such service and not three but four gifts require some recompense...

—Do not, the banbyshn spake to myself, think to protest, sir. Father, this is the proudest of knights, and he bears humility like the double crown. I have taken his pride from him and placed mine own in its stead.

—Daughter, thou tak'st from a wolf its pride and bestow it a lion's. Ah, but I am put to trial; he beareth the silver gorget but is proved grivpanvar thrice again.

The Shahanshah Lleu took up the sceptre of his office, a bull-headed mace of emeraldine jade. He raised it and pronounced, Henceforth, Sir Gvvyn, champion to the Red Crown, shall be sardar and knight champion of all Ymerodraeth. Vispuhran, his sons shall be; the firstborn, Shahryar of Caer Colur when we reclaim it from the foe ¶. The guardians of the west have fallen, and as we grieve Lleon and Danyal, we elevate a worthy line and refresh the blood of our realm. Hail the House of Gvvyn.

—Hail! echoed the vispuhran.

I bowed my head.

—A petition, sire. For my father's memory: of Lludd.

—It is well done! The House of Lludd shall the bards declaim it. Rise, Your Excellency; you are among peers.

And salutations greeted me as I stood, sardar the highest standing within my caste. An ancient honour, little used since the time of Warring Shahs, when the strongest azad were the princes of war. But the sublimation of my issue was of little precedent in my scant learning and, mayhap, a contravention of the Law, but the bards did not speak. Of the assembled, only the shahanshah smiled, and some few officers tapped their chins.

REATHING DOWN MY NECK, Liza was hovering again,
B   and I told her so. She said,
       —I'm not hovering, but what is the hold-up, Mister?
She kneaded my shoulders. It was perfectly normal – it was too
good to be real. All of it, but above all, her. I basked in her signature Chanel freshness.
—I have to be meticulous. A mistake with the drawings will
become a mistake in transliteration. It's also a second chance
to evaluate my placement of the fragments.
    I'd assembled the wax puzzle across three tables – two tablets
per – alongside the drawings, a few KUM long-point sharpeners,
and a dozen pencils the green-and-gold of Fedwyd.
    The glass fishman had slotted into another puzzle across
time. I'd revisited $\triangle 353$; if it wasn't the same statuette, they were
two of a kind. Maaike had all but placed it in my hand, pushing,
prodding me to remember Llesami, but I'd only glimpsed the
bonfire, the horns of

The shahanshah has bid you enter, Your Excellency.
    I was covered in the banbyshn's gifts. A samite tabard, the
red and yellow of Llys, over my new black and white harness of
Lludd. But above all rested the silver crescent of the grivpanvar,
for my burden remained, and as the heart beat, could not let
away. I followed through doors graved with vaughting stallions.
    The high throne was wrought of ivory, alcamyn, and sateen;
Shahanshah Lleu's yellow raiment, the richest of brocades. The
herald announced me, and I stepped forward and knelt under
the eyes of diverse vispuhr ministers, officers, and the bearded
istandar. His Imperial Majesty said,
    —A moment, Your Excellency. Castellan, we must take private
counsel with the sardar and bid all depart hence but bide without
if they have further matter with us.
    A murmur went up, for it was uncommon for the crown
to dismiss the officials in open court. Yet dutiful were all in

attendance, and soon only I, the shahanshah, and such servants as His Imperial Majesty required, remained.

His chalice filled; he bade me rise and take up the gilded cup presented to me.

—We have word, sir, that thou art trothed to a daughter of Shahryar Rhys.

—Aye, sire. On taking my leave from his service, His Grace offered me her hand. I have not met the princess, but the shahryar has extended his welcome, and in due course, I shall make her acquaintance.

—Happy tidings. We raise to thee our cup.

—I thank you, sire.

As did the shahanshah, I raised the golden cup and drank. It sparkled on the tongue like koumiss, its fragrance sweeter than its savour; the past year's winter-mellowed mead was a courtesy between shahrdaran, and I was none. He said,

—If thou marvel'st at this private counsel, we would not have ill rumour leave this chamber, for to the shahryar himself cometh the matter. Tell us, Sardar Gvvyn, doth he in sooth sow seeds of discontent among the peerage, raising foul rebellion against the throne?

I knelt and bowed my head.

—On my life, sire, it is not so. His Grace is loyal to your house and commended me to dutiful service of the banbyshn, that Ymerodraeth may long prosper.

—Then what is the nature of this dissent? For such word as reached our ears cannot be utterly baseless, but mayhap tainted and twisted in the retelling.

—In his words to me, it was the shahryar's wish that the shahrdaran and some others be given voice in the course of the empire: in counsel to the throne.

—What thinkest thou? Do we seem to thee a tyrant over the people?

—Nay, sire.

—But must it not chafe, Your Excellency? His army decimated, his herds made cruel larder, he who ruled a shahdom hath rule now of only a winter palace. We hold naught but the first city against the pertinacious winter, and we fear our Fedvvyd hath become a nest of vipers. We know well the chagrin of the shahryar.

—His Grace is a learnèd man and knows the seasons of Dyrraith and that in the present blight, Ymerodraeth can ill afford fraternal strife. I am a simple knight and abide the azadagi of my fathers; I am sworn to the banbyshn and serve at the pleasure of your imperial house. Command it, sire, and I shall take up the banner.

—Well said, sir, but rise now – a banner must be held aloft ¶. And our fears redressed, come back now the peers.

The doors were opened, and the ministers as had remained returned, and the high officers in their ranks. The Shahanshah Lleu proclaimed,

—Hear now, Sardar Gvvyn, our commission: Take with thee some twenty horsemen by the southern passage and bring us counsel of Fedvvyd and its lands. Thou hast cast down the Pretender and made a trophy of his crown, which even now hangeth in the great hall. We would know the full measure of their dismay and disposition, but with haste, return'st thou by midsummer and delay not to leaf fall.

—I thank Your Imperial Majesty. I shall acquit this duty to the utmost.

The shahanshah appeared well pleased, but Banbyshn Llesami was not. Her chambers were capacious, the floor thick with embroidered rugs, the walls with tapestry; skirted by low shelving for picture rolls; fine objects of obscure purpose; cabinets; vases, tall and small; and the final bloom of spring flowers. Her ladies sat a little apart, a bard standing as he lyred. The hearth burned by day, and the air was heavy with cedar and resinous incense; for vispuhr ladies made a much of the art of incensation, and not a few knights quested at mortal hazard into black forest and mountains high for a sliver of rare wood or a thimble of gum.

Her Imperial Grace was gowned in the emeraldine and gold of Fedvvyd, her father's lost holding, her blonde hair upbraided. She clutched her hands.

—Already, he sends you forth on a perilous course. I am affrighted.

—How now, ma'am? It is no sterner duty than that which you laid upon me.

—It was Your Excellency who made stern my command. A wiser man would have brought me a wildflower of the field.

—I am not so wise at that.

For a span, there was only the lyre's lilting tones, the maids' whispers and giggles, and the rich dark of Llesami's eyes. Soft, she said,

—First, the far reward of Colur, and now twenty men against the demons? Beware, Caer Creu; he means your death.

Caer Creu: the fortress of blood. In the sagas, the black tale of a yielded fortress – a trap with a bloody end. I said,

—We do not seek battle, ma'am, but knowledge of the foe. Marzban Bryn goes in force to the fords, not I.

—Battle will find you.

—It may be so, but there are no demons but men.

—The eaters of men are none. The shahs of eld should have swept them into the sea. If the White Crown does not, the Double Crown will. Silver cannot stay us.

But childless, with no heirs of the body, did any hold the doubled crowns of Llys and Ymerodraeth. She was barren, as His Grace said. High within the keep, her windows looked down over Llyn Tvvyll to the far horizon of my task. She held forth her hand.

—Come, kiss me and begone.

I knelt and kissed the coldmetal of her signet; then, pressed from within; by the three moons that lay between us; by the waiting foe, I kissed too the coolness of her fingers. She took her hand back to her breast, saying naught, and I bowed for my leave, a new weight upon my heart. My first act of treason – and hers, for she let me keep my neck.

After two days of diligence in preparation, with my apologies to His Grace for further delay, assuranced but unmet, I rode forth on the morn; through the martial monuments of the second circle and the narrow streets of the third; against carts moving meat and yoghurt, firewood, and the roots and herbs of the forest. Two by two, twenty handpicked horsemen followed at my back, and such train of spares, packhorses, and squires as wonted for the support of our expedition, which at its utmost, would look upon Fedvvyd's silver walls. Not twenty horse, all told, but five score. These men and lads of Fedvyyd and Llys were strangers to me but in repute, as brothers born apart may be.

Black pranced amid the cheers and shouts of the raman under their broad felt hats, some bearded but none moustached. He was restless, no doubt, for the open steppe and the wallless horizon, but our route lay southwest. First, along the southron shore of

Llyn Tvvyll, then for hundreds of parasangs through the close, horizonless wood. Light on the reins, my hand

on hers. We were alone in the dark with moving pictures, and Liza looked from the screen to me.

—It's not time.

—Time for?

—The wedding. Matters haven't... aligned.

It was one of those period pieces she liked. Costumed dramas. The kind of clothing a woman couldn't put on by herself, and much ado about niceties. Comedic lives that ended with weddings.

—I'm not saying no, she added, just not yet.

She turned her hand under mine and intermeshed our fingers, her eyes midnight pools. I said OK in the momentary lacuna of time. I didn't know what I'd said, not fully here, not fully there. My luck, my reprieve, had run out; I was stretched across the ages, pulled apart from her and the now of us,

for alone came I from the wintry forest, mobled up in the stiff pelt of a brown bear, drawing the rude sleigh of my gathered and scavenged supply, steaming drawn breath. Drawing three spears and arming a nameless sword from the spares, bereft of heritance and honours both. There was no balm of vengeance, for cataclysm offered no redress.

Llys was pale-hued in the morrow light, but my heart could not be filled; I was but a messenger of the dead. Atop the wall, the longbows of the raman, which were no trifle to tribesmen nor armoured knights, were knocked but stayed. The commons were forbid the sword and spear; to ride or lead a horse and, however foolish, to saddle a bull.

Alone came I to the open gates; there, the airs of the city, of cookfires and fresh dung. Little different from Pedryfan in long memory. At the guardhouse, I let the tethers fall to the rutted snow of the road. Many wagons had passed this way and would till dusk.

The gatehouse offered their challenge, for I was the image of a tribesman come to treat. Unfit to appear before Her Imperial Grace, her favour hung upon my arm, and when broken, my arm hung upon it. I proved my tattered and soiled colours, saying only that I must to the shah, and a rider galloped ahead to the Henllys for I was overlate in coming.

I took a post-horse to follow, but there was no gain in urgency: the dead would remain so. The pennons of four houses were proud above the high wall of the first circle. In my delayed return, Llys had entered its winter estate. The dynasty held.

On the height of noon, I attained the Henllys, and in later hours, my patient audience with the shahanshah and court. I was but one of many, for the officials of Vardan and Gorg had come south, attending the shahrdaran, their armies and herds. And all looked askance at my low state, even as I came before the two thrones and knelt before the Red and White Crowns.

Her Imperial Grace said,

—Herald, thou art mistaken. This cannot be the illustrious Sardar Gvvyn, chastised afore in his late obedience to us. I know not this man; pray, what is his name?

—Soft, said Shahanshah Lleu; stay thy fierce hand, daughter. Mark the trials scored upon His Excellency's tabard ¶. Rise and speak, Sardar Gvvyn: reveal Dyrraith as it hath befallen our realm.

There were few tales blacker told by the bards than duty pressed me to tell: Of the sack and ruin of Fedvvyd, of the ring of wood totems strewn with strands of tormented flesh. Of pastures blighted with wisent and yurts, for the Div nation had descended the mountains. Not ten thousand but tens of thousands.

That the magi stood upon the dead Pretender's name; that the Unbelievers – we and all our works – would be cast down and consumed by the daevas; that the Div would reclaim the great steppe – their "promised land". So said prisoners put to question. So they said and cursed us.

Then, I said before all, the Dyrraith of my men falls upon my neck, for it was I who did not turn back with the season. I, who took up the trail of the magi, five score shields, and a dozen captives of Colur, haltered neck to neck. Surmounted five for each, the knights would have fallen upon the foe to succour our countrymen, but I withheld them, seeking the Div purpose as they determined south of Fedvvyd. South, past the deep vales of Ysel, to the black coast of the poison sea.

There, the foe divided, and the magi, captives, and two score shields went forth to a relict fire temple of the age before Cayo Mardd. But half of the circle of figural longstones remained; the rest had tumbled into the sea in years unnumberèd and were lost to the sandy drop. The coast was overgrown with thick boskage, with no manoeuvre for cavalry, and we picketed the horses. I told of the dauntless squires, beardless boys, who stood to take up the spear against the foe, but without harness, I would not hazard them.

The drum of axe on shield called us forward to the wood's edge, the air heavy with salt and smoak. In long squalor, the captives knelt at flint-point beside the towering stones. The charlatans danced, gibbered, and moaned before the fire, and the warriors incited them with shouts and cries. Vengeance on Ymerodraeth. Vengeance for Gueyumar, deprived of his head.

I told of my grave knights, each facing two, who leapt forth from the forest with me, then locked shields in a line, spears high. It was hot work, the foe caught and hampered by the ancient stones, the bonfire before it, and the narrow breadth of the bluff; they could not bring their numbers to bear. The huddled captives cheered in hoarse voices and wept.

Back we pushed the Div – into the very flames – their hewn flesh falling beneath our boots. Back, through the longstones, with no retreat but the brief beach and rising tide. Back into the reeking waters, we drove them, where fish floated up amid a strange steam, the sands washing with slaughter, and Something heaved up from the deep.

—It was fire and darkness, I said; a horror beyond all imagining: a thing that tore at my sight. The sun fled from its power and rage and deafened roar, and day became as night. I sounded my horn, my good men around me, and together we fell, scattered like leaves before the blow. And for a time, I knew no more.

And all in the Hall of Gold were silent. All were still. No whispers among the princes. No signs among the knights. The shahanshah waited, listing, his head bowed under a terrible weight. The banbyshn gripped her throne as if it would wrest itself from her hands, red and gold her gown, red and gold her crown and braided hair.

—A dragon, said the eldest of three bards.

—I cannot say, I replied to him. Its image draws away from my mind, sir, were I upon a cliff's edge, and to gaze too deep is to fall.

His hair white, his voice did not waver:

—Those stony bones – the great toothy skulls – in the gallery do not recount a tale compleat. As the moon and sun, where there is ice, there is fire. The eyes can see the face of a leviathan, can measure the jaw that might swallow a man whole, and the stature of a citadel, but its nature is unanswered. Unanswered lest seen. What you have seen, Your Excellency; for "on the turn of the season", the very earth of Llys trembled twice, and far-flung patrols returned word of smoke upon the horizon south.

I bowed, remiss in propriety.

—Honourable Ovate, Your Imperial Sovereignties, I fear I have seen less than I might and too little to serve you. I awoke alone by nightfall in a narrow dell, in the shadow of a mighty cedar, shivered branches all around, and all the land lay under a blanket of ash, had the clouds themselves burned and let fall wintrous cinders.

But I told not of cutting away my curaiss, crushed by grievous dint, my arm and ribs broken, sore-battered cap-a-pie. I told not of climbing from the trench, my helm lost, of pulling myself up, step by painèd step, with a stout cedar limb; of the ache in my lungs from ash adrift on the air; of the deathly silence that rang within mine ears.

All had been green and thick; with hazel; with elm; with ilex. List, I told my lords, list, for the very earth was struck and wounded. Every leaf, shrub, and stem was grey frosted, then, as I searched, blackened. Then blasted, on a rise where trees were flattened, as if by a great hand, unto a coaly waste of withered life; the land rent and divided, then flooded with the salt waters of Modrvvy Ddu. The sunny vales of Ysel drownèd black.

Of the fell beast, I saw no other trail or sign and cannot say unto whence it passed. I found no staring stone of the fire temple nor any spoor of Div. No other knight of Llys or Fedvvyd. I turned back and sought for any that might live, to find under ash and shattered trees, horses and squires asleep forevermore. Scalded where they stood, their breath stolen. Then,

—I commend them each and all – every knight, every lad – to Your Imperial Majesty, the finest sons of Ymerodraeth. To their kin, I can offer no other amend or redress. Only my shame as their captain. I should be dead with my azad brothers.

—No, said Shahanshah Lleu, our shame is not so easily let aside. It is the shame of a hero to live where others have fallen, of a shah to reclaim lands his fathers won; our duty bears it up. Thou hast brought vital word and again done us great service. Thy brothers-in-arms resent thee not, and thou liv'st on for them ¶. Henceforth, thou art Gvvyn Emrys, the living banner of the five armies, and the dragon shall be thy device.

And thus was my shame fixed for all to see; for all to hear. Emrys, "the immortal". I would carry defeat on mine arm.

Banbyshn Llesami kept a hard grip upon her throne, harder, the line of her brow.

—Ho, Gvvyn Emrys, too proud to mind season or imperial yoke; so proud he smote a mountain, and I doubt not the mountain knew the worst of it ¶. Your Excellency, know you that Llyn Tvvyll has risen three cubits sithence the shaking of the earth, sithence this flood of Ysel?

—Nay, Your Imperial Grace.

—Was the land so torn between Ysel and our pure lake?

—I cannot say, ma'am. No less than a hundred parasangs once parted Modrvvy Ddu from Llyn Tvvyll, and I did not travel afoot to the furthest end of the flooded vales. It may be for His Imperial Majesty to send forth an expedition to ascertain its condition.

—Yes, we shall find us an officer who knoweth the limits of his charge and returneth as his liege hath bidden him.

—Soft, said Shahanshah Lleu. Fifty thousand have descended Mur Mavvr, and

in an empty hall, hospital white, in jarring fluorescent light. I shuddered amid fluidic distortions: Nothing moving. Everything moving.

I hadn't found Black of the Sea among the bodies and ash – he'd been lost in the broad devastation. I remembered.

But dragons were a story for dinosaur fossils, not the Other. Not for madness manifest, for form without restraint, like the Butterfly Nebula made an angel of plasmic hate, wondrous and nauseating in the crushing pressure of its presence. Asag? Vritra?

Something was near, like a shadow rising underwater. My fingers twitched, but there was no spear or sabre at hand. Green doors meant contractors everywhere, and their voices ran together in a stream, too near but unseen. I retreated into the emergency stairwell. Then I waited.

It followed.

—¿Julián, what…?

At Llesami's throat, belying her blue-chip lie, no ABRASAX but the lion-and-sun of Kian. A round silver pendant of similar size on the same chain or the same one in a different light. The same face, now eerie in its frozen expression and the ominous effluvia of the sea. I bowed from the neck.

—Your Imperial Grace. What have they done to you?

—The only thing worse than what they've done to you.

The needles jabbed behind my eyes – the price of speaking a defunct honorific – but I didn't bow to it. I'd pay. I'd keep paying. Issota's accusation prodded me.

—To us.

—To the both of you. You found her.

—I haven't.

—Don't play games. This is…

—Dangerous. I've seen exactly…

—Nothing.

Llesami turned on her heel, leaving me alone in the stairwell. Up or down, there was no safety. No exit.

WILL KILL THEM if they say one more word to you.
And fire your lawyer, whoever it is. I have lawyers.
Brown and Beige had tried to up the pressure, but
they'd put a foot wrong and kicked the bear. Liza was livid.
—They've got nothing, but the DA's office will spend anything
to pin this on someone who can't fight back. I will crush them.
—It's fine; I'll let them know about the change in representation.
She was on speakerphone and couldn't see my placating ges-
ture. Her tone remained sharp:
—We need to have a powwow. Come straight home after

no mishearing, a knocking again called me to my chamber door.
Removed since from His Grace's knight company in the second
circle, I was established within the keep, among Kian's knights
palatine – royal cousins in service to the crowns. Rest did not
come easily upon me, couched amid unfamiliar riches aglow
in hearth light.
I opened the door and bowed.
—Your Ladyship.
Morvydd ap Aryo, High Maid of the Chamber, hung with the
gold chains of her office; hers was the first station of all azad
palace women. Kirtled in red samite, a bejewelled long knife at
her waist, she would throw away her life defending the imperial
person, as I doubted not the azad maids-of-all-work of Colur
and VVydvvyr. All dead.
Her vailèd youth careworn with long discretions, she said,
—Your Excellency, the banbyshn summons you.
—It is late, ma'am.
—Even so, sir, she commands it.
I knew not the cause, not on the fresh heat of her anger. A
single lantern led us through lightless halls and stairs, and a
strangeness came upon me. Cousin to Marzban Bryn, Banu
Morvydd's lineage stood above mine, yet I was assuranced to

the royal blood of Arman, of a measure with Banbyshn Llesami. Unanswered, and with two knocks unreplied, I was admitted into her chambers.

Be it vispuhr maids-of-honour or azad long knives, both, Llesami ap Lleu should never be without attendance, but no court awaited. She stood alone by her high latticed windows and too few candles to illumine her worship. I entered with tender misgiving and, at a distance, knelt. The door closed behind me.
—Your Imperial Grace. What would you?
—Llesa. Here, on this night, I am Llesa.
—Your maids, ma'am, should they not be present, lest suspicion... ?
—I have dismissed them till the morrow. Good Morvydd will keep the watch.
—As I am pledged, I must depart, ma'am. I would not...
—Llesa, and stay, I pray thee. Offer thou no kiss of homage after thy long quest? Am I not thy lady love, as beknownst to all?
She held out her hand. I bowed my head, then stood.
—There is none other.

I would have knelt again at her feet, but her hand rose to my lips. Bare it was of jewels or signet. A woman's hand, which fell into my rough grip. I said,
—Where, then, the prince-consort?
And her voice resonated with all the lonely desolation of Ysel:
—With his catamite: the shah's cupbearer.

She squeezed my arm with fraught gentless, and I kissed her as I ought not have and touched her as I ought not have, and she placed her hand on me as she should not have and soiled her hand and dress, then I knelt and kissed the dewed blossom of her womanhood that I should never have known and kissed it with such suspiring kisses till the maid cried a warning, and I left Llesa more troubled than when I left the ashen graves of my men, O wretch.

I returned to my cold bed and dwelt in thoughts of her. And for a sennight, there passed no word between us, and on battlements and at court was I alone in waiting silence, amid my desolations. And where I had not, I now imaged the gaze of Idvval ap Arshan, prince-consort and marzban palatine, who oft deferred court – said given to the chase of sabre-horned ibex in the high passes – as the shahrdaran petitioned for immediate excurse; or a great demigration, following the grasslands beyond the brackish sea.

The shahanshah sent forth an expedition to Ysel, and spies to all corners, seeking intelligences, but marshalled not his regiments. I had little heart for the practice fields, but from His Imperial Majesty received the white destrier, Carngrvvn, fit for the shah himself; and from His Grace, the princess her dowered harness, and the alcamystres made my fitments.

And followed many tenders of betrothal, though all knew my plight was given, and ever greater did the bride gifts mount. And yea, Vardan made much of a named knight in offers of Princess Essylt and intemperate wealth.

I held my peace, waiting on Llesa's call till I could stay my hand no longer, and on the eve of my meet with Princess Carys, presented myself at the banbyshn's chambers. Banu Morvydd held the pass.

—Your Ladyship, I said, I have come to do homage and suit to Her Imperial Grace.

—Come then, sir, the banbyshn will receive you.

In her cup, Llesa sat among her veilèd damosels; them dicing a game of hazard – knucklebones and a players' board between them – but for two that capered a dance off-tune. The bard playing upon a bowed lyre, some dirge I had no ear for. She looked on me not till I knelt and of her ringèd hand made no presentation.

—Your Excellency, are you yet well and untroubled by your wounds?

—Well enough, Your Imperial Grace, I note them not in your presence.

—Have you tended to your betrothal, sir? Princess Carys is summoned to court and will serve us a fortnight hence.

—On the morrow, I am to have audience with Shahbanu Nasrin and then with the princess meet.

—It is well. Deliver her to our service at the appointed hour, and pray, bestow our love to our good consort's most esteemed aunt.

I stood and bowed.

—As you would, ma'am. By your leave, I will to my duties.

—You have it, sir. But call not again lest summoned or despatched by our father. It is unbecoming the knight of a lady to come forward thus unbidden.

—Ma'am!

Were the banbyshn cut from the high valley ice, she could have been no colder. There was no heart heavier than mine, and it weighed upon my every stride therefrom, but I knew the crown's justice therein.

For by chance withheld from the fullness of crime, from the plunge of the traitor's knife, this was but her mercy in rectification: our rôles set aright, as Law and duty would have them, I away to my new bride, and she, stainless as a banbyshnan banbyshn must be. In service

I pressed Liza deeper, to the limit, to the pulse of heart and breath

nine moons since my troth-plight. After the bathhouse, I girded myself and, with these hands, took up the banner.

Honour. Not that sparkling gem in the eyes of azad lads, plying their practise swords, for mine honour lay with the little ones beneath cold and mossèd stone. Not mine but that of the empire. Of Her Imperial Grace.

Sardar. Knight champion. These were my harness and shield. Too, my office to the house of Arman and the daughter they would gift me. My duty to the line of my fathers and the children to come.

I was shown first to Shahbanu Nasrin, who greeted me like long-absent kin. She was small but in measure, grand in magnanimity, and high of mien; she took it upon herself to present me to Princess Carys, the ladies' apartments thick with incense.

Not so tall as the banbyshn, Her Highness was a pale and slim lass of twenty winters, dark of hair but hazel-eyed above her veil, yet not so white of skin as the red-haired pari. I bowed, but the shahbanu frowned in displeasure.

—Come, your Excellency; kiss your bride. Let there be amity between you. Flighty passions have no place i' wedlock, and chaste inspiration lies beyond its bounds and necessary purpose.

Princess Carys her lips parted behind the diaphane silk worn from her first bleed till the day she wed. I lifted the veil and, in kissing her, was not indifferent. Indeed, her mouth was most pleasing.

—Good, said the shahbanu, now take you a maid and acquaint yourselves.

The winter garden was out-of-season warm, a place of hanging vines and summer colours; alcove and fountain; and mazy hedges to pass within, such that one might not see the palace walls all about us but high above, the arches of latticed glass. The princess herself gowned in purple and white, Arman was named along the great imperial dynasties and kept its colours. A veiled maid-of-the-chamber followed three paces behind, and her bright blade would flash if I raised an ill hand.

I offered condolence of the princess her former betrothal. She nodded, proud head high, hoarsy voice low:

—I knew him but little. Already it is distant, for a path untaken soon falls behind. So Father would say. But I am mazed, Your Excellency: how is it, not a year past you were one of my father's many knights, marzban of an outer fort, but since, you have championed the banbyshn, risen to peer, and here the sardar's azure sash? You supped at the captain's table in Pedryfan, I know not when, and now we are to wed?

—Is Your Highness displeased? Would you have another?

My heart fell, mazing me in turn. The princess laughed and touched my arm.

—No, sir, I will have none other. Kian has fashioned them a new prince, shining and bright, and I shall win him away. Pray, how did Dyrraith turn its face that all in all has come to pass?

—I leave tell-cause to the wise, but would you make a daeva of happenstance?

Her Highness stepped away, light of foot, and recited,

> Like the shadows of fire that dance before our eyes,
> Where are the daevas that rule the ten thousand things?
> Winter follows summer as fallow follows bloom,
> So night follows day and darkness, light.
> Can shadows move the ten thousand things?

I bowed in good humour.

—I am but azad and ill-schooled beside yourself. See you, a sash does not a prince make.

Her fingertips rose to the silver plate on my breast, not new-forged but drawn from the treasure house of Kian, chased and inlaid with gold and alcamyn.

—Grivpanvar. So many exploits, nay, nothing so common as a

prince. The sire of a royal house? Of a dynasty to rise? But I am to court to serve at Kian's pleasure.

—As I, and as Her Imperial Grace commands, I gift you this ring from her hand.

My late errand recalled to me, I presented the emerald ring and knelt. I slipped it on a fitting finger and bestowed a solemn kiss beside it.

—This is my plight, Your Highness. It shall not waver, not unto death.

Princess Carys raised it to the diffuse light and gauged it with awless eyes.

—A year hence and we will wed, and I shall bear your sons.

—Bear what you will, ma'am; they shall be ours.

She said naught but looked upon me sidewise as we continued our garden walk, a secret smile behind her veil, or so I imaged it. Nay, she was not so golden as the banbyshn, but like that ore of silver and gold, "shining and bright" as her throateral words. I noted this quality, and she said the colic had made her speech so as a babe, then,

—Hero of the Ford, pray tell, what is it to be the hero?

—It is shame and regret.

—How now, Your Excellency?

—The hero, Your Highness, is the last man to keep his feet, his companions no more.

—I see, sir. There is kindness in the hero, nay but the captain of war. ¶

The princess peeked at the maid and twined her arm with mine. It was pleasing, and her braided hair smelled not of incense but flowers. She tilted her face up to mine and raised both her voice and veil:

—Her Grace has given her leave.

And so she had, and our second kiss lingered and became warm.

—And tell me of Banbyshn Llesami. Is she cold and cruel, as some say?

—She is the banbyshn and not to be judged by me.

—You love her well.

—I am her knight.

—And you threw down the Pretender for her love and made sport of the fearsome magi. Would any knight do so much for me?

—When Your Highness debúts at court, I foresee many knights palatine taking inspiration and offering pledges.

—Even to the bride of the hero?

—Even so.

—I shall not accept them.

—And why not?

And she kissed me again such that a fearsome heat rose in my blood, and only the maid's cough parted us. And as the light deepened alcamyn, we returned to Shahbanu Nasrin. She said,

—I see the marks of amity and am well pleased. I foresee a fruitful union.

—Your Grace, said the princess, only a fortnight remains ere I must away to court, and in my duty cleave to the banbyshn. May His Excellency return on the morrow?

—No, daughter, that would not suit. Let us extend good and proper hospitality so that he may guest with us this fortnight and along with you to the side of the banbyshn. What say you, sir?

Princess Carys hung then upon my arm, most indecorous, but the shahbanu made no protest.

—I pray you, Her Highness plied me.

And I was more easily overcome than by the burning dragon and its awful power.

—I yield to my bride.

—Ward the princess, warned Shahbanu Nasrin. Let her run not headlong but hold fast the rein; she has all the wit and caprice of the last born, and within felicitous matrimony, one must a steady course keep.

—As you say, Your Grace.

—As I say, but I fear, Carys already has her sway. But betake yourselves to further acquaintance. Away.

The first fortnight of our acquaintance sped, and I found I had gained not a bride but a family: sisters and brothers, nieces and nephews, and some few of the royal cousins that filled the ministers' ranks. And a way opened before me, more than in duty to empire or legacy, but as a man. And some weight lifted from my heart, from the dark days behind, if it bled yet for the banbyshn; but for Carys her garden kisses, from which all other thought fled.

Again, on the last day of my sojournment, we came to our shaded place unspied by windows or the back-turned maid, the

warm air thicker than with late rain, and sitting, Carys her lips
met mine. It was both a yearning and discomfort to caress her
thus, as a sword flexed overmuch, and a pointed cough separated
us, as it oft did, and the maid made courtesy. Carys said,
—Yes, Armani. What matter?
—I must depart but a moment, Your Highness. I pray you, speak
not to Her Grace on it.

The maid fled as if all the Div pursued. I was caught in the
breadth of the princess her hazelled regard and her veilless smile.

I rove her virginity on the shorn grass though it was no fitting
couch, her breasts bared by undone dress, and as I quickened,
she gasped,
—O my Gvvyn, have care!

At Carys her warning, I turned aside almost too late, dismayed,
spent, and dissatisfied in the heat of it, though it were folly to
me and infamy to her. She was flush, her smile content as she
again affixed her veil, though her fine silks bore the marks of our
coupling. I covered myself and the blood of her maidenhead.
—I fear I have besmirched thee and thy gown.
—No matter, I have many more besides; on the morrow, thou
shalt see. Here, my maid cometh, and she will deliver me in
secret to my chambers, where she hath drawn a bath.

The princess kissed me and, laughing, fled with the maid,
whose errand was a ruse. No enticer but enticed, I becalmed
myself; I had made troth-plight, and my wife she would be. Nay,
my wife, she was.

But the chaste kiss of assurance greeted me on the morn,
Carys veiled and furred in ready for her deliverance unto the
banbyshn, who would return her not till the passing of a year.
Their Graces charged me with her safe passage, and on my life,
I swore it.

A wagon bearing the princess her dresses and other vestments
went ahead over the icy cobbles. I walked beside her palanquin,
ready my sabre and rampageous stallion, given more to the tram-
pling of Div skulls than following at hand. His breath steamed
like the boiling springs of Fedvvyd. I said,
—Your Highness is of good cheer?
—So much talk of azadagi, Your Excellency. Is it not natural for
a man to look to the care of his bride?
—So one would think, here, behind these ancient walls, but

I have seen and heard tell of many strange practises among
the hundred tribes, most unfit for the telling. Azadagi is of our
choosing, and like unto the Law that supports it, separates us
from the daeva-ridden savage, whose maidens are chattel rather
than treasure.

She laughed.

—Am I, then, the sardar's treasure?

—A prize beyond worth.

I presented the ancient court to Carys by the grandest of
routes, and so she made her debút before diverse peers as were
in attendance; my particular escort of the princess noted; her
beringed hand upon mine arm. Till scenic delay at its end, I
brought my bride to the chambers of the banbyshn, and Banu
Morvydd received her but barred me from entry and dismissed
me with little courtesy withal.

A knight was but a servant, and with an unclouded horizon and
renewed vigour, I turned to the shahanhah's aides for suitable
commission. They felicitated my betrothment and granted high
office: chief master of the practice halls and fields, of the squires
in their tuition, and the proving of new knights.

My heart wished to seek out the Div, but the shah stayed his
hand, proving merit in this course. War was upon us and might
come on a sudden, like spring storms, should we not sally forth
to meet it. Many had been the years of peace, and many were the
spears lost in the first shock of repentine battle. It was mine to
see the lads ready to win the day against the black tide of sorrow.

In the passing of sennights, I supped oft with my new kin
in Arman's banquet hall, hung with the shields of ages. Alack,
the winter garden, lacking Carys, lacked charm. And I was not
granted audience with her or the banbyshn. And absent court,
in martial observance, granted no glimpse but the fleet images
of dreams. Aye, vispuhr ladies came oft to the shaded viewing
stands to titter over their knights in drill or bout; but he, the
sardar, might not look back. Unless the banbyshn called her
knight, the chief master of the field saw none. Every lad looked
to me and the azure sash.

Thus given purpose, I was bereft of consolation, till upon an
unseemly hour went I by candlelight to the apartments of the
maids-of-honour, to Carys her chamber door. It was not she
who answered but Princess Essylt of the blue eyes unveiled and

in nightclothes that clung, such that the heat touched my face. I bowed, saying,

—Forgive me, Your Highness, I sought audience with my betrothed and no trespass on your rest or modesty. I will away.

—A moment, I beseech Your Excellency. My state is no matter, but know you that Mina, whilom favourite, is discharged from service. Your betrothed is the banbyshn's bedfellow this night, not mine.

—The nights are cold; it is not out of custom.

—No, sir, i' is not. Any maid might serve so i' turn, but Her Imperial Grace is of singular appetites. I cannot speak to i', but Carys cometh not till the dawn, and my bed hath chilled. Hast thou lain alone i' the moon of her repose?

Carys was but a lass. I

sank to one knee, graceless and stiff; there, in her kitchen, with all the azadagi – the "chivalry" – I could muster.

Liza stared.

—Julian, what, how?

—I cashed out my four-o-one-k.

—Come again?

The brokerage rep had thought me insane. The tax penalty alone exceeded my annual salary.

—You're the present and the future, and let's be honest, you're rich. I don't need it.

An absurd yellow diamond beset with emeralds, inspired by the colours of Fedwyd and the ring I'd given Carys. For a single moment, cost had been little object. I held it before her blue eyes with my fingertips.

She was wordless for once. I said,

—May I?

I took her unresisting hand and placed it on her finger. Finally, she said,

—You spent…

—Everything. But there was enough pocket change to pay the mortgage this month. I'm a pauper now.

—This is…

—Yours.

I rose from my knee, which had begun to hurt. Liza held

the upright sabre moon over Llys. Sleepless, I had quit my bed, and there were no other sounds but the wind in my ears, the fluttering of pennons, and the calls of the watch. The nighted steppe lay under mine eye, where herds of horses led greater herds of shaggy oxen, digging the grass from beneath the light southron snows with their hooves – or would by day. All were at rest, and I must return to mine; for my morrow watch within the practise halls, calling sleepy lads to unwavering attention. The sword forgave no lapse.

A lantern rose along the stair to the battlements. No guard but Banu Morvydd, fur-clad, on imperious summons. She led me an ambagiuous servants' path to unknown chambers, knocking thrice, then twice. I entered in silence.

It was a small room, suited to dormitory but spare in bedding and furniture. Only the hearth burned with generous light, and she who waited alone removed her veil. Banbyshn Llesami but not, her tawny hair tight in straight azad braids and garbed in a chambermaid's kirtle. I knelt, and she struck me.

—This castle is mine, and the creeping mouse goes not without my knowing. Faithless knight, have you so forgotten your love that you cast your heart to any chit by the way? We have dismissed Princess Essylt.

—Your Imperial…

She struck me again and again. Raging, weeping, for she was not the banbyshn but again Llesa; she clawed and bit upon me, would she rend and consume me, and locked within her limbs, I could not turn aside.

A DARK PASSAGE WAS OPEN, and eldritch waters bubbled forth, black and oilsome, redolent of a lost world coming again to light in all its fragrant distillation. Liza was the beacon of the present, but she was pushing me into the past through the gaps in her wooden tablets – somewhy evoking a time and place without a written language.

TITANS OF THE FALL, the incipit per Luwian's somewhat flexible syntax. It was a story I knew, not from memory, but set in shattered clay in △353: the destruction of Edin by dragonfire. I tried to imagine it, Llys in flames – to call it up – but nothing came. And Llesami remained an enigma in her hostile silences, the last standing structure of her dead civilisation.

I hung on each graphite line of the translation in progress – to the harrowed strands of Julián – till the present snapped like a pencil tip.

Llesa was frantic.

—I am undone; Idvval hath discovered us.

—Has he to the shah?

—No, but I am afeared, for I will be set aside in the succession, and my place, given to another. I must have the double crown.

Veiled still, she spoke to herself, but repudiation would fall on both should all come to court, and taken aback, I tasted the poison drop of doubt. Of lesser caste by birth, mine would be the headsman's sword – if not the traitor's pit. Then, downcast, she said,

—But beware Princess Carys; she is unfit to wife.

—How now?

It was Carys who should impugn me, for two moons had I proven faithless, stealing by night into the adulterer's bed. Llesa wrung her hands.

—I am loth to speak to it, but we cannot meet thus hence. My maids serve oft as bedfellows, but I have come to know the princess, to know her and her… intemperance ¶. Gvvyn, she is a seducer. Set her aside and bide in thy patience. Bide, and all will be well. Now, I must fly.

The place of our trysting was left unsullied and fireless. We had met twice or thrice a sennight, during the prince-consort's divertments, and but now did Llesa tell of this intemperance, of this seduction; it seemed me of doubtful purpose and ill done. And with this second drop of poison followed the third: had I, in mine intemperate passion, set Carys awry?

Indefensible, this was dying ground, not without but within the great keep, and Idvval ap Arshan held my life in a single breath. But was that not justice; was that not the Law? Where were the red caps, the condign shackles and clanking chains?

I walked free along the great stone halls, lightless but for my tallow taper, and at that skulking hour, came again to Carys her chamber door. She answered my knocking, the fabled daeva of my new spring, of a bright way I had abjured. Forsworn, I was; this said forswearer, mine.

—My wife, have I so despoiled thee?

—Betrothed, come; sit; be at ease.

She drew me in with gentle hands and shut the door, smile untroubled, brow unlined. So clear, her eyes in my candle's light.

—When I learned I was to wed the hero, I sought counsel from my maids, for how could I win you, who smote down shahs and generals for the love of the banbyshn? From them, I learned how a woman may please a man and a man a woman, and ready was I to press my claim when thought lost, you returned Gvvyn Emrys ¶. What custom names and does are divided by a parasang. Her Grace warned me against untimely child ere we wed and that I must take your seed by any other means ¶. Know that Llesa holds us both as chattel and hath taken what is thine and what is mine. But thou art promised me, and I shall possess thee in heart, body, and mind.

—She hath named thee Seducer. A lady of intemperate blood unfit to take to wife.

—And hath she discharged me for this intemperance? Llesa is of my kind, and I play upon her as a lyre. And raising her fingers to ruddy lips, said,—O but she is wanton.

Carys released her bedclothes to the floor, and upon her bared skin, a gold rope bore a many-rayed sigil of the sun. It recalled the shields of the Div, their Sun War, and it liked me not.

—And this idol on your breast? It is no device of Arman.

—Here, high within this keep, Kian hath a hidden temple to the effulgence. East, it faceth the rising sun over Coedvvig Ddu. In the seeming of her devoted disciple, I have drawn the secrets

uploaded the finished text to the cloud. Liza was busy being fabulous somewhere fancy, but her urgency knew no bounds. I'd solved a puzzle but had no answers.

"The both of you": two marked. Edin, the "steppe": the Garden. Correlations in an incomplete picture. The TITANS OF THE FALL were beyond imagining, and the would-be banbyshnan banbyshn, the "queen of queens", wasn't the kind of coruscating alienity that'd boiled the sea right in front of me.

There was no tangible sign of Astaphæus, the eighth angel, but in gold, the radiant Aten. An ancient link between Llesami and THE NAME.

I locked up and took the elevator to the parking level. Heading home to an empty place, but it was Liza's – our – place, and sooner than later, she'd be there. It was myself that I wasn't sure of – if I'd still be now or then.

There was a smattering of posh and pedestrian vehicles despite the hour. I expected no late-night inkblots indoors and stepped back when an elephantine SUV's shadow took shape. I could've cut them down before they drew their guns – if I'd had a sabre.

—This is private property, detectives.

—The door wuz open.

They'd been waiting long enough to unzip their winter coats and unwind their scarves. Beige said,

—Doctor Corbin, it's not looking good for you.

—Tell it to my lawyers, I replied. I'm not answering any questions.

—We're not asking any, but listen up real good. We've got you. The homicides at the MRI place, behind the Institute at your old smoking spot – congrats on quitting, by the way – then your shady little antiques dealer. A few too many coincidences, don't you think?

—All the murders, Brown stepped in. We seen your pattern, Doc. The spiral. Very artsy.

—The FBI…

—Fuck the FBI.

Beige sighed.

—You're at the centre of the spiral, Doctor Corbin, right here. We know you wanted to get caught, and we can help you. Make it stop. If you come in voluntarily, I'm sure those guys with the Hermeez ties can work out a sweet deal. Otherwise, we've got a needle…

Half the lights flicked off, opening portals of chiaroscuro. A silent, sudden dimensional shift, absent the echoing throw of circuit breakers, and prismic shadows burst their constraints in a flicker at the speed of causality. The detectives glanced at each other, and Brown said,

—Spooky, Doc.

—A needle, Beige repeated the threat, with your name on it.

—An' don't worry, added Brown; once you're inside, we'll take turns fucking that pretty redhead of yours. Never had any of that uptown pussy.

—Pfft. Jesus, Louie.

And the air turned red, a gouting, pulsing mist and gurgling, wheezed screams, showering me with incarnadine exaltation. My laughter was a ringing torment of euphoniums, brazen and abhuman, amid the snapping of twigs. Thursic murders, artless and monstrous.

A severed, trousered leg dragged beneath the suv – tearing, cracking – then a voice of layered resonance, young yet old:

—Bless me, Father. I have partaken of the sacrament and bear witness to the glory of your transfiguration.

—Blessings… ?

—Thank you, Father.

Then all was still and dark with the scent and taste of blood, ferreal, electric in my nostrils; I breathed great heaving gulps and smiled buoyant joy with no one to see. And I longed for Liza, for her scent and softness, and that thing – the phone – I smeared it with bloody fingertips and watched my fading lazuli flush.

—Julian? her voice. Julian! Where are you?

She found me somehow, and three white utility vans and a black sedan, glistening with snowmelt, cordoned the scene. Orange HazMat suits piled out, pulling wheeled cases. She was on the phone and called to them without coming closer:

—Get his phone and clean him up. Julian, go with them, and I'll meet you halfway.

Liza reseated herself in the sedan.

—Go on, she said and shut the door.

They guided me into one van, the interior fitted with a stainless stall, a high-pressure hose, and a compressor that made an echoing roar in the indoor lot. I was too tall to stand straight and had to hunch as I was scrubbed till the crimson tide ran clear, then scrubbed again. My clothes were little more than gory rags, gathered up and bagged. I saw no faces.

Blown dry, berobed, and slippered, I was ushered out. Someone had gotten the lot's lights back on, and a pickup truck towing a large tank pulled in. I could smell the caustic. Spotlights aided the HazMat suits, bagging shreds and splinters. Inside the next van, they handed me a tagless tracksuit from a bin of plastic-wrapped bundles, sizes marked, and Velcro slip-ons, likewise. We sped out as soon as I was dressed and buckled in. They bagged the robe, hairbrush, and anything else I'd touched, the plastic marked *incinerator*. They handed me a new phone. Cloned, they said. SIM, IMEI, and memory.

I changed vehicles and met Liza again in a sedan like the first but not the same, like some spy vs spy shell game, as I descended from my exhilarated high and, yes, the sensation of absolute majesty. She held her peace, gripping my hand, till we were alone in a small place on a mucky residential street, midtown, I'd never seen before.

—Why the police? Of all things.

—They planned to rape you.

—I hope they tasted better than they looked.

The place was clean and furnished, the cheap but comfortable, lower end of middle-class. I said,

—What is all this, all that back there?

—I made preparations. I knew your awakening was imminent; I knew there would be blood.

—How? Who are you?

She recrossed her legs, a fluid turn of rich fabrics.

—"The seventh angel sounded, and from above, a Voice as thunder: 'The dominion of this cosmos hath become the LORD's, and of their anointed, and they shall reign unto Aions of Aions.'"

—And you are... ?

—The Voice. The way is open. You have control now, but you could let go, let the monster run wild. Or, if you break the amended rules, then... You know.

If not their words, I remembered the greasy, venomous smiles of the Innominatum's acolytes. This wasn't that. Liza radiated certitude in knowledge and action, not self-satisfaction. I gave her a pointed look.

—New rules, you said.

—For one, you can talk to me without consequences, but only to me.

—What do you know about all of this?

—Everything.

I let the implications steep. Our relationship was no accident. The wooden tablets, no mere passion project. Even the Bowen Trust itself. All were part of the larger game.

Too good to be real? Caught up in the story, I'd lost sight of the board. And Liza, my Liza, wasn't a piece but a player.

—So tell all, I gibed.

I knew it wouldn't be that easy, and she smiled for the first time that evening. She thumbed the ring on her finger. At the family dinner, the Lobster had taken one look at it and said, "Who knew you had it in you? I mean, who knew?" My mother had been especially pleased with Liza's pallor. It would improve the blood, she'd said, but mercifully, not in English.

Liza explained,

—Your amnesia isn't natural. A mountain of experience, more than you'd expect, is hanging over you. Imagine a psychological avalanche landing on you all at once. As it is, you're in shock.

—Shock, from what?

—You turned two people into steak tartare with your bare hands. I've done all I can to help you remember at a safe, controlled pace and expected we'd be ready to talk once you finished the translation.

She said something I didn't quite catch: avatārah, martyāh, in… Sanskrit? Not something I recalled learning, but it sparkled – *mortal men taunted an avatar, and here we are.* Something like that. Like Llesami, she knew what I didn't, and she'd handed me remembrances of things past. I said,

—So you've known who I was all this time.

—Not at first. I saw you once, leaving an art broker. You'd landed a piece I would've wanted, but they wouldn't let me outbid you after the fact. I found out where you worked – to make an offer – but I was… intrigued, I guess, and started following your lectures. It all came together later, Beloved.

A resonance flared like a dying star. It'd lingered, waiting for this moment. I said,

—You've never called me that before.

—What?

—Beloved.

Liza didn't frown, not pretending to think about it. Not playing coy.

—Haven't I.

—Say it in Italian, Beloved.

It wasn't a question or even hope. Something in her teasing directness revived an ineffable loss, and a smirk cracked her poker face.

—In Volgare, Amato?

Even the intonation was correct. Ferrara. Sixteenth century, said with all the lightsome playfulness of a certain contessa. Our relationship; no accident.

—Issota? I asked. O my Issota...

The grief rose in me like a fountain and bubbled over. Then the flood. Her hand rose to her throat, her grimace speaking of pained memory.

—It was cruel how I toyed with you – I knew how you felt or thought I knew. I didn't know myself till it was too late. Julian, what's... ?

Doubled over, I don't know how she understood my ragged words:

—I couldn't live without you.

—You mean...

—I couldn't.

—You... for me.

—I held you in my arms till the end.

Her eyes filled and ran over, matching mine; she crossed the gap. Issota's arms around me, alive, breathing, crying, something forever lost returned to me, and the world would never be the same.

O UTRAGE. BETRAYAL. Liza was right: I'd been in shock. I should've raged at her. I should've torn her little safe-house down, but she'd dodged the hard questions, then put them off.

"Go to work," she'd said this morning. "Your usual half-day. Everything's normal because nothing happened. I'll pick you up for lunch; then we'll come home and talk. If the cops show again, you know the script."

I bided on a bitten tongue. She'd died, opposing l'Avversario to her final breath. Now she was this Voice… Their Voice? And the rules had changed.

She was Issota, but she wasn't the same. Almost four hundred fifty years. A dozen lives, give or take, in pre-contemporary lifes-pans. But I was Guiliano – had been – and I wasn't the same either.

I went through the motions: construction updates; exhibition wheedling. Llesami stepped through our office doorway, and the thread of time caught in its spindle. She'd discarded the vestiges of Maaike: her updone hair recoloured the tawn shade of Llysian memory, her faux glasses set aside. Something had changed. Her frameless eyes met mine and in their night

lay upon the earth, and rising against it, the silvered edge of the veil. My antelucan cogitations wore the stone with circular pacings till I turned, hand to hilt, at the fall of a heavy foot. Prince-consort Idvval nodded to me and, with a curt gesture, dismissed the guards from their watch. He bore no light of his own, but I mistook not the spiral curls of his thin moustaches in the fluttering watch fires. I released my sabre and bowed.
—Good morrow, Your Highness.
—Good morrow, worthy sardar. I heard tell that here is your purlieu of daybreak.
—It is so, sir. If, in your purpose, I am sought, how may I serve?
—Your Excellency has done me great service, and I have come to give thanks.

—Sir?

—The banbyshn is with child, and I am spared a duty most distasteful. I made such intercessions as I could to ensure your interviews remained undiscovered; Her Grace is headstrong and clumsy i' matters of delicacy, like the great bulls of the olyfant routs.

He gripped my arm with a firm warrior's hand.

—But think not to mark on i'. The child is of the imperial house and will not know you. Your service to the banbyshn is abated for a time, but i' due seasons, I should thank you again. The shah would be pleased with no less than three heirs, methinks ¶. Afore long, I shall hold the Field Marshal's baton. Know thy place i' my service. Then pressed he my shoulder, in the semblance of friendly caution, and through his teeth, said,—And know thou Princess Essylt was slain these three moons; on her despatch from court?

—How now? What foe breached the first circle? Why…

—Slain by her father's hand. There was law before the Law, and our ways endure. Vardan hath its honour ¶. Good health, Sardar Gvvyn, and farewell.

—Farewell. Your Highness.

I looked back to the spreading fires of dawn. It seemed the world was burning.

I blinked, and the spell broke. Midstep, Llesami moved through distortions that eddied around me like a whirlpool. She proceeded to her desk, her paper cup of coffee capped with a performative stroopwafel instead of a sippy lid.

And between us, not the void but a boy's voice in the echoing dark, a voice I'd doubted was real. "Bless me, Father". As the mother, the son had suffered; if he too were here – hidden from me – in this time, in this place. Hidden by l'Avversario, hidden by her. She didn't pause between summary question and answer:

—Have you followed the news? Those detectives that were here have gone missing.

—Sounds like a police problem.

—Are human lives nothing to you, then?

Anger unlike any I'd ever known inflamed me: the heat rushed to my face and filled my lungs, lifting me to my feet.

—No; Llesami, I demanded. There is one: what of our child? Why'd I have to find out from Idwal's ghost?

She stared at me, stock still, with the blankest of her expressions, as if she'd frozen within. Then she stalked out, leaving her things behind.

—Llesami! I called after her. Our son!

I brushed my heavy desk aside as if it weren't what it was but took only a single step before my bones filled with molten lead, and no sound escaped my throat as I collapsed in a rigid rictus of agony. The conflagration surged and roiled, emanating through every fibre, burning through me; then it guttered out, and I was left gasping and too weak to move. From where I lay, I could hear her heart beating too slowly, like the pounding steps of a brontosaur, and in her wake, spacetime shivered in nanotremors of gravitation. The very spheres trembled.

A groan caught in my throat, and the merciful dark rose to cover me. I heard Röhm's papers fall to the floor, panicked cries for help, and the approach of that resounding drum, shaking earth and soul; till something filled the emptied space, glowing with soft warmth, a dance of fireflies, spreading life back to my toes and fingertips. A different sensation of movement.

I opened my eyes to Liza's, my head in her lap, an odd ticking in my ear. Blue eyes, but they weren't the same. Not sapphirine but a pale glacier-blue that drew their warmth from her regard. My bearings were contorted, splayed half onto a wide bench seat, under the blanket of my duffle coat, the uptown skyline scrolling past the tinted glass. I found her hand, and she asked what'd happened.

—I stepped in it, I said. I got angry and confronted her. She's always right there; she knows everything and says nothing. They burned me from the inside out.

—That's the temptation, the game. She can't leave you, yet her presence torments you.

—Can't?

Liza caressed my face with her other hand, her ring cool against my cheek.

—Won't, but without you, she can't find me ¶. She wanted power and freedom, and the Rulers gave it to her. So much power she can't afford to sneeze ¶. When I arrived, she was cradling you like an egg; she's the one who called me. She doesn't suspect who I am.

—Neither do I, do I?

Liza's smile reached her cool eyes.

—You've made one connexion; the rest will come. We can postpone our talk until you…

—No. Today. I'll be fine. I am fine.

I kept my cards close, waiting for her to show her hand. Whoever she'd been at the start of the story, she'd become something other. As had I.

Getting out of the car, I was light-headed under the cosmic sway. Large fluffy snowflakes filled the air, enjoying their picturesque moment, the sidewalk cleared of muck and ice. I made it upstairs to a sofa and called it quits, the air thick, not with incense but fresh cut flowers out of season. It wasn't the penthouse of this post-townhouse luxe tower, but in its daylit splendour, ivory, greige, and black, it was anything but lower-middle. Much like her office space, Liza lived within polished marble, warm maple panelling, and an ever-changing parade of contemporary abstractions. Antiquities were hoarded out of sight. She ferried in illicit painkillers, an ice-cold beer, and a laptop. She took the easy chair.

—TITANS OF THE FALL. Your translation looks like Swiss cheese.

—Art reflects life.

—Our lives.

I asked her how she knew about these obscure tablets and their rather Græco-tragic tale of a city destroyed by sea monsters, its three gilded walls ringing of Plato's Atlantis fable and of a princess carried into the underworld like Persephone. She stared up at the ceiling and the private projection of memory.

—I wrote a song once. Well, I composed it; they didn't teach women to write at that time, in that place. I remembered the beginnings then, but I saw no sign of you. Either of you. My family was… long story short, they allowed me music, and I sent out a song, hoping it would reach you, wherever you were:

> Woe to the golden court, for the titans of its fall
> Hath risen, and the very waters boiled in pain…

Still looking away, she said,

—It spread with merchants and pilgrims, but one day, soldiers came to our village. My song had reached Hattusa, and the priests had judged it an offense to the gods and accused me of being a witch that would summon the demons of Ur upon us. My village stoned me to death.

I saw her shoulders twitch and sat up, but she waved me off.

—No, it's fine. We've borne a lot of death; I can shake it off. The important part is that my song survived. It changed over time, but the core is still there.

—The core.

—Yes.

—So Llys was destroyed. By them.

—The old court and empire. Every castle. Every yurt.

—I can't remember.

—You were already

a single blossom threaded upon Carys her bodice, a heart worn without. Banbyshn Llesami's scarlet dress shewed yet no swell of child, but I doubted not the prince-consort's word. There was no mother's joy in her steady gaze, naught but the wrath of the wounded lion. Banu Morvydd put up her blade at the banbyshn's sign and shut the door, and the jovial maids noted but their own merriment as they danced across the floor. The spring festivals were upon us.

In fairer days, the vispuhran would have returned hence to their holdings across the empire, to castles held by lean azad service across the hard winter, and the herds would follow. This year, no departures but the march to war.

Her Imperial Grace drew away to the window, and near upon, I bowed.

—Sardar, she said undertone, you are not welcome.

—I must speak.

—I will not hear you.

—The prince-consort has advised me.

—Speak not to it. I am in his hand, and he would make a shah of himself and deny me my just right. I will have the White Crown ¶. Return to your station, Chief Master.

Three nights had I knocked on Carys her chamber door. Again and again, it went unanswered. I knelt, my face and words low:

—I am dismissed, but my betrothed is kept mistress to Your Imperial Grace.

—To my shame, she made me hers. Set her aside.

The banbynshn's hands were clenched. I raised my head.

—You bade me give troth-plight, and having gone forth, ma'am, I cannot in honour retreat. His Grace may withdraw consent. Her Highness may yet refuse me, of lesser station to herself, even begilded with an honourary peerage. But as you know me, I bear my charge to its end and shall not turn aside unto my death. But if she be unfit, then discharge and return her to His Grace.

—I cannot! she hissed. I will not!

—Then I know who has your love, and it is not I.

—Get thee gone and come not near

Liza handed me a beer that wobbled like rubber in my hand, then sat beside me on the sofa. She wasn't drinking.

—Amata, I said. When did you first call me that? In Padua, it was a memory.

She took a deep breath and looked at me with wet eyes, and I could see the lines of it, etched out of time, of a loss like my Issota, whom she was. She shook her head.

—It's what you called me. Long after the empire was forgotten, we met again in a garden, sharing flowers and songs…

And for a moment, I saw her: Snow-white of the black hair and rose mouth, alabaster pale; her voice, a single line of lyric, distant on the wind, fading.

—I glimpsed… It was you… Domina… Ynes.

Liza covered her mouth.

—Corduba… ante Mauri in illam invaserunt… et…

I held her as she shuddered in memory. It had been my word, my thought, all along.

—Mi amor.

She looked back at me with the grief of thirteen hundred years, a tear-fraught smile.

—My caballarius, my Gothi.

It was me. And it was her. In the silence of our breaths, I could hear her heartbeat as, pleasingly, it thumped for me, and nearby, the faint and tremorous ticking of a tiny clock. It dawned on me:

—You're pregnant.

—Five weeks.

—Marry me already.

In the face of everything. Of the hard questions I hadn't asked, of the answers I didn't want. If her hands weren't clean, neither were mine; if she'd taken on the burden of my crimes, I'd carry hers. Whatever my ultimate origin, we were in this together. She said,

—I told you, Betrothed. Soon.

My persistence crashed upon a single word. I stiffened, loosening my hold, face to face with my suspicion.

—Betrothed? You've never called me that before, mi amor.

She seemed to rise from the pain of Córdova's fall; straightening, she gazed back at me, O the palest sky in her eyes.

—I'm sure I have.

Llesami was right: "You've found her." I said,

—Yes; I remember you saying it many times, my bride across time: my Carys.

—I'm *Liza* now. Carys was a conniving little minx who'd listened to too many romances by the bards. I've grown up since then.

—My Liza, and soon to be...

The hairs on my arm stood on end. Not goosebumps, but the tingling near miss of a lightning strike. In her eyes, the passage before the advent of light, the fathomless crossing. I knew the depth and breadth of it, the subtle shift of her regard. Liza had left the building.

—Little Flea, forever jumping. Mine oracle hath made bond for thy lenience, but bloodwite is owed, and I claim use of thy debt the same.

L'Avversario bit into my wrist with relish, and blood welled around Liza's lips.

T WAS ANOTHER BLOODBATH. Liza dabbed at the
I   stains on her clothes; it was futile. I watched my wrist
stitch itself together in real-time with little more than
an itchy tingle, like some comic book superhero – or a movie
monster. Her grimace was succinct.

—I'll shower first. We'll get a new sofa tomorrow.

A reminder we were both marked? As if we needed it. Nodding,
I said nothing to her withdrawal. We were in this together, but
washing off blood wasn't something we needed to share.

It'd been a strange, lucid moment; in the grip of l'Avversario,
before Liza came to; another déjà vu. The helplessness hadn't
translated across memory. I couldn't resist or lift a finger: a chess
piece on the black, in a tyrannical hold. I'd asked *why*, *who*, and
how? amid their libation.

They'd smacked her bloody lips and, showing red teeth, said,
"We are that we are. I, the dreamer; thee, the dream."

The honking of cars outside brought me back to the corroded
stench of old blood, already tiresome in its recurrence. It didn't
help that I was sitting in it. I

was surpassed. The runners' report: the expedition to Ysel returned in force, but few spears lost.

It was a season of fear. The scouted Div crossing the Bloody
Fords, olyfants harnessed to war, and false cries of Dragon! – on
the horizon, a menace of cloud. Ere midsummer, the battle
would be joined, even if it met at the third wall of Llys, with
sieging waters to flank the victor. The Hall of Gold stood filled
and more, with shahrdaran and ministers of the four standing
houses; with the living maids of their honour – Carys in veiled
attendment; Banbyshn Llesami shewing the first swell of child.

The redoubtable Prince Vahim of Gorg was announced to the
shahanshah's audience; knight palatine and grivpanvar, his bril-
liant harness token of the most ancient pride of Ymerodraeth.

Behind him came two squires bearing a supply cask bound to the hafts of two spears. They knelt, and the prince rose.

—Your Imperial Majesty, we bring news of the breachèd earth and the distant waste that marks the grave of Kian's mighty spears.

For this, Shahanshah Lleu had stayed his hand. The deciding word.

—Illustrious Knight, speak you first on that matter which lies most urgent, and we will counsel on the other anon.

—The sea pours forth, sire, an unstaunchable wound. Ysel is naught but a lesser sea that foredooms Llyn Tvvyll.

A great outcry arose, and questions were cast upon the prince like stones. The shahanshah raised his hand, and silence there was.

—Is there no artifice, no levee of our making, that might avert this flood?

Prince Vahim knelt again.

—I conceive not what awful power so divided the land, but this new river vale, which yields up its dread waters, was rent apart a mile and more. Too deep to ford and too wide for horses to swim. The river bank is glazed with sharded glass, and many are the trees fallen and burnt almost to stone.

—A mile, said the banbyshn.

—Even two, Your Imperial Grace. It is a dreadful thing. Picture rolls have been prepared in our assay of the changèd land. From our surveys, we fear Llyn Tvvyll will a hundred paces rise; for the World Sea does not recede from the far shore, but as a cup without limit, pours ever forth. The ancients, sire, may have had some means...

The prince shook his head. The Shahansah Lleu spoke in his place:

—But we are a fallen race and but one course remains us, for the sea reacheth forth to poison the very heart of the world – and this eternal city, wash away ¶. Nay, my lords, we who came from the east, driving wild herds before us; we who came from the west with the arts of metal and stone; we who brought to rein the great mountain steeds and from base copper wrought alcamyn; we shall not yield to the ravening tides. Here, upon the shores of Llyn Tvvyll, did our forbearers meet, bringing together east and west and lighting the first flame of Law in a world in darkness. We, the heirs of Cayo Mardd, shall not yield to malice and envy nor

give our sons and daughters over to slavery and degradation ¶.
As Llys falls into the sea, we sally to reclaim the west. I, Lleu ap
Esfandyar, bind my house by a bloody and terrible oath: we shall
know no rest till we have scourged this pestilence from the land
and, lamenting tears of mercy, deprived the rabid beasts of breath
to the last foaming pup. The blood of Kian shall not suffer the
Elder Foe to live: this, I swear ¶. What sayeth the third estate?

The istandar nodded among themselves. One stepped forward:
—We are in accord with Your Imperial Majesty, for the depra-
vations of the foe fall most heavily among the many, and none
are unmarked by mourning.
—Give unto the raman our plight and commission, for there
is no further retreat, and every bow must bend for our deliverance ¶. Illustrious Knight, thou hast done us grave and good
service, and all Ymerodraeth giveth thanks. Pray, speakest thou
on the extremity of the quest which has these many moons taken
thee from our lands.

Prince Vahim stood and raised one hand to his burnished
breastplate.
—Sire, we made trial of the pathless wood about Ysel's new waters, and the season changed ere we tasted ash on the wind, and
our eyes fell upon a great waste on the verge of the sea. Its fluvial
inlet is broader parted, by half, than the train to Llyn Tvvyll ¶.
The sardar was humble in his speech, or in his injury, did not
take full measure of the wrath and wrack of the dragon; for its
breadth could seat all of Llys and more besides, and neither beast,
fowl, or flower there reside. No mortal man could withstand such
dread might, sire, and on that, we bear token. His Excellency,
Gvvyn Emrys, is well-named.

The knight palatine beckoned forth the casket bearers. They
placed it before the dais and, with timorous care, removed a
bundled cloth. Unfolding it revealed a sword, misshapen as
if thrust into the forge fires, but the hilt marked its use. The
squires stepped away, as if from a rearing viper, and knelt again.
The prince said,
—Mark you the white hilt, sire. The ivory is scorched, but the
pommel jade remains true. It is my mind that this sabre was
struck from the sardar's hand by the dolorous blows of the great
dragon; this, the proving of that contest. But it cannot be touched,
sire; it yet bears such heat that he who found it in the ash became

fevered and bilious and died of it in a fortnight. It is fell poisoned and should be taken hence lest it sicken the people.

And the shahanshah turned to me, where I stood among the peerage:

—Know thou this sword, Your Excellency?

—Your Imperial Majesty, it is a relic of my fathers, and it sorrows me that it is beyond recovery. It was the last such token after the Long March and the loss of my kinsmen.

—Have our consolation and know that thou art the paramount knight of the imperium. Thou shalt be our vanguard ¶. Let he who cast down the Pretender strike the first blow ¶! Sardar Gvvyn, we charge thee: along with thee a small force, common and peer, that all may have their portion of our due justice, and as we marshal and make provision to protect the herds that provide the commonweal, thou shalt strike and harry the foe in their folly. It is fit that the banbyshn's champion will carry our banner forth. Your Excellency, do you accept?

I stepped forth and knelt.

—Sire, I am ever at your command, and I shall not return ere scourging the foe from the land.

Under the Red Crown, Her Imperial Grace fell into a swoon, and her veilèd maids raised a cry, rushing to her aid, and the prince-consort stepped forth from the peers. The shahanshah took a silver-worked chalice from his cupbearer and presented it to the assemblage.

—My daughter is overcome, for such is the flower of azadagi at its finest. Let every man mark and know its full measure. We salute thee, Gvvyn Emrys.

—You do me too much honour, sire.

—Now, sir, away and exact from the foe, stern payment. Away all, and on the morrow, know the greater part of our mind.

The Shahanshah Lleu stood, and all knelt beside me. In the departure of the imperial procession, I would have set to my duty with haste, but His Grace, Shahryar Rhys, took my arm and myself aside into subdued conference.

—Good sardar and son, I am afeared the shah sendeth thee to thine end. Even the banbyshn is overcome by the peril lain upon thee, for it is plain to all.

—Such peril as this is the azadan's meat and milk; for in the service of Ymerodraeth, of a knight for one or all, am I well spent.

It is a pledge I failed, for many fell and were taken on the Long March, and now shall I take up spear and sword and reprove those who would feast upon the people.

—All merit to thy courage, sir, but I would fain not have my daughter widowed ere her wedding day. Beware the shah; for tyranny may yet shadow the empire, and it is as hateful as the savage horde. By this device, may he seek to purge such dissent as would seek voice in the realm and, with one dart strike two fowl from his sight: peer and foe.

—Hot battle awaits all, Your Grace, and if I may forestall the foul host but a little – and so deliver Ymerodraeth – I will throw this life away, freed of regrets. This war will have in it the proving of many knights, and if I do not return, Her Highness will choose a prince among them.

—Beware, my son, the foe before and the friend behind.

—By your leave, sir, duty calls.

Already could I hear the trumps,

the vibrations passing through me. Llesami was nearby and coming closer. In my hand, a wavering cup of black coffee, half and half on the kitchen counter, midmorning sun through the broken clouds. We must've slept in. I could hear the shower and smell the steaming water and floral soap.

The sofa was still a horror show – hours, not days, had passed. I shuffled to the entryway, neatened my bathrobe, then opened the front door as Llesami reached for the bell. Her look was oblique.

—May I?

I wasn't up for another confrontation, but she was here and dressed to impress under her open coat, but she thought "Liza" was a patron of the Institute. I stepped aside, then shut and locked the door.

—Is there an emergency?

—You haven't answered your mobile. I left messages.

—I didn't hear it ring. Maybe it's silenced.

Liza entered in a powder-blue bathrobe, patting her au-burn-wet hair dry. Her brow furrowed at the vestibule conference. Llesami apologised for the intrusion.

—I needed to speak to Doctor Corbín for a moment. I couldn't get through.

—I turned his phone off.

A deep chill settled over me as an awkward silence fell, Llesami in the hot seat. I saw no source for the draft, and as Liza reached us, she folded and flipped the towel overshoulder.

—We needed privacy without interruption.

—I beg your pardon, but might I have a moment, Mizz Bowen?

—You've had many of my moments, Llesa. Won't you call me as you once did?

—Carys?

Llesami's voice was rich with yearning and repeated loss, and envy struck my heart; the thin, daggerlike green serpent from Issota's mural. Liza's voice cut:

—No, no; it was, "My sweet Carys." "My heart." "O my Carys… "

—Don't shame me.

—Is that all that's left of your so-called love? Shame… ?

My limbs grew leaden, and I tried to shake off an odd lethargy that settled in with the chill, snugging my already tightened robe. The two closed, nose to nose, sparring with a wounded and ancient intimacy.

I had no ears for words they meant for each other, but vertigo struck me a resounding blow across the face. Unable to turn from them, I slumped to the floor sans motor control, unable to move or even breathe – like a corpse, but for the moment, alive and awake.

—What did you do! Liza shouted.

—I did nothing; it's the Tyrant.

—No! The ban is lifted. Release him!

—I cannot. I haven't…

Liza grappled with Llesami but was brought to her knees, mastered like a cub facing a lion, the opulent inlaid marble flooring cracking beneath them as the room shuddered. Unmoved, Llesami said,

—Don't make me hurt you.

I couldn't breathe – couldn't, but no, that wasn't right. I didn't respire like orb-bound things that swam and crawled and jumped, but there was a thumping strain for oxygen, and my lungs wouldn't open. Then I remembered and gulped heaving breaths and forgot again, the memory slipping my grasp like a shadow.

—Stop it! Liza cried. Don't kill him, not like this, not for those detectives!

—It's not me; it's the Tyrant. You can't be together!

Another ragged breath drew into my lungs, torn between the doubled presence of my body and something other, of central air and a distasteful cold, of the fractal weft of thought and myriadfold dreams and a cosmos that bent to will alone. It wasn't me, and with that tiny sip of air, out choked,
—What...? Who are...?

I AM

My heart faltering, Liza sprang backwards, up and over me in some move out of an old Hong Kong action film, minus the wires. She breathed life into me but gave me no compressions; she could hear my heart steadying as I could hers and our child's. Llesami countered,
—What have you done?
   Liza spoke between pauses for air:
—I am the Oracle and bride to the anointed... I was shriven, and the way is open.
—What! How?
—All this time you've searched... for even more power... but I could search too... It was under my nose...
   Llesami struck the floor with one fist, raising a cloud of powdered marble.
—Carys!
—The Div were the key... I followed their path... and became THE GRINDHOUSE KILLER... –a means to an end... –but you already guessed that.
   And then Llesami wept, a strangled mime of weeping; for all of its anguishment, there were no tears.
—No, my Carys. Don't give in to them. Come back to me.
—So there's your love... Too little, too late... And it's Liza now... Carys is for your slaves... your comfort women.

—Please…

—This is my destined rôle, you… could claim me yours forever… or take my place… and be with Julian… Now, release him… or choose, and strike one of us down for good.

The pressure in my skull reached the bursting point, redoubling, my eyes filled with stars; then redoubled again, ablaze with a mad fire, spinning at the centre of the spheres: power without mind but alive, trapped and terribly alive. I knew THE NAME, and it howled its horror against space and time. Then it was gone.

My limbs returned to me, and within the glut of air, my chest heaved as if I'd sprinted a thousand yards. I was spent, and the chill beyond the room did not leave me. I wanted to sleep, even on the cold marble, even in the dust. Liza rested a hand over my heart but looked above me.

—See? I knew you had it in you.

—It wasn't me, replied Llesami; I'm powerless. Why won't you believe me?

—Yes, as powerless as when you snapped my neck in Veshali. As easy as snapping your fingers.

—The men had gathered to hunt the rakshasa. You were out of control, and they knew it wasn't a tiger; they knew they were hunting something that walked on two legs. You would have slaughtered most of them before you died in pain. I had to end it, but I would never torment Gwyn. He will never serve the Tyrant, and neither will I.

—Serve? We are what we are, Llesa. Would you save him and damn the world?

—There's a possibility.

Liza's fingers knotted in my robe.

—A false hope.

—No. I won't let you be monsters forever. No matter what it takes, I will free you both. I swear it.

—Llesa, you lived one human life. Less than thirty years, wasn't it? You've been one of the Ogdoad for thirty thousand, yet you cling to this human mask. How close did you come when you stamped out the last of the Div? – every man, woman, and child that survived the holocaust of Llys. How close were you to letting your humanity go? Cast away this shell and become Astaphæus.

—You cannot see me like…

—Go. Ascend your throne or don't. Leave us to find our eternity:

Julian and I have something important to do. I won't spend it in the waiting room that is your memory of Fedwyd while you take what you need from me. How many times have I had to forgive you? You made me your slave, then killed the monster your lust made. And I forgive you.

—I... I'm...

—Sorry? A parting gift, Astaphe. Do what the three did to Llys, and the seed of power within you will bloom; then the Greater Shear will fall away, unable to harm you. It doesn't even have to be this city. Any major city will do. Now either use it and destroy one of us or get out.

I didn't watch Llesami leave; I could only follow the sounds of the closing door, quieting sobs, and the seismic throbs of her heart as it receded. Liza's eyes met mine, warming.

—Come, Betrothed, I can't move you without manifesting, which could have other consequences for the mortals in the building. The hunger can be difficult.

I tried to sit up but sagged. My limbs were rubber and had no strength. My voice just as weak, my mouth strange to me, I formed each word with care:

—Everything... you said to her...

—Don't worry; she wouldn't actually destroy either of us. Not in a million years – a literal million. She hasn't the spine. In a way, she is powerless.

—But you said she... she killed you.

—She reset the game is all. That thing around her neck is a kind of weapon, and if she uses it against one of us, we're gone for good. But she can splatter either of us with a wave of her hand and has, many times: whenever it's taken us over. Whenever we lose ourselves.

It. My words were the softest exhalation, deep in my throat:

—How long have we been monsters?

—We've been many of them. The first werewolves, the last windigo. Ghilan, ogres – tales to frighten children. For a thousand generations.

I couldn't grasp the number – it couldn't be what she meant. I prompted,

—So Llys fell... ?

—Thirty thousand years ago. That's how long she's watched us, how long she's kept us penned.

★

HIRTY THOUSAND YEARS. It was a gap I couldn't com-
T   prehend, pushing the gilded city back into a remote
darkness where the Other had extinguished its light.
I'd no recall of the war elephants of the Div. I could picture
the arched tusks displayed in the Hall of Judgement but not
a single living tusker on the steppe: the Mammoth Steppe of
the Last Glacial Period. An excision so neat I'd missed it and
its implications.

Of a Silver Age before the Bronze Age of my long studies,
dwelling in the decayed remains of a mythologised Golden
Age. Tottering in its senescence, unattested in its erasure. Liza
squeezed my hand.

—We know. We know what's worse than existential dread – than
an empty, meaningless universe. Something is out there – something is here – and we've been noticed ¶. The Div were the fragment of a dream. You and I will take Gueyumar's place in that
dream, in their vision for mankind. That's our bloodwite. He
was shahjahan and magush: you'll be one; I am the other. Unlike
him, we are filaments spun from ἐγώ εἰμι, one and inseparable;
we stand below the Rulers but above humanity ¶. You know
what is coming. We are the only salvation, the only protection
they have ¶. I've opened the way for us, and you've awakened to
yourself, but there's a time limit on this grace period we've had
together. Soon, you'll feel the call to a high place where you will
claim the kingship. There's no turning back, but we'll gain the
authority to save Man.

ἐγώ εἰμι, Ego Eimi, "I AM". "Authority" – ἐξουσία – resonated
from the Mysteries; this had been long in coming. I prompted,
—ἐξουσίαι?

—Yes. When the Rulers reäwaken, Ymerodraeth will be reborn
through us and our children: a new Millenium. I thought we
would have more time to prepare, but when you feel the call,
you must go.

The unspoken catch in her sales pitch prompted me, in turn:

—And what happens to Llesami?

—One of us has to lose, or this game never ends.

I gathered my recovering strength and sat up, pulling from her light hold. It was clear.

—You're planning to kill her.

—She's had a geologic age to move forward on her own. Maybe she'll act now that she's finally in danger ¶. You showed them everything when you joined with them – it's no accident that I was taken. Now we are linked forever, Beloved.

She pressed herself to me and kissed my shoulder, my neck and, warming, the chill shed from my skin. I responded to her despite my weakness, unconcealed by my robe, and she unknotted my bathrobe belt.

Liza shifted onto me, right there amid the rubble, but I resisted, pushing her back. She clenched my arm with a strength not unlike Llesami's, snarling,

—You're thinking of her – after she tried to kill you. I'm the one carrying your baby!

Shaking my head increased the vertigo. I began to say, "It wasn't…" but faltered as I watched the blue drain from her eyes like the fall of dusk, sped into an eyeblink, a green flash, then a fiery orange-gold. Blue that rose again in her skin, the bones of her face distorted, pressing forth: the wrythen mask of rage itself, her voice pealing with layered resonance:

—You are mine, Julian.

A nimbus-like smoke gathered around her head, black, writhing, serpentine. A crown of seething thorns. Savagely, then, Liza bit me.

Every muscle seized in an agonising spasm, and my jaw clenched tight. I fell back hard; then she was atop me, biting again and again. My veins filled with fire, liquidised fire, burning down to my toes and into the roots of my teeth.

She straddled me, and I throbbed inside her with a painful pressure. The mouth I'd kissed innumerable times was a smudge of blood and lipstick; tubular fangs jutted over her underlip, dripping hot amber.

—You shall have no other before me.

And then I knew the layered echo of her voice, throaty Carys within Liza, doubling and reverberating – within a flame-haired avatar of Kali. It seemed there would be no end to it, no release, as she ground against me with the force of a car rolling over my pelvis, her clawed fingertips fish-hooked into my flesh. On and on it went till her rage spent itself: dawn relit the blue in her eyes that faded from her skin, and droplets began falling on my bared and bloody chest.

—I'm sorry, I'm sorry, I was so angry...

She clung to me, her apologies running together:

—You'll be OK, she said; you're stronger than you think, and it will wear off... it will ¶. But you see why we have to end this. I would never hurt you on purpose; sometimes... sometimes, she drives me insane.

The blood was mine. Liza cleansed and treated my wounds after tearing away the ruins of my robe, then covered my nakedness with a blanket and placed a pillow beneath my head.

—I'd prefer to move you to the bed, but...

Instead, she lay with me on the floor, her head on my shoulder, as we sometimes slept. My priapism wouldn't subside, a beacon of throbbing discomfort rubbed raw – my empowered healing envenomed. She sang the Luwian song I'd never heard in a language I'd never lived – a lamentation for Ymerodraeth.

She came and went as I slipped in and out of consciousness and found her sleeping beside me. Sometime in the small hours, the venom loosed its hold, and my limbs began to twitch. I listened to her soft and steady breath for another hour or more, clenching my fingers till some sense of strength returned. Slowly, shakily, I shifted away from her and out of the makeshift bed. I wobbled to the bedroom and dressed, taking my wallet but leaving my replacement phone. She might've installed another tracker.

I understood the monster – the reflexion of my rage in the parking lot. My reflex was to tuck her in, would've been, but I slipped out and locked the door, pausing at every sound. The elevator ride was short, yet I expected visions of Llys to rise on its brief descent. I reached the street still present, in the surreal flight from the one I'd yearned for. I needed to find Llesami.

There was an ATM in the corner store,

Morvydd stepped away, holding an oil lamp, but the door did not open further; the gap held like the gate of a contested fort and me in full harness. The banbyshn's whispers passed between:

182

—Sardar, the hour is late, and it is unseemly that you should call upon my chamber.

—Nay, Your Imperial Grace, I whispered in urgent return; the hour has passed. The sun rises, and the enemy is upon the field. Black fires have been marked from the walls; there can be no further delay. I must away lest the foe bar our foray.

—So it has come.

—Aye, ma'am. Think not ill of me; my sword has ever been in your service, even when you knew me not. Only thus can I prove my love.

—I doubt not that in the face of all peril, the unconquered knight, Gvvyn Emrys, will return – covered in such glories as will spell new legend – and claim his bride ¶. But wilt thou not grant me this one boon and release her? Release and let me keep her at my side. Thou hast my love, ever, but I am… bewitched, and in it, my crown stands imperiled.

—Make suit to His Grace, and mayhap…

Her sob troubled my heart, and I raised one hand to the stout red oak, heavy-banded with alcamyn. Her voice was rent with anguish:

—The shahryar hath refused me and advised that, on my coronation, I may take thee unto mine esteem and imperial council, placing you both within the Henllys and Fedvvyd. A fox he is, and my father gathers the hunt even now ¶. Bethink thy love, and in the patient measure of time, our separation shall find surcease, and we will be rejoined in felicity; we and our autumnal fruiting. But betimes thou must release her.

—I pray you forgive me, ma'am; I am your humblest and most unworthy sword, and I will never falter, retreat, or turn aside from you. Every regard I send to our child, for I may not know them in this life.

The door shut,

but could feel her heartbeat from the sidewalk, the high rise wavering above me, serpentlike. At least I was on track despite the gaps. Llesami buzzed me in, no sleep in her voice.

She waited in her open doorway, wearing the slouchy pyjamic things the younger set thought was activewear. It suited her wry tone, if incongruous with her imperial poise and luxuriant surroundings:

—It's four AM.
—Do you even sleep?
—That wasn't my point.
—She's planning…
—My death; I know. Come in.

Questa papessa, as Issota had said. "This popess", Llesami's billionaire's eyrie was a night-and-day contrast with Liza's. I got the big view on stepping in, the constellated city lights below ending at the void of the sea. Books and artefacts dominated the surfaces, and Llesemi gestured at a scarlet sofa, the room steeped in faded incense, linen-rag paper, and old leather.

She prepared two polished goblets: mead, she said, scented with rose petals. I turned the cold metal within my hands, the mouths silver-lined. Unasked, she answered part of my thought, explaining we'd rediscovered alcamyn a century ago: an alloy of beryllium and copper. Prompting me to ask about the glass fishman – but that, she said, she'd taken from the "invisible college" devoted to "the outsiders". Of a kind, but not the same statuette I'd taken from the fire sabbat. Some relics of the Div had survived the pogrom – her word.

Llesami smelt the traces of venom, and I explained without explaining. She didn't ask why I'd fallen. I didn't say.

She sat across from me, alone on the loveseat. Bound together, held apart. She froze for a time, her dark eyes on the intricate weave of an Iranian carpet, as inexpressive as a doll. A jewellike machine?

—Carys has set something in motion. Something dangerous, and I don't know if I can stop it.
—Without stopping her, you mean.
—I can't. I won't.

There was no denying her feelings. There was no denying Issota's anguish; her soul invaded, she'd said. I recalled Crowley saying something odious about astral rape, but I hadn't given him more than a cursory glance. It was hard to filter the Other from his ego and his unapologetic legerdemain. Still, I remembered hearing it as if I were present while he played to the room.
—That astral–dream projection thing you do…
—Astral? Llesami dismissed. Are you familiar with the Egyptian concept of bau? It's a limited manifestation of my will, of my latent ἀποκολοκύντωσις. It's not a dream, per se, but a bubble

reality. A bubble within the bubble within the greater matrix – there are astrophysical constraints. Your πνεῦμα is trapped, but your νοῦς can radiate past the event horizon, so to speak.

ἀποκολοκύντωσις, apocolocyntosis or "pumpkinification". A sly callback to Seneca, pending her transfiguration into a new tyrant. However dry her humour, none of this was funny. Not to my πνεῦμα, pneuma, or νοῦς, nous. My "soul" and "mind". I asked,
—Have you tried it on Liza?
—No. I didn't know. I never know.
—Unless I reveal her to you.

I could've surfed on the pressure wave. Llesami evinced little through gesture or microëxpression, but her emotions manifested like barometric changes.

It sank into me and settled into my ribcage like a breached ship coming to rest at the bottom, and the green viper swam through. There was a dark side to her power, and hazardous potentialities, given her enduring passion for the Princess Carys of Arman, whom Liza claimed was a childhood phase. It pricked me with fangs of its own.
—And what expression is that? asked Llesami.
—Jealousy? I don't know.
—Shouldn't I be the one? You've put a ring on her finger again.
—You pushed me away.
—I had no choice. You think I've felt nothing for you? I, who suborned the servants for our secret rendevous; I, who sought you out of all the knights in the imperium and came to you on your favourite watch? I who have come to you from the ends of the earth, across a dark age I'd thought would not end until the walking fish came from the sea and allowed us to raise cities again – to reinvent the wheel.
—I remember the Stone Age. I saw with the eyes of a þyrs before I understood what it meant.
—We can't talk about it.
—We're past that, Llesami. We've been trapped in the same pattern since Llys, but the monster is here now. This is the endgame.
—You think you can control it? I've watched over you, Gwyn, generation after generation, but the Tyrant can cloud my vision ¶. I wasn't there when you were reborn from her body in Frisia – when you marauded north and across the Danish marches as mother and son. An entire life, in torment, with her – as þyrsas,

to use your word. The fairy tale champion and the beautiful princess: accursed, reviled, and hunted down by lesser men. I only saw the aftermath.

—I... I remembered.

—I know.

It was there, like an itch beneath my skin, waiting. "We are that we are" didn't tell me how it'd come to this. How it'd come to be. A filament "spun from ἐγώ εἰμι" with a bottomless thirst for blood. It, the ultramarine avatar of l'Avversario, Gwyn Emrys – and every life thereafter – warped within its weft. It, I was. The ache began behind my right eye, an almost gentle warning, but I forged on:

—How many times have you had to... stop us?

—Carys remembers too many. I tried to be merciful.

—She's angry.

Llesami's voice was brittle:

—She hates me now, I think, to do what she's done; the suffering is driving her mad. You've both suffered so much; it's unbearable.

She lifted the amulet from behind her nightshirt.

—With this, I can deliver one of you from the cycle of death and rebirth. Or if you follow the path she is laying out for you, it will destroy me and release me from this eternal... prison ¶. But however we choose, only one of us can find deliverance; the other two will be damned for all time as the highest servants of the Tyrant. Forever monsters bound to the false gods of the Div. For us, of Ymerodraeth, there is no greater capitulation; for we would become the Div as the Pretender would have wished them to be ¶. No, there must be a way I can save you both – one that doesn't involve abandoning what little humanity remains me.

I turned the thing around in my head. My cup was empty.

—Then why are you in Egyptology? It wasn't for me.

—It's for all of us. I've spent much of the last few centuries in academia, as far as they would accept women, searching apocryphal archives and old libraries for clues ¶. I always find you eventually, and I left my doctoral program in Rotterdam when I discovered you were here. Doktor Mikkelsen gave me full access to the Institute's resources, on and off the books.

—Find anything since you bounced me off the walls?

—Hints. Allusions to an inutterable name hidden within the Living Aten. Some have glimpsed what they described as "the

Aten of Atenu". Others have heard fragments of a manifold name – THE NAME emanating from al-nur al-a'zam.

My Arabic hadn't improved, and I raised my brows at the last. She glossed,

—The Supreme Light.

Carys's words came back to me: "a hidden temple to the effulgence". Less suspicion than revelation. I prodded,

—That which is effulgent.

—Yes, the first daeva.

—It was you, wasn't it? You transmitted the irradiance cult to Holocene civilisations.

—I wasn't wrong. You can't predict where genius will take hold, what will be revealed, or by whom.

—You've been using them all this time.

Her remaining humanity became an uncomfortable question: it wasn't Man she was fighting for. Her tone remained bland, factual:

—Our κόσμος is like a projection, a bubble of reality, as I said before. And at the radiant of all emanation, something beyond madness is caught within the web of its own spinning, all-powerful but impotent ¶. The outsiders cross κόσμοι the way we would cross an ocean. If everything is possible, somewhere out there, then they are one extreme of the possible. But the power that manifests our κόσμος is alien to their power; if I can access it, then I could challenge the Tyrant directly. Even drive the outsiders from our bubble – that's a part of this game, too ¶. While the Supreme Light is immanent within mankind, those of us touched by the outsiders are... contaminated, corrupt, incapable of enlightenment. We must look for its signs in them.

κόσμος, κόσμοι, "cosmos", "cosmoi"; the scale was beyond my reach. Llesami was on the cusp of a titanomachy. With Greek emphasis, I said,

—Would mankind even survive μία τιτανομαχία? You're playing with fire – an unspeakable fire.

—What choice do I have? In my search, I've only found that THE NAME has fifty-five notes, and even the fragment I acquired omits the vowels. It's a dead end thus far.

—Sixty, I said. Sixty syllables. Sixty spheres. Fifty-five is a corruption, or a lie bandied about the Mediterranean since Aristotle.

—You found something, or have you recalled... ?

—It. I found it: THE NAME.

She sat up.

—Sixty tones…? Where!

—That's the bad news.

Her posture sagged a hairsbreadth, and the pressure dropped a few microbars.

—Of course, there's bad news.

—I'd smuggled them out of the Institute, but someone broke into my apartment.

—Did they take anything else?

—Only my work on a Gilgamesh tablet, but I'd stored them together. Why?

—The invisible college; that filth does what they can to keep tabs on you. Your Foundation is a front. When did they contact you last?

—Not since the Gala.

—The college has gotten better at avoiding me. I never change, but they can't stop me. They can't even use it. All they can do is try to hide it from me.

She sighed, that pressure-valve blow, then sank back. I asked,

—Why do you keep saying *tones*?

—It's not a human sound. THE NAME is sixty syllables, but in one chord – like hitting sixty piano keys at once. A single discordant vocalisation. It's not clear if even I can speak it in this form.

—If you have to ascend first, it'll be a pyrrhic victory.

—Do you expect me to say Carys is correct? I can't give up, and I won't know until I try. Why did you keep it from me?

—Was I wrong? Why'd you keep *him* from me?

I described the voice in the darkness, and she bowed under an unimaginable weight. I asked for his name, and the seconds passed like hours till she spoke, her words not brittle but broken glass:

—Medrault. He yearns for you. He yearns for you and is never far.

—What did they do to him? Thirty thousand…

—The outsiders are removed from technology as we understand it; their bau is transcosmic, and the least of them are a terror beyond imagining. When the waters of Llyn Twyll began to boil, I knew something was coming and gathered as many as I could to flee the city by a secret subterranean route ¶. Three rose from the lake like mountains, like volcanoes erupting in webs of arcing plasma and billowing clouds of steam. Some fainted or vomited or went mad at the sight, and we who could not turn away watched as their voices crushed the air, the shockwaves shattering the treeline at the distant lakeshore. Then they rained blue fire and lightning down on Llys and everything nearby ¶. I didn't see it all; the Div found us, led by the magi. I was taken... into the sea. I can still hear Carys screaming for me as they carried me away. Medrault... He was...

I shushed her. It was too much. We'd borne too many deaths, as Liza had said, too many horrors. The pain sharpened, threading my eye, and I blinked to keep it from watering.

—You should get some rest. If you can sleep.

—I can, but I don't care to. Sometimes they sing me such terrible and beautiful songs. Sometimes I want to walk away from all of this. To sleep and forget, but I can't forget about you and her and how much you suffer every day and how people everywhere suffer because of what they've done to you. I can't...

I shushed Llesami again. I said I'd go to a hôtel or something, but she told me to stay for now. I settled into the guest room, golden-yellow shades of the Henllys, then lay in the dark with all that wheeled through my mind, like galaxies in the void. I bolted upright at an unforgotten chalky squeak – *skree skree*

would have thee set me aside, keep me mistress; and remarry thee, illustrious sardar, on the death of Prince Idvval. She would have us both.

Princess Carys was yet in her nightdress, and I stayed her hand lest she cast it away. Time was the matter, and even these few words dear bought, but I stayed my urgency at their import.

—How now? asked I. He is hale and well.

—No man is hale against an arrow, and all will muster in the coming battles.

—She speaketh such treachery?

—Ward the prince-consort or warn him. As thou refusest her, the banbyshn will yield to my father's wishes upon her ascension to the high throne. I shall be kadbanu of Lludd, and thou wilt sit on a council of my father's devising. To wed her mak'st thee a consort in her house and not the prince of thine own.

—And she keep my wife as mistress? Thou wouldst have it so?

—I would.

And so was I sore put upon, for I should neither warn nor ward His Highness, lest the empire fall into his hands. Nor might I set aside she whom I had made wife in nature if not yet in Law. Princess Carys, it seemed, clearing the hazard board, would win the game, and so she spake:

—No fear can touch me, Betrothed. Ride forth and send the Elder Foe to their invented gods in nothingness. When thou return'st, we will marry, and the House of Lludd shall rise among the great houses of Ymerodraeth ¶. Away, Your Excellency, and return to me, thy bride. Thou art mine immortal.

And in our parting embrace, I held that the banbyshn and I were equal fools and treachers to

avoid or disclaim the inarguable source. Goosefleshed, my hair standing on end, I followed, opening the unlocked door with reckless caution, and there Llesami slept, turned on her side, little blanketed in her vulcanic warmth – *skree skree, skree skree,* the sound of her grinding teeth.

M Y BROKEN BONES AND TORN LIGAMENTS knew too
well the crushing power of the Other, of Llesami as
she'd become, a seed in germination. Not yet the seventh angel, yet subject to human wrath.

I reached the sidewalk uncontested, in flight for the second time in one night, and made for the subway, hands in pockets. The sun was late in rising, the sidewalk treacherous with ice; there were few braving the early morning commute. Bitter it was and cold.

Her heartthrob remained stationary behind me, and while she and Liza dreamt, I envisioned what lay ahead: THE COMING OF SUMMER AND LIGHT.

"The ſea with ſier, the Element with ſmoake, | Which gods and monſters from their ſleepe awoake", said I to the wind burning my ears and muffling my voice; Markham, not Shakespeare on this slippery stage. Though I was no philologist, or whatever, to have that on my lips – the past was bleeding through.

Railroad spikes of pain hammered through my eyes, and I stumbled,

my sabre fallen out of reach; my spear pinioned. My horse whinnied but lay still. Banbyshn, I have failed your worship.

The sound of ten thousand braying olyfants vibrated the piteous earth, and it rose above me, a leering darkness, whorling and ridden with lightnings. I could hear its voice, grumbling, muttering – like a man half-asleep but roused in insensate vexation – underlaid with mocking tones that pummelled me as would fists with waves of roiling force.

The dead lay about and behind me, charnel smoak yet smouldering thick with blood on emberous coals. Mine eyes could nay be doubted nor believed, for what herb craft had been wrought that such visions might form within the mind itself? The seers knew not my name, but I did not forget their kind, these elder magush of the fire temple. These greybeards led no van to war but wormed the black heart of the Div nation, and the nation has come. Long had been our search as we struck and harried the horde that came in its bands, bearing sun-marked shields, to encamp before the sea-doomed city, where you, I knew, watched in my stead. They impelled the serpent coiled before Llys and raised up to strike. We came upon them even as they supplicated the rising waters, daevas, and dragons, as like to summon forth a dream or storm.

My fingers knot in the tawn summer grass instead of your tresses, which I will know nevermore. Through-smitten by the arrows of my countrymen, my bones were broken by the fall. You have turned me away, but I am forever your knight, and I will never yield my love for Your Imperial Grace nor the favour you bestowed upon me; it will band my sword arm till mine end.

The darkness expands beyond my sword, a bridge of flames but not flame, spanning out or within, unto a chasm of hueless delirium, spelling nightmare and abomination as smoak from fire; its vituperations made manifest as it would burn my very heart and eyes with the sight of it, but were it apparition or not, I would not be broken so. I yet grasped for the blade that I could not reach.

For you, O Banbyshn, I will not yield unto the last breath. Every deed since our parting, every blow struck or taken, to my final moment, is for you. I can think of none other and long only to be at your side.

O, if I could but see your face once more. One more smile, even as you look upon fair Carys, in your love for her. Know her no mischiefful girl, but a shahbanu born, and we were both played upon her board. I have reached its end.

But a fallen sword retains its bite, its will straight and to point, and I am your sword, Banbyshn. I will cut to the last. Even struck by friend and not foe, for the shahanshah raised his hand against me, as His Grace did warn, and in our destruction of the caballed seers and sacrifiers, our archers turned their arrows upon me and my Fedvvyd-bred steed, taking us unawares from behind.

They laughed as horsemen fell before them and their long-bows, and one proclaimed, "Your pardon, sirs, but he that plucked one shah's crown may pluck another—a double one at that—and no knight here may bear witness." And it was thus, in mortal peril of the Henllys itself, that we fell to among ourselves, and on my sabre and spear their blood met with the Div's, and the untended altar fires belched forth their ill charge into the air, feeding it seemed on the hate between brothers. Last, amid the dead and dying, Carngrvvn and I tottered, smote through many times, and together we toppled before the rising dark, though dazed that I saw only light.

I remember yet, how you first came to my sight, always so tall and straight you were, even amid our retreat, the shahanshah's household gathered round as you were a fire that gave them warmth and strength. You did not see me, one knight of many in the shahryar's van, but even then, your bearing inspired mine own, and I bethought myself unto you as we rallied again and again, till our horses flecked with foam, till our arms we could no longer raise, flinted arrows a bittermost rain against us. Again and again, the reavers came, striking the dolesome column night and day, bent on rapine, slaughter, and ravishment.

But as we ranged forth, stemming hither and thither the dark tide that would wash over us, then our herds, my kinsmen lagged, storm-blinded, and the Div fell upon them, the elder put to axe and spear and our youngest raped away into the night. Long did I scour the tempest to find that which remained after cruel sport, savage feast, and violation.

I was left alone, Banbyshn, and only you remained within my heart. Alone, I raised a cairn over my dead, over the little ones whom I had failed. And tears, too, became rain in my beard, for no man could bear such a thing. The path of vengeance was closed by storm, and in duty recalled, and in defeat and desolation, I returned to the march; only in my service to you could I live on, even though you knew it not.

Your image I upheld before me, and before your eyes, the shahanshah named me *grivpanvar*, any honour yours. My sword served you, and no other, and mine eyes saw and sought none but you.

Could I describe the great mystery of your arrival on my dawn watch? How confounding you were! And you claimed the life already yours: the heart that belonged to none but you. I have had more of your love than befits one such as I, and in my jealous heart made mind of some claim, but such is the weakness of Man. Better ten thousand arrows than we should part as we did.

O this black and fœtid whirlwind, that it should lie before me and not behind, that I might turn one last time, to see the sun reflected on the first circle of Llys, to see the northmost parapet where I know you stand amid your maids, in the hand of our seductor. But the enemy lies before me, and I cannot turn away. Your sword shall never turn aside, and if shattered and trod under boot, it will bare its shivered teeth and bite.

You will be banbyshnan banbyshn ere long; though I shall not see your crowning, its glory lies within my fading sight: I hold it within my feeble fist. The delusive heart has been cut from the Div serpent, and though the shahanshah proved treacherous, the people will scatter the savage rabble; for dismay will find their ears anon, and this foul cloud disperse as the embers succumb, untended. It is done.

I cannot recall a fairer sight than when I first beheld you and shall know none other as the creeping darkness makes its way closer. O phantom! Its laughter called me to stand, to rally again and assay its might. But I waited, biding as the grasses wither and die at my fingertips, whether it be a curse upon the earth or a pollution of the mind. Though warmth leached from my hands and sensation from my limbs, though lanced by my broken ribs, I made breath itself my spear and spat into the eye of darkness. This phantasmic foe was worthy of naught but lowest contempt, an illusory god as the Div would reverence.

And the befouled land heaved under a loathful recoilment, my laughter yours, in my final breath, mocking the invidious mocker, even if a spectre raised within. What for but to scorn one's own weakness and folly?

I rose and fell, the bridge of flames passing beneath me, my last thought of thee, my Llesa, and regret. Then the braying, retching, raging darkness surged over and around me, and the darkness was

forced myself up, disinclined to cause a scene, but with envy-less ears that didn't hear and eyes that didn't see, no one even glanced my way. I didn't lose any skin but suffered a hammering headache and cold, wet hands. I almost took a header down the subway stairs.

The jaundiced glare below stung my eyes, even as a tugging turned my head. There was nothing but dingy tiled walls. I found the subway system map, and it became clearer: the line west to the last stop; then, I didn't know. "You'll feel the call".

Liza. Llesami.

One had killed the other innumerable times, and the other plotted her destruction in turn. One was carrying my child, and the other was the mother of my son. The passion between them, the wounds of it, the soap-opera tragedy, was a win for l'Avversario in their twisted game.

"A high place", Liza had said. A coronation. A way to end the cycle, but I couldn't bring harm to Llesami. They couldn't push me that far or anywhere near. Not even for Liza. When I'd had nothing else, I'd fought for the banbyshn. Fought to the bitter end. I would go to this high place and spit in their eye again; l'Avversario would learn that Gwyn Emrys did not yield.

I paid and walked to the platform to wait; it wasn't quite de-serted. I shook it off; oddly enough, I felt stronger, the floor stable beneath my feet. I listened to the cablelike quivering of the rails before the steel-on-steel screech of the approaching train's wheels; the embarkment, a Rubicon taking me out of my life as Julián, knowing, as in my parting from the banbyshn on that final dawn, that return was unlikely. There were no goodbyes.

The subway car was better populated, and a man standing near the doors jolted back as if stung by static when I brushed past him. "Damn, man, that's freaky." I glanced at him but kept moving. As I sat, I drew a few more looks, but most remained in elevatorlike isolation, one person watching whatever aloud on their phone. Then more glances. I looked to my reflexion in the glass, against the dim tunnel lighting, and eyes the vivid scarlet of fresh wet blood stared back at me from my face.

Change of plan. I disembarked at the halfway mark. High street shopping wouldn't be open yet, but I picked up a cheap pair of Ray-Ban knockoffs at a drugstore; then I sat in the park, another hobo with nowhere to go till ten.

I started with a hair salon, well, three to find one with a spot for a walk-in. I gave a girl with macaw hair carte blanche to cut and recolour mine as she saw fit. I removed my sunglasses, and she stepped back.

—Fuuck, she drawled. Where'd you, like, get those contacts? They kind of glow, like, fluorescent?

—Online. Hollywood prop.

She was inspired. I walked out with nineties Club Kid hair, then burned too much cash on garish clothes to match and a duffel bag. A strong impression, but the wrong one. The police were sniffing around, and I had to avoid them – for their own safety.

I backtracked midtown to a cheapish motel for a shower, tossing my old clothes in the trash. Llesami could've found me but didn't. I cat-napped with one eye open, then checked out late for a midnight Greyhound going west, leaving my new car behind. A last ATM pull was tempting – I needed the cash – but the camera would capture my new look.

"A high place" could mean anything but the submerged, scattered, and sea-washed rubble of Llys, and an entire hemisphere lay due west. My gut told me it was far but not across the sea, like a direct circuit connected me to my destination, and it tingled the soles of my feet.

My second seatmate was a little too chatty, and I gave him a red glare over my sunglasses. We reached the Appalachians in sweet silence, the outhouse stench of the onboard toilet, and the aroma of someone's stale BLT. The mountain air was less sweet than fumy, with pickups and semis belching black smoke. X didn't mark the snowy spot.

I dozed in the station and took the next bus heading towards the Rockies; I'd learned to sit up front. I had too much time to think but too little information to deduce answers. L'Avversario had destroyed most of the Div in their purge of Ymerodraeth, leaving a few stragglers to Llesami's vengeance. The bloodwite was little more than a sardonic joke in that light, but history was full of tyrants – their atrocities and jaded appetites.

I'd failed to die, and in crossing the bridge of flames, I'd exposed Llesami and Carys to l'Avversario. It was on me to find a way out for them.

The pull west was steady, then uncertain in Limon, Colorado, before the rising white shoal of the Rockies. The wind blew southwesterly, away from the ski slopes and down towards New Mexico: the desert plateau between me and Mexico proper. It didn't feel much farther, and my cash could stretch to one more leg.

Just as well, for the monster was alive and awake. The sweetish scent of cold bacon and warm cheese: it'd followed me for days, from bus to bus, but stretching my legs in the cold air outside the Greyhound, it faded into the wind. Then I knew: the scent of the other passengers. To the monster, they were ripe meat, like Parma hams fed on whey.

The horror of it was that I felt no repugnance. No disgust. In a thousand generations, how many times had others paid my penances in pounds of their dilacerated flesh? I ran my finger over a map as if I were dousing for water and stopped on the tingly, itchy irritation of a mosquito bite. So I rode once more, thinking the thoughts of Gwyn Emrys but with thursic appetite: on what I'd become. Of what I'd been for thirty thousand years, across a thousand stories.

The final leg left me at Gallup, in the high desert near the border with Arizona. One of my last twenties went to a Walmart sleeping bag. The rest I held onto for water.

It was cool, not cold, and free of snow. I didn't need my bearings; it was that way, and I began to walk.

H UNGER CRAWLED UP MY THROAT, unappeasable, against Arizona's parched and blasted landscape. No romanticised dunes gleamed against a featureless sky, no undulating waves of white gypsum, but badlands of scrub and stone, dried clay and dust, stagnant cloud.

Each day I grew stronger, longer of stride, freer of breath – the aches and pains accreted over the years scraped away by the miles between me and my office chair. Or by something more sinister.

Some part of me knew this land; there were pockets of sand elsewhere, but this was creosote, mesquite, and agave. This was Burroughs' MARS: a place for monsters, venom, and a monster's hunger for Man. I swallowed the pangs to use the truck stop markets that served the highway I was tracking southwest. I couldn't fathom how Liza had controlled it every day. Then, considering her practised cleanup crew, perhaps she hadn't at first.

Two backpackers I stumbled on lived only because they stank of soy-corn chemurgy. Vegans, or vegan-adjacent eaters of animals in plasticised effigy. I couldn't get away fast enough.

Then I trespassed on the trailered property of some prepper with a penchant for the word "faggot", living on his outpost of isolation from a society that didn't miss him and wouldn't notice his absence anytime soon. He was too fat and slow to use the guns he postured with. My skin shimmered blue, but I snapped him in half without partaking of long-pig. I could smell other meat inside.

I traded my less-than-ergonomic duffel for one of the unused mud-brown backpacks in his collection, a tarp, and all the packable food I could carry. He'd stashed his cash and, of all things, gold coins in the places a thief would look first. I traded my cheapo sunglasses for the waspish wraparounds that'd looked absurd on his porcine face. The veil of night had thinned before my new eyes, and the glare of day had sharpened.

Trailing me southwest, light snow nipped at my heels, laying a thin dusting over the red land. I made camp for the night, checking the area first for fire ant nests and the like. Those were bothersome even for a þyrs; a single fire ant inside your ear is a whole bad night unto itself.

I lay me down beneath the complete horizon, one unencroached by buildings or man-made structures of any kind, my back to the earth, looking out through cracks in the breaking cloud. Out and not up into deeper space, to the kaleidoscopic rotation of the spheres; the expanding emanation; across the weblike fabric of the cosmos, the great prison even the Supreme Light couldn't escape. I couldn't see, couldn't've known the greater geometry but for the Other's drowsing eyes. We were legion, my adversary and I.

Listening to coyotes yowl in the distance, I dropped off to reäwaken, shivering hard in the dampened cold. I gathered what bramble and brush I could find and lit an acrid smoky fire. I could leave off sleeping so long as I didn't freeze, but then the fire spoke to me:

—For your bride. I watched them raise a black vortex with the blood of the other maids: they cut their hearts out one by one ¶. I hear them. I hear them crying for their fathers. I called for you, but you were waiting for me on the other side ¶. When I was the only one left, they flayed me with their stone knives, with joyous laughter and exalted faces. I saw them dancing in my skin before they threw me into the blackness. Then I became the vortex, and there was no pain, only cold and...

Sleep did not find me again, and the fire burned low, a fading whisper. It was a lot to take in, a lot to think about. Together, we'd journeyed here from Edin. Alone, on my desert passage, I was minded of THE RUNNING MAN in his flight to an unexpected elevation. A high throne.

As bright as it became under the clearing sky, the wraparounds were worth more than gold. I didn't come across any rattlesnakes over the milder days of the following weeks, but a squad of javelina couldn't get away fast enough.

I crossed from the brush-covered hardpack to a dilapidated gas station that waited on an intersection empty of traffic. A single black sedan with tinted windows loitered at a pump and had since I'd spotted this place from down the road. It wasn't suspicious; it was obvious. A German luxury tank could only be here for one thing: me.

The door was unlocked, and I sat within to find myself face to face, not with Liza, but with the Foundation's pet Puffin. Inside or out, he was a public face for the invisible college. I interrupted whatever canned pleasantry he'd prepared:

—Give me some water.

Pellegrino sat on ice like Champagne. He prepared to pour a glass – I reached over and took the bottle.

—O yes, he said; it is dry out there, isn't it? You've led us on a merry chase, Doctor Corbin.

—Don't waste my time; get to the point.

He did that nervous liplicky thing.

—Ahem. You've been most difficult to locate. You're a person of interest in certain notorious serial killings and the disappearance of two police detectives, and your sudden departure has raised suspicions. While there isn't a manhunt, per se, the FBI is looking into your whereabouts. Our resources are extensive but not unlimited, and while we are doing our best to provide a buffer, perhaps we could lend more direct aid that would serve the will of the Innominatum.

I could smell it on him and wondered how I'd ever missed it: incense and charnel smoke underlay the functional detergent fragrances and artificial musks, his breath reeking of wintermint menthol, whiskey vanillin, and long-pig roasted over an open flame. I took off the sunglasses.

—Mystes, I said in pealing words that came to my lips; the way is open, and the Bridal Chamber prepared. As two rise, one falls; and starred is the coming of the Father, Son, and Voice. Bloodwite is claimed, and its full due will be paid in trinity.

—"And his eyes like a blazing fire… " How may I serve, LORD? Please! How may I serve!

I pointed to the west.

—Speed me, but come not to the high place.

—Your will, as above, so below.

The Puffin had no idea what lay below but muttered to himself, tapping on his smartphone screen in the probable absence of any cellular signal. I ignored him as I could. The hunger, the trek, and the frigid nights had gotten old. I'd needed a warmer sleeping bag and one of those ground pads.

We weren't going in precisely the right direction, as the crow flies or the backpacker hikes, but near enough. The badlands' peaks and dells gave way to sweeping hills and dales, wider roads, and heavier traffic. Trucks descended from the vast stepped pit of an open strip mine into the spiralling juncture of interstates. Westward, we passed rest stops and ranch houses to discover an isolated town raised over one of the glaring, rocky ridges, "Dilmun" on the exit sign, a quarter mile back.

—Here, I said. Leave me at the town.

—Yes, LORD, will you be needing... ?

—No.

We caught the exit. Here and there, abandoned boats sat amid creosote on the steepening hillsides. A black and grey fifties TV small town with deep, dry canals with a row boat lying on the concrete bottom. We were a good four thousand feet up in a region with the least rainfall in the nation and no large bodies of water.

R
E
F
R
I
G
E
R
A
T
I
O
N

–antiquated signage from before the euphemistic *air conditioning*. The houses huddled together with metropolitan density, parked cars lining the pavements, but there was little traffic and no pedestrians. Defunct rails, lying across dry-rotted ties, crossed rusted bridges to nowhere. At the right spot, I told the driver to pull over. The Puffin was anxious.

—Are you certain there's nothing... ?

—Yes.

As we pulled to a stop, I put my sunglasses on and dragged my lifted backpack closer to the door. He knelt on the floor with awkward difficulty in his suit and tie, then bowed his head.

—"And he placed his right hand upon me, saying, 'Fear not. I am the first and the last, the living one who was dead; behold, I live to the Aion of Aions... ' "

I raised my right hand, saying,

—Don't get ahead of yourself.

His skull cracked open like a walnut, brains spattering the windows. I drank from it as a cup, licked my fingers, then stepped from the car and shut the door. It pulled away without haste. THE NAME was too dangerous for Llesami to get her hands on, but I hadn't forgiven the theft of my tablets.

The pull was unambiguous: straight up the San Francisco–steep hillside and over the top. But I'd stopped here for a reason.

MOTEL
VACANCY

A weathered grey building. Unpainted but for the signage, with the cast of coastal New England on a mountaintop.

A wan girl with yellow hair leaned on a stool behind the counter, brass keys hanging on hooks behind her. A rabbit-eared TV sat in a corner, off, with nothing to show, and a tinny radio played brassy tunes my childhood friends' parents might have called "square" when they were kids.

She looked at me with watery colourless eyes: grey but translucent through her fishbowl spectacles. Skinny, babyfaced, and as pale as if she hadn't seen the sun her entire life, in a place where the UV burn was eleven on a scale of one to ten, she took a brass key from the wall and slid it across the counter without a word. I took out my wallet, but she gave an alarmed shake of her head and pointed at the key with one knobby finger.

I found the room without difficulty, and it looked clean and comfortable enough after weeks of sleeping in the dirt with scorpions: the king-size bed fit for three, the greying towels coarse enough to sand wood. I hung my clothes and ran myself through the shower.

The scent of roasted meat preceded a knocking at my door. Another pallid blonde, fleshier than the silent receptionist, waited with a small dolly, a covered platter atop. Towel-kilted, my sunglasses on, I said,

—I didn't order anything.

She gestured within, under the same vow of silence; they were probably related. I sighed and stepped aside. She set it near the small side table, then lingered amid an air of uncertainty. I wasn't prepared to tip, but taking inspiration from one of Liza's action flicks, I presented the girl with a fifty-dollar Eagle. She raised her hands in denial and stepped back. Sunglasses off, I said, —Don't offend me. Take it and go.

Unstartled, she looked down from my "eyes like a blazing fire", then took the coin with hesitant apprehension. She made an odd gesture, like the Urdu adab in reverse, before exiting and shutting the door.

I sat down to meat with a side of meat. Greasy-looking beef ribs. A whole roast chicken. What looked and smelt like brisket and a sliced pork heart or similar, sapid and tender.

Two things were clear: First, I was expected. Second, they knew there was a monster in the room – showing not fear but reverence.

For all I knew, the girl was an offering like ἀνδρομέδα, "Andromeda". Her gesture recalled the impish Bastard's genuflexion before Signora Leonarda in the Palazzo Ginori – but the Puffin hadn't signed before me. Likewise, the queerness of the town was underscored by his evident ignorance of it. L'Avversario had pawns unknown to each other.

Full but unsated, I rested, half-awake, in that deep Other-lethargy that weighed on my limbs at times: images of Liza, Llesami, and even the place of my long exile. Given the lavish funding I'd left behind, Röhm had probably replaced me with little difficulty.

Morning itself was the only creeping disturbance till another knock found the dolly I'd pushed outside returned with a platter like the first: a round dozen eggs replacing the brisket. Shame; I'd liked the brisket.

Alongside the platter was a white card.

CHAPEL OF THE LORD

Ministry of the New Kingdom

It went into the circular file, printed with a street address that meant nothing to me and no other writing. I clad myself in aired out-clothes and shouldered my pack, leaving an Eagle for housekeeping.

The front desk was untended, the radio off. I left the last three coins with the key and stepped outside. The wind blew thrice over me, saying,
—It comes. It comes.

C·P·SERRET,
GRENDEL
VVEPT,
XXI.

★

T HE END WAS NIGH. Not in the town itself but nearby, somewhere beyond that hill.

I located a mom-and-pop grocery store, which wasn't quite empty. A cashier. One mother and child. All of a type – subterranean dwellers of the mountaintop – though the cashier was the first male I'd seen, lanky, lean but stooped, with a bulging Adam's apple.

My hydration sack was topped up, but I collected a basket load of luncheon meats, cheeses, and bread, till something coiled itself around my leg. Little-girl arms attached to a little blonde girl, a hint of blue in her big pale eyes. She stared up at me as if she would drink me in with them, and for a moment, two little girls were standing in the same spot: one was meat for the monster, the other, the knight to die for. But there was only one little girl and one man-monster. Her mother was frozen behind a half-filled cart, the blank aspect of fright.

I set my basket down and gently led the wayward waif back to her mother's side, who made an awkward half-sign as if she wasn't sure if she should. I took the basket to the cashier, who shook his head and nodded to the grocery bags. I didn't bother and loaded the pack instead. I only caught his homage reflected in the glass door after turning my back.

At the crown of the hilltop, I found a white-picket church with no steeple cross, a rather opulent wedding arbour before the open doors, thick with lilies and roses. The Chapel of the Lord, as if I could've missed it. A narrow red carpet stretched beneath the arch and down the short steps. I would've pressed on, but a red figure beckoned me. No small-town pastor, but a man in the vestments of a prelate: a bishop or patriarch.

As I passed beneath the arbour, I could see the vesture for what it was: a mockery. Hung with chains of gold skulls, the red fabric woven with abstract patterns – curious geometries that caught at the eye – his mitre was ovoid and leaned back on the head, mimicking an elongated skull.

He signed, bowing, then backed within. I could smell it: the sea and decay, ammonic and pungent. Three red nuns, whose headpieces covered all but their eyes, attended it within the nave, pressing wet sponges to its suppurating bronze scales. A trail of pustulant slime dulled the polished floor, smoke and old blood lingering somewhere beyond it.

An enormous "walking fish" bearded with webbed spines, its limbs and face half-fashioned in gnarled mimicry; its elongated fish-toad form contorted into hunched bipedalism by a callous hand. It wheezed, its gills flapping with horrid futility. Its rolling eyes were neither fish nor Man but bulging gelatinous globes of yellow anguish. It clutched a sheathed sword; at a glance, the replica of a common horseman's sabre from Ymerodraeth.

It gurgled and hacked, its voice a pained and desperate wheeze of stuttering phrases. A tongue long dead; he, not it: Dagon. Uan. οάννες.

The sword had been taken from the Black Sea, where dead Llys lay scattered and forgotten under hundreds of feet of water. Scattered within a true dead zone, without oxygen or aquatic life. He offered me the sabre, repeating, "The trial, the trial… "

My hands yearned for it, and with this clear warning, I took it from his spiny, crabbed fingers. I turned to leave, but he outstretched a pleading hand. It shook with palsy. "Mercy, LORD. Mercy… "

Bowing, the nuns backed away. Wise of them, I let it rise: that itching tingle beneath my skin. That surging charge, as if my lungs swelled, the light becoming brighter, and I felled him on the draw stroke. He flopped to the floor and kicked twice, his final huff a long sigh. The scabbard was new, as I'd thought, but the sabre was not. Alcamyn of the Llysian forges, bright and new-polished, the cloudlike temper line gleaming black.

The nuns prostrated themselves, and the magus genuflected, his face ecstatic, blue reflected in his silver eyes. A daeva made flesh; I was not inclined to be kind and wiped the blade on his sakkos. It would've been easier to rend them all than to stalk out as I did. To release it and be Gwyn Emrys. I wiped the saliva dripping from my lips – I couldn't do that again anytime soon.

It left a bad taste in my mouth. There was no demiurge among the would-be Rulers. This wasn't their world, and judging from Dagon – from Modarette, Liza, and Llesami – the outsiders didn't create anything. They chose to warp and distort what was. There had to be some leverage, some way for me to come to grips with l'Avversario. Some way to wrestle with the unnumbered angel.

I descended to the vacant weedy lots on the other edge of town, crossing an empty road that zagged where I felt the call to zig. The serrated ridges and scraggy ravines northwest looked like nothing less than a labyrinth. A trial – a minotaur? – therein. The railroad took its own trail into the badlands, southwest, opting out. I descended, sword in hand.

High noon announced itself with unforgiving brilliance. I cast about, sunk in a direction-sense that appeared to lead me in a spiral or to circle back on itself.

Hanging my tarp from a cactus, I sat in the shade. I hadn't come all this way to chase my tail, and after a long pull of water, I drifted into a floating drowse. I'd been called lord thrice but in two languages. Issota had revealed "Báal"; then Dagon had: a name of dread, exaltation, and despair. I mused till startled by rock skittering over shale, then sprang to my feet with novel athleticism. Watching my visitor's circuitous, loping approach, it was clear he'd wanted me to notice and had made it easy.

I recognised the tawn-skinned Mordarette, as we'd known him in Ferrara, sprouting into the semblance of young man-hood, longer of limb and as lean as a greyhound. Like me, he'd dressed for the city instead of a hike in the desert. He stopped a nonthreatening distance away, then raised his shades like a knight's visor.

—Father, you are lost. I will show you the way.

The voice in the dark. I acknowledged what I'd suspected from Llesami's partial explanation:

—My son, name yourself

He grinned at me: the Div had filled their teeth, but his were triangular piscine needlepoints, glassy white. Piranhalike; I don't know how they fit into his mouth, and the pity of it pressed my face. He said,

—In her sorrow, my mother called me Medrault ap Gwyn, the final son of the imperial House of Kian, the firstborn heir to the House of Lludd. I am Shahryar of Caer Colur, of which no stone remains. Known to some as the Bastard ¶. Come, Father, ere mother arrives. She is full wroth and bears the power of your unmaking. Leave all; we must away in haste.

He had his mother's eyes, eyes that had seen the Deep, but

my dark, almost black hair as it'd been then. He also bore the fragrance of the sea but with less weight than her. He looked like what he should've been: a boy born of the confluence of far-ranging tribes that met thirty-five thousand or more years ago on the Pontic steppe. My midnight inkblots by day.

—How do you live? I asked.

—As the wolf that came to shepherd the sheep. It has always been thus. Now follow.

Medrault turned and ran uphill at marathoner pace, lightly, kicking up little dust, and I left everything I'd gathered but the sword. He led me out of the Charybdis of crags by way of a rock crevasse I'd overlooked twice, requiring a sideways squeeze to get through or advanced rock climbing skills to go over.

A new valley view opened, revealing a wide plateau of desert grasses, a singular tree at the centre, and an Old West ghost town proper towards the other end. He stopped at an outcrop overlooking the vale.

—A road? I said in disgust.

Cursored by the black sedan driving away, back into the hills, and trailing a cloud of dust. He crouched.

—Yes, Father. The townfolk use it.

I sighed. Half a day in the desert, and there'd been a road the whole time. That road. Medrault pointed to the tree:

—There is the place of trial – they await you. I may go no further till bloodwite is satisfied. Quickly now! Mother comes.

I could see two dots by the small tree and sprinted down the steep animal track to the field, all out. In moments, I began to make out one figure menacing the other, black hair versus red, on the other side of a tree infected with winter-blooming mistletoe.

No minotaur, but a Div warrior brought forward in time, waving an Aztec sword like a cricket bat edged with obsidian blades. It was a bit high-tech for a Div. He was dressed not in hides but in blue jeans and red flannel, his face and bared forearms scarred by their ritual bloodletting. A strange enough sight as I'd ever seen.

He leered, spouting gutturals. Liza stood her ground, arms crossed. Under a light jacket, she'd accentuated her baby bump with a crop top, as if she'd dressed for a casual brunch with other Society moms and not the end of our world as we knew it.

—I'll put that splinter... ¶. Julian, you're late!

Her double heartbeats were music to me. I rounded on him

in a flash, sabre drawn – the þyrs at my fingertips, but I withheld it. The Div stepped back two paces as he levelled his war club, designed to crush and maim the enemy for better sport later. Like any club, it could kill, and correctly applied, it would snap my slender sabre.

A single sabrous tooth protruded from his carious mouth: silver and scalloped with occult engravure. He laughed at me in an exaggerated and overbold gesture to himself, drawing my eye to the cord of white beads that hung loose around his neck.

I'd not forgotten the Div's debased tongue – a hard-won lesson of the steppe. He declared with pride that he of all the tribes had been chosen by the anamaka, for he'd made a sacrament of my clan. In my defeat, would he become shahjahan, my bride his, and on its birth, would he sup on our child and again taste the sweet young flesh of my kin – so much sweeter than this local meat. He gestured back towards the town.

He named himself Blood Dragon, or Red Dragon, or some-such epithet; returned after a night and a day within the Abode of Seven Colours – said with all the grandiosity of a primitive mind undeveloped since thirty thousand BP. L'Avversario had released him for this final showdown. In the right corner...

A flashing star fell by daylight, like Soviet video footage I'd seen of an ICBM reëntry, and I held my breath till it turned at a sharp forty-five-degree angle, leaving a contrail straight as an arrow, heading this way. Llesami. I might've laughed in his face; even if I failed to kill him, they'd be scraping his remains off the moon. I might've laughed, but my little ones, I couldn't forget their contorted and bloodied faces as they'd lain discarded in the pulsant rain like boneless dolls. And on his neck hung their baby teeth. This was a blood feud and, perhaps, justice.

I tossed a fragrant red-gold bough of mistletoe at the feet of my ancientmost foe – he hadn't seen me pluck it in passing. It was a prototypic pattern, echoing back across time from this moment. And the little girl I'd just met, how many like her had he...? The sword came alive in my hand.

But l'Avversario had remade him, his breath a methanogenic fume. His rubberlike limbs flopped and folded, and I fended his heavy, whirling blows with the base of my blade. Liza had stepped away from our contest, saying something pointed about my hair, but I couldn't spare her a glance. The Div was without finesse but unpredictable, and the sonic boom reached us as we circled the tree, stone ringing a brazen bell.

Llesami fell from the sky to land with balletic ease, unsinged by the plasmic fires of her descent. There was no cratering impact or pluming dust, only the pressure of her presence and pulsing heart. Liza was herself:

—Now, Llesa? You're too… Then her voice echoed with grumbling contempt, not Carys but Other-voiced, resonant within the abyssal chambers of my mind:—Three contesters stand before the Tree; the shears are awakened to their purpose and may not be turned aside. To the Tree, the Warder is bound, and flight will avail none but forfeit. Bloodwite is claimed, and two will serve in the stead of one and his promised line. None other shall remain.

Puppeted in entheos, she gestured towards we duellists.

—Know this, Banbyshn of Llys, the Warder-borne Lesser Shear cannot sunder our Oracle. We assure her place against all save one. Should Warder or Sardar slay the other, the Greater Shear wilt be thine unmaking, lest thou first strikest mortal blow and take our binding service onto thyself; whereupon the Lesser will shear the remaining contester, if but one. This is our compact, and it cannot be undone.

Llesami gripped Liza's wrist, demanding,

—End this, Carys! Gwyn found the key: I can save you both.

—Didn't you listen? said again-Liza; the bough is cast. He's committed to us and our child ¶. Julian, finish him! When the low places have washed away, this will be our Eden.

—It won't be our Eden, said Llesami. It will be theirs.

—It already is, Llesa. Liza kissed her, then stepped back, wresting her hand free:—Farewell my noontide brightness, my eventide flame.

The glance I spared them cost me a resounding blow to the left arm. The silver pendant at Llesami's throat gleamed with lancing harshness in the afternoon sun: eyes raised, arms still at her sides. She was waiting to die.

He mocked my broken and bleeding arm, but I didn't need it for this; my sword was single-handed. Gwyn Emrys, as I'd become, was no easy meat. But in my lust to kill him, in my vendetta, I'd placed Llesami's life in the balance. If I struck him down, she would fall too.

The Warder wasn't a threat; he was a foil. Bait. The memory

of those tortured bodies had been delivered with purpose. The pain across my upper arm was bracing: even if I was Ba'al, Ba'al was not me. I knew what I had to do.

—Llesami! I will hold him. Kill the Div, then keep and protect Liza.

—No! cried Liza. Our baby needs you!

—She'll care for you both ¶. Banbyshn, do it! Do it now, before I weaken.

Her champion beyond death or dismissal, my life, my fealty, was hers, and any worthy cavalier would lay down all to hold the pass. For her; for Liza, for our child, everything till this or any other end. I had not failed. I was ready.

And Llesami screamed then, a scream of such anguish that even the Div paused with his club raised. A thunderclap shook limb and leaf, a dazzling bolt of lightning rose from the ground to the sky, and the tree burst into flame.

> The sound of dry snapping twigs –
> A whole bundle bursts at once
> Liza's gagging hiccups
> Flops in the dust,
> Llesami's arm purpled to the elbow,
> Purple with syrup blood;
> Pulsing in her small fist
> Drops to the dirt, twitching,
> It crawls like a slug

He raised his chin in bellyful laughter. Fool. My arm needed neither will nor heart. His sword hand came away from his wrist, then his head from his neck. I cast my sword into the yellow grass, smoking with his corrosive blood. A rank green flame gushed from his gaping maw, the silver tooth glowing white, and his head incandesced with the rushing hiss of a road flare.

And Llesami spoke, Other-voiced in turn, an irremeable curse:
—Hail, Gwyn ap Lludd. King.
—Hail, rumbled and echoed thundrous in celestine octaves.

The faint ticking faltered to a stuttering stop. Out of time. I dropped to my knees at Liza's side. It couldn't be.

IT COULDN'T BE.

Her face was slack above the gouted ruin of her chest, her arms and legs akimbo. Two heartbeats become none.

—What have you done? I said. What have you done.

—I saved her soul, said again-Llesami. She's at peace. Sundered from the Tyrant, freed from the cycle of death and rebirth and the yoke of eternal servitude. She will not return. I have taken her place, Your Majesty, and speak as their Voice now ¶. Our son is coming.

—You should have chosen her. You should've chosen them.

She put her arms around me from behind, and strange tears ran down the back of my neck, as cold as rain.

—I did. This is our sacrifice for her. Her long years of suffering are ended, and in her place, we will bear the great struggle to come. She is no longer a monster, and the child will not suffer what Medrault has.

In Llesami's eyes, she'd pulled me into perdition for her Carys. It was my in-extremis decision reflected back at me. I understood, but the hurt of it was too great. I said,

—You're cold.

—The bomb they placed inside me is spent. Now I'm like you: a tendril hanging from the intercosmic man o' war ¶. Medrault must do what I could not, but in time, they will tempt him with the eighth throne. I'm sure of it.

She squeezed my arm. I was without words, and a remembered sensation passed through me, shivering me: Grendel weeping alone in the darkness, not for his – my – mortal wounds, but for in gaining all, I'd lost it too.

A thousand doors stood open, and the sea of memory crystallised with bedazzling glitterance, the thousand facets of a single carbuncle, and within the torus of flow was bound another: her, we, binary stars in eclipseless union. Like candlelights playing upon a thousand eyes, I AM beheld us, and we were.

—It is done, whispered the smoke. Away.

Medrault arrived at the split and scorched tree without urgency, then knelt before us and signed, a new tugging in my bones. She dried kenotic tears.

—We are to the Inverted Palace, sire. All is in preparedness.

—Yes, Your Holiness, said I. This chill likes me not, and I am wearied. Our rest will be brief, and we will return on a fairer day. Summer is nigh upon us, and eternity is a small thing.

—Father! I will show you the way.